FILES OF THE
MISSING

FILES OF THE
MISSING

Book 2—Gray and Armstrong
Private Investigations

Eve Grafton

To order additional copies of this book, contact:
Xlibris
1-800-455-039
www.Xlibris.com.au
Orders@Xlibris.com.au
792321

Eve Grafton was born in Western Australia and grew up proudly Australian. After her marriage, Eve lived in many countries across the world until their children's education made it necessary to return home. Later in life, they owned a small hobby farm, where they became practically self-sufficient. Now they live in Perth, in Western Australia, and Eve writes novels to replace the many other hobbies she had over the years.

1

As James Armstrong entered the office, he sighed in relief, looking around at the smart room with his mother-in-law's beautiful paintings on the walls and the smart furnishings with which they were surrounded Gray and Armstrong were successful so far. Both Percy Gray, retired police officer and James Armstrong agreed they were doing well.

They had been busy every day, closing the office on Saturdays and Sundays. Kate Langford, an ex-policewoman, had been taken on to help out as an investigator, and Alicia, the wife of James, was their receptionist–consultant.

One of the current jobs being investigated was Percy's. He had received a call from the police force to follow up on a missing child. The police had no clues and had passed the job to Percy, stating that the boy, aged fourteen, had left home two weeks previously, after an argument with his mother. He was invited to attend a party of a seventeen-year-old boy whose parents allowed alcohol at the party, and Mrs Warren would not allow her son to attend. The missing boy, Jonathon Warren, had packed a bag and left home after the argument, and after two weeks, his mother had not heard from him and was quite distraught.

Percy had been investigating the story, but after asking at the school and various friends of Jon, he had not come up with any clues to the boy's disappearance. Jon was still missing. Percy called James in on Sunday morning to pick his brains. Alicia asked if she could come to the discussion, and afterwards she would go to the shopping centre next door until James was ready to go home.

After setting up coffee and biscuits in the meeting room, they sat down to discuss the situation. Percy said the school had been on a break for two weeks, so he had followed up teachers in their homes. They knew nothing of Jon's disappearance, although they were able to give the names and addresses of his friends. When Percy spoke to them, however, they were not forthcoming with any information; when Jon's name was mentioned, the boys had clammed up. Percy had a photo of the boy and checked at bus and rail stations and around the town to see if anyone had seen him, but this also came up negative. He felt he was not getting anywhere, and the boy was still missing.

Alicia smiled. 'Percy, have you asked if the boy has a girlfriend?'

Percy looked startled. 'He is only fourteen, Alicia, a bit young to have a girlfriend!'

'Ask his mother. She may know about it, although I bet he has not told her.'

Percy rang Mrs Warren, Jon's mother. She said he had never spoken about a girl to her; he was only fourteen, and that was a bit young for a romance.

'Which of the boys whose names you gave to me was the closest to Jon, Mrs Warren?'

She gave Percy three names and said, 'They have been friends since they started school and are inseparable. Like most boys of their age, they went everywhere with each other. I asked them, and they knew nothing of his whereabouts.'

Alicia looked at the partners and said, 'I think you will find he has gone to his girlfriend's house. Perhaps the parents are not aware Jon is there. This happens a lot when both parents are working. They lose sight of their children and what they are up to when they are at work all day. When they come home tired and the kids go off into their rooms and do not allow their parents entry, they grow apart without noticing what is happening.'

Percy said, 'I asked the teachers if they had noticed anything out of the ordinary, and each of them said no. Surely if there was a romance going on in the school grounds, they would have noticed something?'

'There are a lot of teenagers attending the school, Percy. It would not be hard to move off from the crowd to have a few private moments, and with so many in cahoots, such as his friends must be, you are not going to learn anything from them. They would be hiding their friend from the teachers.'

'Wow, things must have changed since my boys went to school, Alicia. I cannot imagine either of my two sons having a school-ground romance at fourteen years of age.'

'I personally did not,' said James, 'but I did know some boys who were chasing girls at that age.'

'I am looking at it from a female's perspective. Seeing as school resumes tomorrow, why don't you go back to the school with a romance in mind and ask the teachers once more and chat with those friends of Jon's again, keeping in mind the boys who were closest to Jon.'

'I got short answers from the teachers previously, Alicia. They were abrupt with me, as if I was accusing them of not doing their jobs correctly, and the friends were not forthcoming at all.'

'Were the boys anxious for their friend, Percy? It sounds as if they were not, so they know where Jon is! Why not let James try, Percy? You know he is a master of interrogation, with all the experience he has had. The teachers will give up and say they cannot watch everyone, but with James' gentle persuasion, they may even recall that they had noticed something. Take Kate with you, James. The boys will be trying so hard to impress her they will give up their stories in no time at all!' Alicia laughed; she enjoyed goading Percy.

'You are probably right again, Alicia, like you usually are. You are right about Kate. She was good in the "good cop, bad cop" situation. I am pleased we took her on. She has turned out to be a real asset to us. I can see a bunch of teenagers being impressed by her. As for James, he is more the age of the teachers than I am and will impress them with his interrogation methods, which he always makes out to sound as if he is so interested in what they have to say. Okay, I will set up the appointments for tomorrow morning for James and Kate to speak with the teachers and have a conversation with the boys. You can see I am bowing to your superior female knowledge of the world again, Alicia.'

She laughed. 'Okay, Percy, I will go into the shopping centre until you and James ring me to say you have finished work for the day.'

'What a clever lady you have won for yourself, James.'

'I appreciate her, Percy. She is smart and good-looking—and a good cook into the bargain. I have indeed done well for myself.'

Alicia smiled at them and walked to the entry of the shopping mall adjacent to the office, giving them a wave as she left.

* * *

As Alicia walked through the shopping mall, she had a strong feeling she was being watched; she turned around, looking to see why she felt this way. There was a woman who looked vaguely familiar staring at her. She smiled at the woman, who then walked towards her, saying, 'Alicia, do you remember me?'

Alicia looked at her curiously. The woman did look familiar, but she could not place where she had seen her previously. The woman said, 'I am Sandra Jenson, now Dunstan, since I married. It has been a long time since we saw each other, but you have not changed.'

Alicia was shocked. The woman who called herself Sandra Jenson was a school acquaintance from many years ago, but she was unrecognisable to her now. This woman looked at least ten years older than she should have. They had been in the same classes in secondary school but had moved around in different circles of friends after school hours. Sandra had been a beautiful young woman, very popular, with many young men always around her, while Alicia had been a more retiring student, more interested in books than beaus.

After they graduated from school, they often came across each other at many of the watering holes around the town, though Alicia did not drink alcohol and was left out of the popularity stakes because of it, whereas Sandra was always present, with a man in tow and a glass of wine in her hand. They were friendly but distant in those years. It seemed such a long time ago.

Alicia had left town to take up a career as a flight attendant, first in Gatwick and then in London, so she had been away from the city for several years. To see Sandra looking so lined and weary now was a shock. She also had a little girl by the hand who looked very much like Sandra would have at the same age; she appeared to be about four or five years old. Sandra introduced her daughter as Jody and said she was four—tall for her age, as Sandra had been also.

Alicia looked from mother to daughter and could see the likeness. Sandra had been a beauty from the time she was very young, and Alicia could hardly believe this woman was the girl she remembered. Time had not dealt well with her. She did notice that Sandra was slightly off balance as well, not the upright girl she had been, and she was also hesitant, which Alicia could not remember as a characteristic from her younger years. Something was very wrong with Sandra, Alicia decided.

Alicia asked if Jody went to school. 'I am homeschooling her for now' was the answer.

Sandra asked Alicia if she lived in town permanently now, as she knew she had been away for several years.

'Yes, my husband and I are back in the house with my grandmother, and I help her in the bookshop. We have been running it together, since my grandmother broke her arm in a fall, which made her a semi-invalid. Thankfully, Granny is improving, and I am now working in my husband's business. She will be able to manage, as we have taken on someone to help out in the shop on a part-time basis. James and I live above the bookshop, in a lovely apartment, so we are handy when we are needed. My husband is a big help, but he has his own business to run, so he cannot spare too much time for the bookshop.'

'I noticed you in the private investigations office as I walked past it to the mall. Is he the good-looking one with blonde hair and blue eyes?'

Alicia looked curiously at her, remembering her as a young woman always with a man in tow, and said, 'Yes, that is James. We have been married almost two years now.'

'Congratulations. He is certainly handsome.'

'Yes, he is. We are very happy together.'

'I am pleased for you, Alicia. You were not one for being led astray like so many of us were with drugs and drink. We always talked about you being a little Missy good shoes but it has paid off for you. You look wonderful, not much different than when you lived here before you went off to fly with the airlines. I now think you were the one doing things the right way. You did not need all the drugs and drinks like many of the rest of us, so you do not have an addiction like me. It has worked out well for you. You look full of good health and happiness, and I envy you for it. I hope my daughter will grow up to be like you.'

Sandra abruptly turned and walked away, leaving Alicia staring after her, disturbed by the conversation. She had to agree that she was obviously doing much better than Sandra! It had been such a shock to her when she had realised who the woman was, and she wondered if it had shown on her face.

She went on with her shopping, but somehow her happy mood had evaporated; she found herself wondering about the circumstances that had changed a beautiful, vibrant woman into the broken woman she had just met. With her changed mood, she decided to give up on her shopping and wandered back to join James and Percy in their office, where they were still discussing various cases. When they saw Alicia looking so sad and upset, they quickly found her a chair and made her a cup of tea and asked what had happened to make her look alarmed.

Alicia described Sandra Jenson to them. James said, 'I have seen that woman peering into the office several different times in the last week or so, looking as if she was trying to find enough courage to come in to talk to one of us. Next time I see her, I will walk out and greet her to find out her problem. She certainly has one, by her appearance. I would say she is on drugs, but that is not something we can fix for her. There must be something else worrying her.'

'She seemed so unhappy, James, but I have no desire to get tangled up with her. We were not good friends at school. We moved in different groups. I never invited her home to visit. I knew Granny would not approve of her. My memory of her was that she was like a model or actress moving around with an entourage of other girls and lots of young men, and she was their leader.

'She was very beautiful in those days. She always showed her ancestry must have been Viking, by her looks—tall, blonde, and so lovely. So seeing her now and knowing she is the same age as me makes me feel strange. I cannot believe the change in her, and she seemed very bitter. What sort of life must it be for the poor little girl who stood so quietly by her side while we were talking?'

'Do not worry about her, Alicia. There is nothing you can do to help. If she wants any help, she can come into the office, and Percy and I will help her out. You do not want to be troubled for her. Leave her behind. Whatever is troubling her, she has brought it on herself, so do not think of her again.'

'Are you going to be very long here, James? I think I would like to do something to try and clear Sandra from my mind.'

'We are just finalising things now. Sit here for a few more minutes, and I will take you home.'

'Thank you, James. I am so lucky to have you to look out for me.'

'My darling, we look out for each other. That is what being married means, and I hate to see you so disturbed.'

*　　*　　*

On Monday morning, James and Kate went to Jonathon Warren's school to interview teachers and Jon's friends once more, leaving Alicia and Percy to hold the fort at the office.

A telephone call from a woman asking for James Armstrong came in at nine thirty. Percy explained that James was out of the office and should return by eleven and could not be called earlier, as he was on a case, suggesting that James could call back at that time. The caller gave a number and the name of Jack Whistler at London Police Headquarters. Percy was curious, knowing James had been offered a job in Jack Whistler's department before taking up Percy's suggestion of the private investigation partnership a few months previously.

James and Kate returned at eleven, as expected, and James was also intrigued by the phone call. He hesitated to make the return call and left the message on the desk while he filled Percy and Alicia in on their school excursion.

Being the first day back at school after the holidays, Jon had turned up for classes, along with his girlfriend, Tina. They had spent the two-week break at her house, unbeknown to her parents, spending the days freely roaming the house and the evenings locked up in the girl's bedroom, making sure they organised food for the evening before the mother returned from work.

On weekends, they had gone on bus trips to various locations, with Jon wearing dark glasses and a hat as a disguise and carrying a walking stick to finish the look of an older person, and no one had questioned them. The girl's parents were totally unaware of what their daughter had been up to. The youngsters bluffed them, Jon exiting the house by the back door and knocking at the front door, asking for Tina to go out on an outing on the weekends. They told all this to James, giggling and holding hands, just like two children doing mischief.

James could not help laughing at the young teenagers' escapades as he described to Alicia and Percy. It showed great imagination on the part of the children how they managed to delude the adults. Not once did Jon profess any consideration about how his parents must have felt. James said he tried not to laugh with the young couple at the time of the interview, and tried hard to keep a straight face while telling Jon how his parents were so worried about where he had gone to, thinking of abductions and all the terrible things that could have taken him from them.

He also told the boy of the cost of the investigation for the time he was missing—not only money but concern and fear for the son both Mr and Mrs Warren loved. He was pleased that his words had some effect on the boy, with him saying that what was a joke for him had caused his family heartache. It had sobered the boy up, and they had left him thinking of what he had done.

James ended the story by saying Mrs Warren was going to the school at lunchtime to see her son and work things out. That was the end of their dealings with the missing boy.

Percy breathed a long sigh and said, 'I think I am getting old, not realising how grown-up youngsters can be nowadays. In my day, this would never have happened. At fourteen, they were still children, although they often finished school and started work when they were fifteen or sixteen. But back then, mothers did not go out to work, and spent more time with their families.'

'These are still children, Percy, not thinking of anyone else but themselves. Can you imagine how Tina's parents are going to feel when they hear this story? I think it is totally disrespectful of the two young ones, to their parents and their teachings of decency. I personally think they should be taken before a magistrate to be talked to about what terrible worry and concern this has caused Jon's mother. However, our part in the story has now finished. It is now up to Mr and Mrs Warren to talk with Tina's parents and work something out. I am glad to hand it back to them.'

'Good work, James, and you too, Kate. At least it is a happy ending.' Percy stopped for a moment to think and continued, 'Well, perhaps it is a happy ending, but I can see more worry ahead for the parents. You were right once again, Alicia. I bow to your superior knowledge. You had better make your phone call to Jack Whistler, James. I, for one, am very curious about it. I told the secretary you would ring at about this time.'

'Yes, Percy, I am curious as well. I hope he is not going to tell me Sahib is on the loose again. He is the nasty piece of work from the passport-smuggling scam we solved last year, we had arrested. I doubt it, because he must still be incarcerated for some time yet. Alicia does not need the worry, with all the other worries she has with her grandmother and the bookshop.'

'The only way to find out is to make the call, James. I will leave you to it,' Percy said, leaving the room.

James dialled the given number and asked for Jack Whistler, the liaison person with the police force in his previous occupation.

'Thanks for ringing back promptly, James. I have been asked by my boss to contact you about a job, if your partnership is interested.'

'I am willing to listen, Jack. What is it about?'

'There is to be a visit to the Isle of Wight by an Indian diplomat, although it is a private visit, not an official occasion. We have received a request by the Indian party to visit the island, as it seems the present person's great-grandfather came as a child with his father, who was entertained in an official capacity in the time of Queen Victoria and was gracefully received. He had taken many photographs and the present man's father is writing a book about his relative, with reference to that time, and wants to visit to get a feel for the place. It will be a private visit, nothing official about it. However, it is a problem for us, as we have a crisis with the whole police department on the island coming down with a bad case of the flu and therefore not able to monitor the visitors. We have a choice of sending down a crew from London or asking you and your team if you are interested in stepping in. I understand that you have two ex–police officers on your staff, so they would be knowledgeable on protocol for these occasions. Do you think you would be able to do this? We do not expect any trouble. It is really just having a presence when the party arrives.

'They are booked to travel on the Wednesday morning ferry this week and return on Friday. It would be a bit of a holiday for you and your wife. I remember she knows a little of the Indian way of life, so she could be helpful in watching out for them. We would include her time in the pay packet, of course, as a consultant.'

James laughed. 'I am not sure her knowledge goes that deep, Jack, although I will ask her opinion, as she is very good with people. I will have to ask her if she feels up to going. Can I ring you back after lunch to confirm all this? Her grandmother still needs care, so we will have to work around that. I will also have to ask my partner and employee if they are willing to do it also. We are a private firm and do not operate like the police force, where you are told where to go and have no choice in the matter. What do we need to know about accommodation, et cetera, what do you visualise as monitoring the visitors?'

'We have notified the local historians, and they are organising a high tea on Thursday, after Osborne House is closed to the public at 5 p.m. We have a historian showing them around the house and grounds before the high tea, including the Swiss house used by the royal children when they holidayed on the island. Luckily, this was recently restored to its original condition—it had grown into disrepair over the years—and is now open to the public. The group particularly wanted to see it, as the person the book is being written about was a child during the official visit and insisted a similar little house be constructed in his own gardens for him when he returned home. The historical society has gone all out to make it a good visit, up to even wearing clothes from the period of the official function.

'I suggest to you that you meet the party at the hotel they will be staying at, perhaps inviting them to tea on the first day—included in your expense account, of course. Offer your services if they need them, but do not necessarily tag around after them. This is a private visit by them, and the only other offering from us is the high tea at Osborne House. The rest of their time is up to them to arrange. Your presence on the island is really only as a replacement for our sick officers, so a casual visit at the house while they are visiting would be a good move. The visitors do not need to know of any other officers around the island. You will be in civvies anyway and will not stand out.

'Perhaps you could go through the house before the party arrives, to make sure it is safe. Your team could sit in another room and have tea at the same time, just as a precaution. I will leave it to your discretion as to how much time you put into it and what you see when you get there. I have one good fellow on our staff who knows the island. I will send him along in case you need to make an arrest. I will also send a companion with him. So with you and your two staff, it makes five to manage the three days, which should be enough.

'If there are major complications, which I cannot see happening, you will have to call the local fellows from their sickbeds to help out. From what I can gather, the worst part of their influenza is over, but it has left them feeling very weak. So unless it is an emergency you cannot control, you will be in charge, and the five of you will have to manage.'

'That all seems straightforward, Jack. I will get back to you about two o'clock, after I consult my partner and my staff member here and my wife. The only part I can see a problem with is closing down my office for three days. I will have to work something out for that. Okay, leave it with me for an hour or so.'

'Good man. The chief sends his regards. It was his idea to contact you on this. You certainly made an impression on him.'

'I am not sure what to say about that. Our partnership is working out well here, and I think we will be in front by the end of the year. There were expenses with setting up, but we have not been at a loss for work to do. We needed to take on another person to help out, as there was so much work offered to us. There is plenty to keep the three of us busy, and my wife helps out as our receptionist.'

'I am pleased it is working out for you. Okay, James, I will hear from you about two o'clock.'

James put the phone down and went to see Percy and Kate for a conference on visiting the Isle of Wight. They stated they had both been there many times, as they had been brought up in the area. It was only a ferry trip away, and it was a nice place to visit in summer; the weather should be fine Wednesday to the weekend. They both knew Osborne House; it had been Queen Victoria's holiday house in her day. It was one of the favourite places to visit when you were on holiday on the island.

They wondered about leaving the office unstaffed for so long. After some discussion, it was decided that James and the two London policemen could manage well enough on Wednesday. Kate and Percy would come to the island on Thursday, closing the office about midday to be there for the Osborne House viewing and high tea, and stay over for the early morning ferry back to the mainland on Friday.

James and Alicia would go on Wednesday, invite the visitors for afternoon tea, and on Thursday, attend the house showing and high tea, with the team in an adjacent room to the visitors, and escort them back to their hotel afterwards. They would stay on until the visitors went back to the mainland, and they would follow on the next ferry. At this stage, they did not know the timetable for the arrival and departure of the party by ferry.

Satisfied with that, James went with Alicia to tell her grandmother about the proposed working holiday and asked Granny if she would like to join them. Alicia liked the idea of showing James around the island. She knew it well from her childhood and had many summer holidays there.

Granny asked to be excused from the trip, saying she would mind the shop. She could manage until Friday evening with the help of Caroline, the girl they had taken on for part-time work when Alicia went to work at the investigation business. They all agreed that was a good idea, and Alicia and James would be back to help in the bookshop on Saturday.

James went back to the office and called Jack Whistler and relayed the timing of the team arrivals to him. It was agreed and bookings for the ferry and hotel would be made by Jack's office. He would arrange for the policemen to arrive so that James and Alicia will travel on the same ferry. They would arrange a hire car also, making it large enough for the six people to fit comfortably. James added that his partner would be bringing his own vehicle, as he could travel from home to the ferry and have the vehicle available if anything came up that would make him require transport while on the island.

'We have booked your party in to stay at the same hotel as the visitors. This way, Alicia may be able to pick up vibes from the party if they are unhappy about anything. The names of the two policemen are Sergeant Ken Johnson and Constable Josh Waters. Ken is the one who has been to the island and knows it well, so he will be the driver of the vehicle. They will hire the car and drive down to Portsmouth to meet you and take it on the car ferry so they have a vehicle when they land. Thanks for doing this job for us, James. We often have jobs in your area, and perhaps we can send a bit of work your way in the future.'

'Thanks, Jack, we will be happy to do anything at the moment. We have not turned anything away yet, but by the way things are going, we may look for a fourth person to help out soon. It never occurred to me before trying this job out how much work is available. I quite like doing the police work. There is usually a more interesting facet to it than finding people and doing insurance work, so I will look forward to anything you have to offer.'

'I will send you an email confirming all the dates and times and the names included in the Indian party and hotel bookings as soon as we have finished the arrangements. Good luck, James.'

2

licia was quite excited to be included on the Isle of Wight trip. It was some time since she had been there, and she had always loved the summer holidays she spent there as a child. She had learnt to swim in the ocean and played on the beaches while her grandmother sat knitting in a deckchair and watched her, chatting with mothers while their children played. It was a lovely period in her early life. Now she would be able to show James around, and felt thrilled by the thought of it.

She went through her clothes, decided on wearing to the high tea, the dress that she had bought for the opening-of-the-partnership cocktail party, and packed her bag. She wanted to look right; and was aware that the other ladies in the group would be wearing rich embroidered saris, and she did not want to look dull beside them.

Caroline was the person Granny chose to help her in the bookshop. She was a regular customer in the shop, and they liked each other; so when the thought had come up about having an extra person in the shop while Alicia was working in the investigations office, Caroline came to mind straight away. She was in her thirties; quite attractive, with blonde hair held back most days with a ribbon; and well dressed. She had stated to Granny that she would work the times her son was at school; wanting to help her friend, Valerie, out and thought it would be interesting in the bookshop. They eventually came to an agreement about the amount she would be paid. She would start at ten each morning and leave at three, as these were the busiest times. Alicia was very pleased with this arrangement, and going with James to the island made easier for her, with no need to worry about her grandmother while she was away.

The fax came through, with the ferry times and tickets for all of them to be picked up when boarding, and James and Alicia set off early for the Wednesday appointment so they would be in place when the Indian party arrived at the hotel.

They travelled by coach to Portsmouth, and on the way, Alicia said, 'It is so nice to get away from the office for a short while, and I love the Isle of Wight. You will like it too, I believe. At this time of year, it is a lovely holiday experience. I am looking forward to showing you around.'

James answered, 'You are right about getting out of the office and away from the city atmosphere. It is perfect weather to be holidaying in the sunshine, and it is always nice to go somewhere different. This sounds idyllic: sunny weather, lovely beaches. What more could we ask for? And our accommodation and meals paid for, as a bonus. Even this coach tour is comfortable, and we are seeing the countryside at its best as well.'

The coach pulled into the Portsmouth dock area, and as arranged, Ken and Josh, the two policemen, were at the dock when they arrived. They travelled together to the island on the ferry and to the hotel. Ken appeared to be about thirty-five years old, and Josh in his early twenties. James liked the two men on sight; they were a friendly couple, looking forward to the few days on the island. The hotel had been booked so that they could move straight into their rooms without any waiting time. James went to speak to the manager about lunch or afternoon tea, whichever the Indian guests preferred, to be served in the dining room.

When the Indian party arrived, amidst some flurry (as there were twenty people in the group, which included several young children), James and Alicia went down to meet them in the foyer before they went to their rooms. Crossing the floor from the lift, James said, 'Blow me down, if it isn't Stumper from Oxford!'

Alicia looked around and back at James and said, 'Which one is Stumper, and how did he get that name?'

'His name is Jameel, and he was on my cricket team at Oxford while we were at university there. He was a marvellous bowler and was clever at stumping players out, so he picked up the name after his first half dozen was stumped out. He was a merry chap who took congratulations well, knowing he had earned his reputation. He always smiled his white-toothed smile and said "Thanks, boys" each time he got someone out, as if it were the easiest thing in the world. He is the tall good-looking chap there with the small boy, who must be his son.' James went forward to meet Stumper and received a warm handshake and a hug.

'This is unexpected, James, but a pleasant surprise. What is your part in our welcome?'

'I have been requested to look after you in a friendly way by the police department, as their officers are recovering from influenza at the moment. My orders are to make sure you are comfortable and to invite you for lunch or afternoon tea today to get acquainted with the hotel and my staff of carers before you wander off into the wide blue yonder by yourselves to tour the island. I understand that you will be shown around Osborne House, where your great-grandfather attended a reception with Queen Victoria. It was her private holiday home, and she received a few people there while in residence in her later years. The house showing will happen on Thursday, followed by high tea in the residence, with the island heritage group attending wearing the fashion of that period when your great-grandfather was here for his official visit those many years ago.'

'I greatly appreciate your attention, James. Is it a coincidence that we know each other, or was it set up this way?'

'Pure coincidence, my friend. I run a private investigation company with a partner in one of the cities on the mainland, close to the island, and I was contacted because I was available. I am also known by the London police, in a friendly way, as a detective. I have worked for them previously.'

Jameel responded, 'You are a lawyer, aren't you? How did you get into the private investigation business?'

'It is a long story, Jameel. Perhaps we will have time to talk about it later on. Meanwhile, I am to invite you to lunch, if you would like it, or afternoon tea, if you would like to wait awhile. May I introduce my wife Alicia?' He held out his hand for Alicia to come forward.

16

The handsome Indian turned to Alicia and said, 'I am pleased to meet you, Alicia. I can see you have a happy marriage. He is a reasonable man, your husband. We had many happy celebrations after our cricket games. He was the batsman and I was the bowler and we managed to bamboozle the other teams comfortably.'

Alicia looked at her husband. 'You did not tell me you played cricket, James.'

'Only at university, Alicia. I have had no time for it since, and it does not look like I will be playing again.'

'That is a shame, James,' said Jameel. 'I always thought you would be batting for your country, and I looked at newspapers expecting to find you in the visiting teams.'

'No such luck, Jameel. There was always someone better than me!'

Jameel looked past him and said, 'Here are my wife and son, James. Meet my wife, Indira, and my son, another Jameel. He is going to be a bowler as well, by what I see in the garden when he plays with his friends, but he is a bit young yet to be trained up.'

Indira shook the couple's hands, looked at Alicia and saw an attractive, self-assured young woman, and an immediate friendship was struck up.

'We want to know if you would like to have lunch with us now or would like to join us for afternoon tea. We have to advise the manager of the hotel, and he is waiting on us for a decision. What do you think, Indira?' James asked.

'I think afternoon tea at about three o'clock would be better. We had a big breakfast and have been nibbling ever since, and I think your mother, Jameel, would like a rest. She is looking a bit peaky after the ferry trip. It was not rough, but she imagines all sorts of horrors as soon as she steps on to any boat, especially a ferry.'

'That is a good decision. We will move off and allow you to rest in your rooms, and we will see you down here in the dining room at three o'clock.' James and Alicia moved to where the manager of the hotel was waiting patiently, and the visitors moved to the lifts to go to their rooms.

The manager was pleased the decision was for afternoon tea. It was nearing the lunch hour, and a group of twenty extras would be a bit hurried; his relief showed that a more leisurely afternoon tea would be immensely better for all concerned.

As James and Alicia moved away from the group, Alicia said, 'They are such a handsome couple, James. How well did you know Jameel previously?'

'He was in my cricket team, and we met up for practice twice a week in summer and played the matches together. This usually was followed by drinks in the bar and a meal. During the winter months, the team practised indoors so that we kept up with our fitness schedule. I knew him for the years we were at university. It was a good friendship. He is a nice fellow and is easy to talk to. He was a little quiet at the beginning but grew out of that quickly in the friendly atmosphere of the cricket club. It must have been very strange for him when he first arrived, but he soon became one of the chaps. After all, we were all mainly from somewhere else and settling in, and after a while, he was like everyone else there. I do remember the forays we made into the town to find Indian restaurants, where we allowed him to choose from the menus. We did have some great times together.' James smiled at the recollection of happy days and friendships.

James and Alicia went for a drive around the island with the two policemen to see the sights, and they arrived back in time to dress for afternoon tea. James told the two men that they were free for a couple of hours and that they need not come to the afternoon tea, because he knew one of the main visitors from his university days and did not expect anything out of the ordinary to happen. He said he would appreciate it if they turned up for dinner at 7 p.m. as a precaution, but he did not expect anything to upset the party; the four of them would sit at the dinner table together.

James told them that they would have to take turns being on duty during the night, each alternating a turn sitting in the foyer in case anything was needed, with Alicia excepted, of course. They could read or drowse during this time, but no liquor could be consumed. The others agreed to this, saying it was fair, as each one would get adequate rest in between.

James volunteered to do the first shift, from the end of dinner till midnight, and then Ken would do midnight until 4 a.m. and Josh the rest of the night until 8 a.m., when they would meet for breakfast. Josh could go back to sleep in the morning, and Ken could take James to Osborne House to check the grounds and get their bearings and come back for lunch. They would all be on duty for the afternoon foray, with the visitors going to the house with their heritage hosts, and James and the policemen going earlier to make sure everything was as it should be. Percy and Kate would have arrived by this time; they were expected at about two in the afternoon and would join them at Osborne House. Percy had his own vehicle, which would be an asset if something untoward should happen.

Each of them agreed to this plan. The policemen seemed to be enjoying their mini holiday. Josh had not been to the island previous and he admired the huge cliffs and the beaches and the yachts sailing off the Cowes shoreline, saying it was like a picture postcard. The day was sunny and warm, and everything looked shiny in the sunlight. It was a lovely day to be at the seaside, they all agreed.

Jameel asked James and Alicia to sit at their table for afternoon tea after introducing them to the rest of the party, which included his mother and his father, who was the person writing the book. The rest of the party was made up of Jameel's sister and her husband, his younger brother and his wife, and two cousins and their wives, who had never travelled overseas. Each couple had a servant and at least one child, making up a party of twenty altogether.

James felt a little overwhelmed, with so much chattering amongst the crowd of visitors. The family sat at the tables nearest to Jameel, and the servants sat with the children at a little distance. All seemed to be talking at once in what Alicia said was Hindi, an Indian language.

Indira heard Alicia say this to James and asked how she recognised the language. Alicia then told of her monthly trips to Mumbai as a flight attendant for approximately two years, saying she had picked up a love for the food and the lovely silks available in the markets and the smells in the spice market. She learnt a smattering of Urdu and Hindi because she had a knack for languages and could use it in the marketplaces.

Indira and Alicia went on chatting—they were much the same age and felt friendly as soon as they met—leaving James and Jameel to chat about their previous school days at Oxford University and what they had been doing since leaving it behind them.

James told of the passport mystery he had solved, wherein an Anglo/Indian, generally called Sahib, his code name, engineered the stealing of passports and jewellery from the homes of Indian/English citizens and used the passports to illegally substitute others' photographs on them and sell them for illegal entry into England. Jameel was very interested in the story, saying he was now in the diplomatic service at home. He had nothing to do with immigration but met with officials often to discuss these types of stories circulating.

He could now report back that it was a true story and that the offender was locked up on the British side. He would check what had been done on the Indian side and send back a report to James. They exchanged addresses and phone numbers, with Jameel saying it would be good to stay in touch, especially since their wives seemed to have made a connection. He nodded at Alicia and Indira chatting comfortably together.

James laughed. 'Yes, Alicia seems to be able to make friends wherever she goes. She is a happy soul, and people are attracted to her.'

'Indira was shy when we first met but has come out of her shell since our son was born. I am glad she has made friends with your Alicia so quickly. She usually stands back a little until I nudge her forward, and this time she has done it herself.'

'That is a good sign. Now that she has done it, it will be easier for her in the future. She is a beautiful girl, Jameel. You have done well to win a lovely wife and have a son to be proud of.' James turned to Jameel's father and said, 'Have you started writing your book, sir, or is it still in the preparation stage?'

'It is well into the preparation stage. I have all the facts in order and boxes of photographs to choose from. I retired from public service twelve months ago, and I have had this book in mind for many years. I came across a box of photographs, many featuring Osborne House and this island, when we were cleaning out my father's rooms, and that made up my mind to write his memoirs. He died several years ago at the age of ninety-eight, a fair innings. He was in the diplomat service, as was his father, and now Jameel.

'It was the photographs of Osborne House that captivated me when I looked through the box. My grandfather was only a child of about seven or eight at the time he visited here with his parents, but he was obviously taken with the place, the beachside, and the sea. Where we live is a long way from the ocean, so when he saw the children playing on the beach and swimming, he was obviously intrigued.

'He also loved the idea of the royal children's playhouse, the Swiss chalet here, and he took many photographs from all angles and wanted a similar house built in our familial home grounds. His father capitulated and built the little house for him, which, I might add, is still also standing today, built to his specifications from all the photos.

'I also have played in that house. We did not have the seaside joys, but the chalet was built on a lakeside at our family home. As children, we swam in the lake and also fished for our supper, so we enjoyed it immensely. It was a wonderful childhood that many would only dream of. I was overcome when I unearthed those photographs, and I talked my son into bringing us here to see it in the flesh, so to speak, so I could write the story with the joy of my grandfather's feelings included.'

James smiled at the other man's story. 'It is a lovely story, sir. I hope you will not be disappointed. You have your own grandchildren here with you to help bring back those memories, and the story should be an easy one to write. The children's chalet has been in disrepair for many years and has only recently been renovated and opened to the public, so you are lucky. I have been told it is as it was when the royal children played here, although I personally will be seeing it for the first time tomorrow. I have only read reports of it until now.

'The house was used as a convalescent home for war-injured officers in the military during and after the world wars and has not been a royal residence since Queen Victoria died. She died here in the house, and her funeral procession went from it to Windsor. Her son donated the house to the state as a naval training college after her death. I believe the main rooms are still kept up as they had been when your grandfather visited, although most of the rear rooms have been modified to fit the officers' accommodation into the space.

'The gardens and the outside of the building are much the same. Also, the beach areas would have remained the same, so you should get a good idea of what fascinated your grandfather as a child, although by the time he came, there would have no longer been any royal children to play with. They would have been grown up and married and would have gone to fulfil their destinies in other parts of the world.'

'You do not come from this part of Britain, James?' asked the older man.

'No, sir, I grew up close to London and moved to Oxford to attend university, where I met Jameel. I worked in London for several years after my university days and then moved south with my wife, who comes from a close-by city. Her grandmother was involved in an accident and has become a semi-invalid, which we hope will pass in time. However, she needs our help, so we stayed.

'The idea to become a private investigator was impressed on me by a friend when I left London to come to be with my wife and her grandmother, and it appears I will be staying for many years, as our business is growing every day. It was my association with the London police which earned me this interval of keeping you safe and happy.'

'We appreciate your help, James. My son, Jameel, has spoken highly of you from the time you were in Oxford together. I was pleased to meet you after he told me of your exploits together. It is a real pleasure to know you. It is difficult for foreign students to settle when they come to your country, and your friendship meant a lot to Jameel at the time.'

'Thank you, sir. We were a good team when we played cricket together, and the friendship remains between us.'

'So he told me. Perhaps you will appear in his book when he writes his own story.'

'Most certainly, sir. We had some good times together, as young men do. However, most of us have to separate and go about the business of earning a living and raising a family, so we lost touch. But Jameel now has my address, and I have his. If our paths cross again, we can make contact.'

While this conversation was taking place, Alicia was asking Jameel's mother why she was so troubled by ferry trips; she had appeared quite distraught when she arrived at the hotel.

The older woman hesitated a moment. 'This is not something I talk about often, because it is so upsetting to my family. It stems from when I was a girl attending college. Each day I went by ferry from one side to the other of the Ganges River, to and from school. One afternoon, after school was over for the day, I was waiting in line for the next ferry to arrive, as we had run to catch the four o'clock ferry but missed it. Standing on the jetty, we, mostly schoolchildren, watched as the outgoing ferry, the one we had missed by inches, was struck midstream by another boat travelling swiftly up the river and not watching what they were doing. We all saw the ferry go down with everyone on board, many of our school friends amongst them.

'It was very traumatic for us. It could have been us on board. We had only missed it by a short distance, and a lot of our friends died that day. This picture comes back to me each time I see a ferry crowded with people, and I am afraid I still go to pieces all over again all these years later.'

Alicia saw that Jameel's mother could still see it happening all these years later, and she said, 'That is terrible. I can see why you do not like to travel on ferries. No one would forget a thing like that! Did you continue to travel to school by ferry after that?'

'No, my parents were horrified by the tragedy and changed my school so that I did not have to cross the river. It was not such a prestigious school we changed to, but I was happy not to have to travel by ferry again. I now try my best to avoid such means of travel if I can. My husband did not think to tell me there would be a ferry in our itinerary on this trip.'

'Perhaps he forgot to mention it. It is only a twenty-minute ride, and our waterways are well monitored. You will have to travel back the same way, so try not to think about it. Do not look out of the boat. Chat with someone. Holding a child may help. Their chatter will take your mind from it.' Alicia felt very sympathetic for the older woman and wanted to help her.

'Thank you for your kindness, Alicia. I will have to try that. I know in my mind that it is not likely for another accident to happen. I will have to try hard to overcome my fears. It was a long time ago, but it is something not easily forgotten. It seems to be stuck in my memory, and each time I see a ferry, I relive it. My husband is usually kind enough to not take ferry rides when I am with him, and I think it is only that this particular journey has caught his imagination and caused him to forget my fears.'

'I can fully understand your problem. I am sure I would also still think of it each time I was on a ferry, but I have been on these same ferries many, many times and have not had an accident yet. I am sure you will be safe. If you are really sure you do not want to go on the ferry, there is an airport, mostly with small aircraft flights. You would have to separate from your family to fly. Perhaps you could go with your husband and pick up the rest of your party in Bournemouth.'

'You are a sweet girl, Alicia. I do not want to disrupt my family with my horrors. I do not speak to my grandchildren of the sunken river ferry and my friends who died that day, as I do not want them to be frightened too. I will take your advice and hold one of my grandchildren on the return voyage. I am aware how much this visit means to my husband, so I will try my best not to upset the applecart by making a fuss.'

It was a very congenial atmosphere, and it was the children who broke it up, saying they wanted to go to the beach again. The party moved off in their hired vehicles, leaving Alicia and James to have a rest before dinner. James wondered if the policeman, Jack Whistler, had known of the association between Jameel and him. It seemed too much of a coincidence to him that his friend from Oxford was the visitor he had been asked to accompany!

3

During dinner that evening, the police party table was abuzz with the fact that James was a school friend of Jameel. They had not been told anything about the Indian party by Jack Whistler, but they agreed that it was too much to believe that the chance of them being old friends and meeting was a coincidence.

After dinner, James went to his position in the foyer, and the evening passed quietly. Sitting in the foyer, trying to concentrate on the book he carried with him for his vigil, his mind went once again to the 'coincidence' of meeting Jameel, and he decided that it was not a coincidence after all. The London officers wanted him to bring up the Sahib story with the diplomat, to find out what was happening on the Indian side of the stolen-passports case. Yes! He decided he was right about this. He took out his mobile phone and sent an email to Jack Whistler:

> *Please send the report of the Sahib case to me by fax to this hotel prior to early Friday morning when the party leaves the Isle of Wight.*

He knew that Jack Whistler would know what he meant.

* * *

Early next morning, James asked Ken to drive him to the local police station. The police sergeant on duty greeted them and said that he knew of James's presence on the island and that the local police force had been stood down for James to take their place monitoring the Indian party. James asked if a flu epidemic had passed through the police station recently. The policeman looked at him oddly and said, 'Yes, they had the flu a couple of weeks ago, but everyone is better now. Thank you for your enquiry.' Ken and James looked at each other, and Ken said to the man behind the desk, 'May we have a private number for the person on duty this afternoon in case we have to contact you, please?'

The man on duty wrote out a number on a card and handed it to Ken, who had previously identified himself with his badge. When they left the station, they stood and looked at each other, and James said, 'It appears I have been set up.'

'It does look that way, James, but believe me, I was not aware of it. No one mentioned anything but what you already know. It seems it was left to you to make your own decisions on what to do.'

'It is okay, Ken. I know now what it is all about, and I should find a fax for me at the hotel when we get back. It is about an old case where I ran up against a smuggling gang between India and Britain. I believe that your superiors want me to pass the information I know on to my friend, Jameel, who is in the diplomat service in India. This is an unofficial way to get the information to him. I sent an email last night asking for a copy of the case, and I guess I am right to expect an answer this morning. By doing things this way, we are not making an official request. It is to be only a conversation between friends. Clever people, your superiors.

'Someone must have looked Jameel up when they knew he was coming to the Isle of Wight. There was no need for us to welcome him. It is a private visit for his family, and I wondered why we were called in. They obviously talked it over and saw that Jameel had attended Oxford University. After all, he had spent several years in Oxford, and it would have shown on his passport. When they saw that information, they tied it up with me attending the university during the same period and guessed we knew each other, hence their roundabout method of passing on information. I am sure they have guessed that I have already mentioned it to Jameel.

'I have worked with your boss previously, so I presume they now think they own me. Okay, we will do what they want me to do. I will just make sure they pay my bill when I send it, but I cannot press Jameel to investigate the case when he returns home. There is a limit to friendship.'

Ken nodded. 'It is an ingenious way to get you to do something for them. As you say, there will be no record of a request for information except an email and a fax message to you, which will go unnoticed in the records. They must know you well, James. How have you gone against them in the past?'

James did not look worried. 'I worked in another government department for several years scouting jobs, which I handed to Jack Whistler with the answers and usually a conviction for their records. They did offer me a job in their department. However, I needed to move to the south coast for personal reasons, and I turned them down. I have been working as a private investigator for several months now and find I enjoy the diversity. Some jobs are a little dull, I have to admit, but I like that I have a choice of which jobs to take.'

'I think it is most policemen's dream to act as a private investigator. As you say, we do not have a choice of which jobs we do in the force,' said Ken.

James looked at Ken and said, 'Would you be interested if I invited you to join us sometime in the future?'

'I am no longer married. My wife left two years ago, tired of being a policeman's wife and the hours we have to work. She said I was never there for her. I do not have to ask anyone's permission nowadays. I do love it here on the South Coast. I love to sail. I never get enough time off in London to sail and fish as my father did and enjoyed and I always vowed I would do that someday. Yes, I think I would like that, James.'

'I will keep your phone number, Ken, and if we decide to expand, I will give you a call. I like the cut of your jib, as they say in sailing terms. It will not be for a while, as we have only been operating for less than six months, but the work keeps coming in.

'We started out as a partnership. You will meet my partner Percy Gray tomorrow. He is a retired police detective, it was his dream, and he talked me into it. My wife, Alicia, is our receptionist and consultant, so we are somewhat a family affair. We have since taken on another ex-policewoman, Kate Langford. She will also be here tomorrow. I can see a time in the not-too-distant future when we may need to expand and take on another person. I may be out of line speaking to you like this so early in our business, but things are certainly moving for us. The three of us are flat out keeping up.'

'It sounds good, James. I will give it some thought so that when you contact me, I will have an answer ready for you, one way or another.'

They continued on their way to look around the grounds at Osborne House but found nothing untoward. There were gardeners working on the flower beds, and they told the pair that they would finish up at three o'clock, as they started early in the morning. Everything looked peaceful, so they returned to the hotel in time for lunch. James was right about the fax; it was handed to him along with his room key when he enquired.

Josh was ready for lunch, so once again, the four of them sat at the same table and chatted amongst themselves. They gave a wave to Jameel and Indira when they came to the dining room as James and his party were moving out. When he passed his friend, James said that he would see them later at Osborne House for viewing and high tea.

James told his team that he would meet them in the foyer at 3.30 p.m., because 4 was the time the heritage group would pick up their visitors; James and his party would go ahead to check the house out prior to the Indian party getting there. Alicia was going with the Indian party, in case of any emergency amongst the women or children, as she had a calming effect on people. James said it was her airline experience coming to the fore. Whenever there was a crowd of people, she always managed to look like she was in charge, and people followed her example.

Because there would be other tourists viewing the house and grounds until five o'clock, James thought it a good idea if she kept the Indian party in sight until the other tourists left, only leaving their party to have the organised high tea in the Durbar Room. This was the beautiful room where Queen Victoria entertained visitors, and it was unchanged from her time there.

They were aware that the heritage group was expecting them, and they had set up a table in the alcove adjoining the Durbar Room for the police party. They would be able to see their visitors from there but would not hear them unless a clatter was made. Alicia was impressed by the organisation. She had only been there until five o'clock on previous visits, and usually on the weekends, when they had jugglers and food stalls and other acts set up on the grounds. It had always been fun for her to visit.

When the high teas were ready to be served, Jameel asked James and Alicia and the rest of his group to sit at the table with them, leaving the servants and children to take the anteroom table. Jameel explained, 'The servants are uncomfortable sitting at the main table with us, and the children usually play this time of evening. Their amahs will have more control over them at the smaller table.'

He added, 'It is such a pleasure to see you again, James, and to meet Alicia. I would much rather sit at the table with you than a squirming bunch of children. Your group of officers is welcome also, and as your masters are paying, let's enjoy each other's company!' He introduced the police party to his family and explained his association with James to his family members.

By this time, Percy and Kate had arrived and joined the group, and Percy said quietly to James, 'You will never be able to surprise me again after this tea party. Did you know Jameel at university, James? It looks as if you have been set up by your high-placed police friend.'

'That is the conclusion I have come to also, Percy. Ten points for picking it up so quickly. It took me a day to work it out for myself. I think the surprise of it slowed me down considerably,' James said with a laugh.

They enjoyed the company and the tea, with everybody saying what a wonderful experience the Durbar Room was and how special it was to be dining there. You could still feel the majesty that the room held.

As they were packing up, Jameel said to James, 'Do you still want me to look into your Sahib affair, my friend?'

'As long as you do not put yourself in danger, Jameel, I would appreciate it. When we get back to the hotel, I will leave the folder of the case at reception for you. Keep in mind that we consider the leaders of this gang dangerous, so watch what you say and to whom you say it. I would hate to think I have set you up in any danger. I have always enjoyed your company, and my employers have seen fit to give us this time to catch up, for which I am grateful. I hope to see you again next time you visit the UK, Jameel, and Indira too. It looks like your wife and Alicia also enjoy each other's company.'

'I have never seen Indira get so friendly with someone so quickly. I am sure this will be an ongoing friendship, and we will see you again sometime in the future.' The two men shook hands as they parted.

4

When they reached the hotel, Percy and Kate were shown to their rooms, but first Percy said to James, 'Could we have a drink in the bar? I have something to relate to you. Also, Alicia needs to come, as it involves you both. I will ask Kate to come also, as she knows what I am going to say and Alicia may feel better with her company.'

James was alarmed. 'Is it her grandmother, Percy? Is she all right?'

'Nothing like that, James. Valerie is fine, although a little confused at the moment. Bring Alicia, and we will tell you a story.'

The four friends adjourned to the bar and sat down at a table. Percy ordered drinks all round before starting the story he had to tell.

'Come on, Percy! What is it you have to tell us? You are making me anxious!' Alicia looked concerned, thinking her grandmother may have had another fall.

'Your grandmother is fine, Alicia. There is nothing to worry about in that direction. You both must remember the woman who spoke to Alicia in the shopping mall? Well, she came into the office yesterday morning, about eleven o'clock. She asked for you, James, and was very disappointed you were not there. Her name is Sandra Dunstan, and she said she had been to see Valerie, expecting to speak to Alicia. Valerie explained that Alicia was on the Isle of Wight, having a holiday for a few days. Sandra said she had left her daughter with Alicia's grandmother and said she wanted to explain to you what it was all about. When I told her that you were away with Alicia until Friday, she burst into tears. She said she could not wait until Friday, so she told me why.

'Sandra Jenson, which is her maiden name and the name Alicia knew her by, is married to Aaron Dunstan. Both of them took drugs socially only, dating from early in their acquaintance, but it became worse after a car accident that occurred while Sandra was pregnant with Jody. The airbag had exploded, pinning her in the car, and it had injured her back because she had leaned forward to protect the eight-month baby in her womb. She had been cut from the vehicle and rushed to the hospital for the baby's delivery. Aaron too was injured when his head hit the driving wheel. He had broken two vertebrae in his neck, and he also had whiplash. He was never the same again afterwards, often being laid low because of headaches caused by the accident. Sandra was in a lot of pain from her back after she was allowed to go home from the hospital.

'During her stay there, she had been given morphine for her pain. Aaron also took drugs for his headaches. Previously they had only used drugs in social environments, but after the accident, they were given prescription drugs to ease the pain they both had, which became addictive. For the past year, they had tried taking methamphetamine, as it was easier to buy locally, but they decided it was too drastic and stopped taking them and stayed on prescription pills.

'Aaron had not been working, and their income was low. Over time, he started getting nervous that they could not afford the drugs, so he suggested she have sex with strangers for money. She heard a man called Bull and Aaron talking. She heard Bull say he was not very interested in sex, but he wanted the little girl for photographs. Sandra then told us that her daughter is four years old.

'This Bull had taken to calling in to see them often over a period of a few weeks. He had been a part of the group in their youth and had tagged around with them but had not been seen for some time. He saw Sandra and Jody in the shopping mall one day and followed them home. After that day, he would turn up at their home without invitation quite often, becoming a nuisance to them.

'At first Aaron would not accept Bull's request for the child, but Bull said he only wanted to take her photos so he could look at her photograph when she was not there. He would pay £500 for the use of her for a weekend, and they would get her back intact. Sandra said she heard interest in her husband's voice and got frightened of what would happen to her little girl. It was bad enough that her husband had suggested she have sex with strangers, but to involve the child was frightening for her. This is why she has been hanging around our office after recognising Alicia and realising she works at our office. Alicia had told her it was her husband's business place.

'She said if she went to the police, her child would be taken off her and put into care. As a child, Sandra's father had beaten her mother over a drinking problem they both had. She herself was put into care by the authorities and hated it. She was beaten every day and ran away when the man of the house started to fondle her, even though she was only eleven at the time. Not wanting this to happen to her daughter, she was looking for a place where someone could look after the child, Jody, while she went into a rehabilitation clinic to get off the drugs.

'Poor girl, she looked desperate. I asked her what she wanted us to do for her. She had left her daughter—Jody is her name—with Valerie, telling her that she had spoken to Alicia, who agreed to look after Jody until she came back from the clinic, maybe in three months, maybe six months. She was not sure, as she had not tried previously to keep away from the drugs, needing them for the pain in her back. This was the story told to Valerie, although it was not all true, as Sandra had not asked Alicia about looking after Jody.

'We took all this down on tape while Sandra was talking, and Kate typed it up and got her to sign it before we let her out of the office. We asked what she was going to do now that she had left Jody with Mrs Newton. Her reply was that she was going to get on a train and go to a clinic. Sandra had been waiting for a place to come up, and they had rung her that morning and could not afford to let the place go to someone else, which would happen if she did not go that day. She seemed very agitated and in a hurry to get away and seemed to know where she was going. I guess she must have known there are clinics in the bigger cities around here and also in London, but did not say which one she was going to and was gone from our office and was up the street towards the train station before we had a chance to say anything more.

'We decided not to ring you, because we could not do anything about it. Sandra had already left Jody with Valerie, and we did not know where she was headed. It all happened so fast, so we decided it would be better to tell you in person today. I went to see Valerie after we closed the office last night, and as I said earlier, she was a little confused because Alicia had not said anything to her about having the child. Jody is a quiet little girl, and she sat and looked at picture books most of the day and coloured in other books she had brought with her. Valerie has made up Alicia's old room in her house for Jody, and they seem to have accepted each other. Jody fits right in.

'Your grandmother is some lady, Alicia. Sandra had told her some of her story, so Valerie was working on how to change the looks of Jody in case her father came looking for her. She already decided on a haircut and perhaps some hair colour. Jody is a child who wears only jeans and T-shirts, so Valerie is planning on buying her some pretty little dresses and ribbons for her hair. Don't be surprised, Alicia, if you see a lookalike child copying your childhood looks by the time you get home. I think your grandmother is enjoying her role as a great-grandmother already!'

Alicia and James looked at each other, appalled, but then Alicia shrugged. 'She did seem like a quiet child when I saw her in the shopping mall. What can we do about it? Sandra is right, because if we call the police, they will hand the child back to her father. Goodness knows what hell awaits her there. The other thing they might do is put her into care somewhere, and it could be what Sandra thinks of it—another sort of hell. We can keep Jody. We do not know what this Aaron Dunstan looks like, he could be one of the customers in the bookshop, for all we know. So if he does come looking for her, we should change her appearance.'

'You sound philosophical about it, Alicia. Have you accepted the child already?' asked Percy.

'What choice do we have, Percy? It has already happened. I will not hand her to her father. That would be criminal on my behalf. I could take her to the police and tell them the story, but why haven't you done that? You were a policeman, and Kate also came from the police force. You know what happens to children and the proportion of them who are abused in their foster homes.

'Let us give Sandra the six months she needs to get her life back and come for Jody. Jody is a child that seems to be self-sufficient. She would need to be, brought up by two drug-addicted parents. I would say she dresses herself and gets her own meals sometimes when her parents are under the spell of the drugs, and she probably does some of the housework as well. I will wait until we return and see for myself what kind of child she is. What do you think, James?'

'Like you, I cannot hand her back to her father, knowing what he intends for her with Bull. As to foster homes, they are not all bad. You have to be unlucky to draw a bad one. I do know one or two children from my school days who were in care, and they seemed normal. If you, Alicia, are prepared to look after Jody until her mother returns, it is okay with me. As Percy said, your grandmother seems to have accepted the situation already. We will talk it over with Granny when we get home tomorrow and see what she has to say about it. You have been quiet about it, Kate. What do you think of it all?'

'I think Sandra may find she will need a bit longer than six months for rehabilitation. She seemed to be a real druggy to me, and I think she has been taking drugs for years, by the look of her. She has been through some tough times. Although she is the same age as Alicia, she looks years older than her. It is not easy to get over an addiction. We have seen many like her, haven't we, Percy? They are clean for a little while, and then something upsets them and they slip back into the drugs scene again.

'Sandra has had a shock, with her husband willing to sell Jody to this Bull person. This may be the thing that is keeping her focused. I personally think the child would be better off in a foster home. She would have a chance there, but staying with her parents, she has no chance at all. By not reporting it, you are just letting Aaron Dunstan and Bull off the hook. They should go down for child pornography at least!'

Alicia and James both looked defeated, and James said, 'What do you think, Percy? Should we report it to the authorities?'

'Yes, James, I agree with Kate. You are taking on Sandra's problems, which are of her own making. Having the child for six months is only going to make it a harder decision when she returns. You may not want to hand the child over on her return. And Kate is also right about the child pornography. We have to find this Bull person and hand him over to the police.

'I think you should take it to the police and make out a custody authorisation for Jody. If this is long-term, you may be able to manoeuvre Sandra in some way to let you keep Jody and give Sandra rights to see her from time to time. That means that the child will be safer altogether. Also, as for telling the police about the father, we can take Sandra's word on that. We have it in writing, and she has signed it. That will put the father out of the picture to getting custody of her.'

James sighed. 'Well then, that is the decision. We will go to the police when we return with Sandra's signed form and tell them about how we want to have custody of Jody long-term to protect her, deciding whether to hand her back to her mother if she reforms.

'The main point here is to pick up Aaron Dunstan and Bull, whoever he is—he is obviously a paedophile—and to get them both locked up so they cannot do any more harm. I bet this Bull has a computer full of child pornography. Once we find him, it will be an open-and-shut case for him! I am not sure what they will do to Aaron Dunstan. He has not done anything wrong yet, except being on drugs. They are prescription drugs, and it is only his wife's word that he wanted to sell the services of the small child.'

Percy nodded. 'I think that is the best decision, James. It is not a nice scenario, but we have to think of the child. Sandra has become a victim, but she made those decisions herself. She has not tried to remove herself from her situation till now. The child must be the prime consideration on the whole thing, and we shall all try hard to get you the authority to look after her, if that is what you want. With both Kate and myself standing up for you, we should manage to do that, but ultimately, it is up to the child welfare people.'

'Thank you, Percy. I can see you are right, and if we do not do something about getting Jody in a happy environment I can see more trouble ahead for her. At least while we have her in our care until Sandra reforms, we know she will be safe. I note your mention that drugs may play a part in the long term for Sandra. I think you are right, and we should ask for long-term care of Jody, allowing her mother visiting rights when she cleans up her act.'

Alicia said, 'It makes me want to cry when I think of what that man Bull wants her for. There are some selfish and terrible people around. To do that to a small child is unthinkable.'

'At least Jody is safe with your grandmother Alicia. All her mothering instincts came out immediately when she saw Jody. I think Jody is in love with her already. When we saw her, she was holding your grandmother's hand and looked quite happy to be there.' Percy smiled at the recollection.

'We will be home by midday tomorrow. Jameel and his family will be on the nine o'clock ferry, so we will be on the next one. That will fulfil my duty of care, as requested by Jack Whistler.' James sighed. 'I will write up my report to him while I am on the ferry, to finish that obligation, and send it off as an email as soon as we get back to the office. I have done what they asked and what they did not ask but expected, so that is the end of it for me.'

'So now you are expected to be a mind reader, James! That puts you in a bad position, having to ask Jameel for his help. I think it unfair of headquarters to put you up to it.'

'Ahh, but they did not put me up to it, Percy. There was no mention of it anywhere. It was only a conversation between friends. However, it was good to see Jameel again and to meet his wife and his parents, even his extended family. We enjoyed their company, and I think they reciprocated. Don't you think so, Alicia?'

'Most certainly, James. Indira and I got on like a house on fire. I think we have made friendships that will last.'

'See, Percy, friendship was what it was about,' James said with a grin.

*   *   *

The following morning, James watched as Jameel, his family, and his servants left the hotel for the ferry. Alicia, James, and the two policemen then left the hotel and went for a last look around the island before arriving at the car ferry, where they were booked for the 10 a.m. departure. They eventually arrived home around midday, walking the last few minutes from the ferry to the bookshop.

As they went through the door of the shop, Alicia's grandmother came to meet them, holding the hand of the little girl Alicia had seen in the shopping mall with Sandra. Her grandmother said to the child, 'Say hello to your new mummy and daddy, Jody.'

Alicia looked at the little girl, now dressed in a flowery dress and with ringlets in her hair. In Alicia's eyes, Jody looked completely different from the child she had seen with Sandra. She said to her granny, 'Let's have a cup of tea in the nook, and I will talk to Jody about things. James has to go back to his office. He will pick up the papers her mother signed, and we will make an appointment to see the child welfare department people. Percy was going to make an appointment for us when he arrived this morning. Kate and Percy arrived back on the early ferry, but we had to wait until the Indian party left before we took the next ferry. Has everything been okay until now?'

'Yes, Alicia. Jody and I are getting on well with each other. She likes her dress. She told me she has not had a dress before, only jeans and T-shirts. I think she looks lovely in that dress, don't you?'

'She certainly does, Granny. You do look lovely, Jody. Dresses suit you. We are going to hide you with us for a little while until your real mummy comes for you when she comes out of hospital. Everybody will think you are our little girl. You have blue eyes like your new daddy and you are tall like him, so people will think you are our little girl. You are going to stay with us for quite a long time until your real mummy is better. First of all, we have to go and see some people to get a paper that says you can stay with us. We will do that this afternoon and see if it is all right. Are you happy to be here with Granny?'

Jody nodded. 'I love Granny. She is so nice to me, and she talks to me. Where we lived before, there was no one to talk to except my real mummy. She used to sleep a lot, so I had to play by myself,' said the little girl.

'You may have to play by yourself, Jody, but there will always be someone here looking after you. We will take you to school in the New Year. You will love that. I always liked school. There are other children to play with, and you will learn to read and write and do lots of interesting things.' Alicia smiled at Jody.

The child took her hand and said, 'Thank you, Mummy. I would like to go to school.'

'Good girl, Jody. You have learnt to call me mummy already. That is very clever of you! I can see we are going to enjoy having you with us.'

Caroline came over to them and greeted Alicia and took the little girl's hand and said, 'Come, Jody, we will read a book together.' She took the child to the children's section of the store.

Alicia and her grandmother looked at each other and smiled. 'That is the first hurdle over' said Alicia.

'You seem to have decided to keep her then, Alicia. Is James also compliant?'

'When we heard the story from Kate and Percy, We agreed that we would keep her as long as possible. It is really up to the child welfare people to agree. Poor child, she must have had an awful upbringing up to now. We are going to try to adopt her if we are able, for her safety. We both agree that we cannot let Jody go back to her parents. A future with them would be short anyway, once the child welfare people hear the story and what her father had planned for her. Even if Sandra comes off the drugs, we all agree that the welfare people will be on her case. We think they will not allow Jody to live with her again because Sandra has been on drugs for so long now, and her chances of going back to them are great. She will probably only be granted visiting rights from now on when she returns.'

Granny nodded. 'It is amazing that the welfare people have not picked up on it so far. Sandra must have kept her daughter a secret. Usually someone would report it. I think next year, when Jody starts school, someone will come to visit. You cannot keep a child locked up permanently.'

James asked if Alicia could attend the child welfare appointment, saying that Jody also had to attend so that the welfare people could assess her. They would also be visiting the house where she would be living, perhaps today or tomorrow. Alicia had expected this, so she was not too worried about an assessment. The fact that the mother of the child had left her there spoke volumes for her future care, according to the person James had spoken with on the phone.

* * *

Percy and Kate had taken the paper that Sandra signed to the police department, and an order had gone out to bring Aaron Dunstan in for questioning. As they had no idea who Bull was, they first had to question Dunstan about him and where to find him.

When he was brought into the station, the team looked through the windows of the interview room, out of his view so that he would not recognise them.

When Dunstan was interviewed, he gave his employment as a freelance journalist who worked from home and travelled for jobs. This surprised James, although Alicia said when she saw him that she remembered him as a dapper young man about town in the days before she left town. He was always with the crowd around Sandra in those days. He did not appear so dapper now and denied all that Sandra had said in her litany to Percy and Kate. He looked guilty when it was mentioned using his wife for sex sales, and he was adamant that this had never happened. It had been a joke with his wife when they were short on money because he had lost his job. He spluttered when his daughter was mentioned, denying that he knew the Bull person mentioned in the report.

He looked so guilty that none of the watchers believed him. Perhaps he had not yet sold his daughter to the paedophile, but from the panicked look on Aaron's face, the intention was there. He refused to disclose any knowledge of Bull to the policemen, even though he was pressed. He demanded to know where his wife and daughter were now, looking angry at being questioned.

At the end of the session, the policemen said they had to let Dunstan free, as they did not have a crime to keep him locked up. Percy took the policemen to one side and asked if his team could follow the connection up and find Bull so that he could be charged with paedophilia. Percy said he was sure that contact would be made by Dunstan to warn Bull. They would follow him and keep watch to see what would happen after he was dismissed from the police department. The policemen agreed, signing a release for Dunstan and giving an official report form to the private investigations team to follow up on the case.

Alicia and James went back to the private investigations office, while Kate and Percy followed Aaron Dunstan.

Alicia said she was glad they had decided to look after the little girl. She believed Sandra's story after seeing the interview. 'He looked pitiful when the selling of his wife for sex was brought up, and he became quite talkative, saying he never did that. He said he had joked with his wife that it was an option when money was low, but it never happened. What a dreadful person he has turned out to be. And when his daughter was mentioned, that look of panic was an admittance of guilt, if ever I saw a guilty person. His look gave him away.

'I know in my mind that Sandra is partly to blame for this predicament. She should have left her husband long ago, but the craving for drugs must have been too hard for her to make decisions. She took the easy way out by doing nothing until now. I feel sorry for her in a way but can't get over the fact that she was bringing up a child in such a terrible situation. I cannot see the welfare people allowing her access to the child again. It would not be fair for the little girl to grow up in those conditions.'

James nodded. 'I agree with you, Alicia. So we have our first child in the family. Granny seems happy to look after her while you are working. Therefore, at the moment, it is alright. We will have to wait and see what the future holds. Your grandmother is getting old, Alicia, and has a bad arm. She may not be able to manage for long.'

'I think Jody will look after Granny, James. I think she has been caring for her mother most of her life. Sandra does not seem very strong to me. She obviously still has pain in her back, by the way she stood and walked. She is fully reliant on her drugs, from the look of her, so I think their roles may have been reversed, despite Jody's age. She seems to be very grown-up for a four-year-old. I know we have not spent a lot of time with her, but the way she presented her case to the welfare officers greatly impressed me. I do not think she will be a worry to us or to Granny in any way.'

'Yes, Jody does appear to be independent. I agree that it probably comes from having had to care for her mother. She has not had the opportunity to be a child, as she has had to grow up quickly. I hope we can bring some fun and games into her life while she is with us. She will enjoy the Monday children's day at the bookshop.' James was referring to the Monday morning session for toddlers in the bookshop and the afternoon session for older children.

Alicia smiled. 'I would like to find a playgroup placing for her so she can be with other children her age. From what I understand, Jody has never mixed with other children. She has begun to feel at home with Granny and us very quickly, but she should learn to interact with her own age group. I will ring around this afternoon and see if I can find a group who will take her. I might have to take a short break from the office to take her and bring her back each day. It shouldn't take too long. I will deduct it from my hours worked for the business.'

'You are taking this all in your stride, Alicia. Well done! I have not had much to do with small children, so I have been leaving it up to you to make the decisions, give me a nudge if you think I should be doing something extra.'

'You are doing fine, James. I watched Jody while you were talking to the welfare people, and I saw that she admired you. I think you have already won brownie points with her. Her expression of how happy she is with us and Granny won the welfare people over. I do not think she will be too much trouble to us while still a child, but knowing both of her parents from their youth, we may have some trouble if she follows their example as she gets older.'

'By that time, Alicia, she will be following your example and Granny's too, so her mindset should be different from her parents.'

'I hope you are right, James. Her mother was a real be
youth, and Jody looks very much like her. I think it's a disa
a way to be beautiful, as the wrong sort of people become ..
you. It certainly did Sandra no favours. Aaron was an attractive young
man about town also, but look at him now. I feel disgusted with him.
They were two beautiful people, and they have sunk to the depths in
such a short span. It was all of their own making, and they should not
have brought a child into their world.'

'Children do not have a choice of parents, and Jody seems to have
made the most of her situation. She is being very stoic about the loss
of both Sandra and Aaron, and she has settled in with Granny as if
she has always been with her. There may be flashbacks occasionally,
but she seems to be managing very well at the moment. I must say, I
am surprised that she has accepted the change in her life so quickly.
You were about the same age, Alicia, when your parents died in a car
accident, and you have no memory of them. Perhaps Jody will forget
her upbringing and settle in with us completely.'

'I was five, James, when my parents disappeared from my life, and
I cannot recall them at all. Hopefully, in time, Jody will forget her
parents.'

5

Percy and Kate came into the office and went straight into the kitchen to make themselves a cup of tea.

James asked how they had got on with the chase of Aaron Dunstan.

Percy said between sips of his tea, 'Sorry, I need a drink. We have done so much walking today. We followed the man when he came out of the police station, and he walked about a block before opening up his cell phone and making a call. We were not close enough to hear the whole conversation, although we walked past him and heard him say he would meet the person on the other end of the phone at the train station in twenty minutes.

'We kept following him, and he went to a block of units and came out of a ground-level unit to the street wearing a jacket and hat and walked towards the train station. We were still following when he stopped and went into a shop, so we went on to the railway station to get into position to see who he was meeting there. I took some photographs of him speaking on the phone and coming out of the unit and wearing the jacket and hat, and I was able to get in a good position to take a photo of the person he was meeting at the railway station. Kate can take it from here.'

James looked at Kate enquiringly, and she smiled. 'A bit of a breakthrough. I recognised the man Aaron met. He is Andrew Bullock. I arrested him about two years ago in a toilet at a park. We had been called by the father of a young boy who was photographed by Bullock in the toilet block. We confiscated his camera and found several photos of young children on it. He was charged and went down for six months. It seems it did not change his predilection for young children. The name Bull must be a nickname for him, a shortened form of Bullock.'

Percy went on. 'I took quite a lot of photos of both men. I will show you on the screen. No one can deny that it is not the same two people, Dunstan and Bullock.'

He projected the photographs on to a computer screen, showing Aaron walking from the police station, walking some distance before talking on his phone, going into the block of units, and coming out again with a jacket and wearing a hat. There were more pictures of him going into a shop and then arriving at the railway station holding the hat, so the photographs showed him both with the hat and without; in both cases, it showed clearly that it was Aaron. There were other photos of him meeting up with a soft-faced, chubby man with reddish hair, whom Kate identified as Andrew Bullock, and of them talking together for a while and then jumping on a train as it was about to pull out of the station.

They were all clear photographs, as it was a fine, cool day without rain, and they came out showing clearly the features of the two men. Percy said, 'We think they took the London train. They both had passes, so they did not need to buy tickets. We cannot say for sure that they were going to London. They may be getting off at some stop before that. We were too late to get on the train, as we did not have tickets, so we gave up the chase at that point.'

'You have done well, Kate and Percy. We now have a name for Bull. If they have gone to London, it gives us time to get a warrant to search Bull's house and computer. I saw that he was not carrying a laptop when he got on the train. I will look up his address. Percy, can you get the warrant? You know your way around the system better than me. If we can get it, we will go and see what we can find. Do you want to go with Percy, Kate, or shall I go to search with him? The computer stuff we want to find is probably encrypted, and I could deal with that.'

'I have some work here, James, that I have left half done. It is better if I finish it off while it is still fresh in my memory. Unless you do not have the time?'

'I would like to finish this Bull person off as soon as possible, Kate, so it is not hanging over little Jody. I am sure Sandra will appreciate it too if we can finish the story for her. She was so agitated that she absconded and left Jody behind, so I think what she told you is true. I will make time to do the search.'

* * *

Percy organised the warrant to search Bull's flat. The address was easy enough to find by checking police records of his previous sentence. Percy also organised a constable to go with them in case it would be necessary for them to make an arrest if Bull came back while they were searching his flat.

While they were waiting for the warrant to be issued, James told Alicia what they had found to date. She asked what would happen next, and James explained that the search would be done mainly on the computer they would find in Bullock's flat.

She suggested, 'Look for paper photographs, and look in the freezer for backup discs as well. If Bull was only sent to jail for six months previously, there was obviously nothing found in his flat, so he must have a good hiding place. If anything had been found on his computer, they would have given him a longer sentence. You will have to search well.'

He looked at her admiringly. 'That is a clever observation, Alicia. They must have done a search previously. Where else would you suggest to look?'

'Perhaps in shoeboxes at the back of the wardrobe and in his spare shoes. Backups are not very big nowadays. They could fit into hardcover books with pages cut out or could be slipped behind books in a bookcase, perhaps in a tissue box—those sorts of places. He obviously has them hidden. They were not found, so he must have an innovative spot for them. I am sure he must be a paedophile, from Sandra's description of him in her case file. Just remember the passports hidden in my airline bag. Something like that could be a good spot.'

'We will look with that in mind, Alicia.'

Percy came in with the warrant he had been sent to pick up and with a constable in tow, introducing the constable as Tony Walton. He asked, 'Are you ready, James? We need to get going before Bull comes back.'

'I am right behind you, Percy. Let's go.'

*   *   *

They were gone for two hours and came back triumphant, saying backup discs were found in Bull's wellington boots, behind a suitcase in the wardrobe; the boots were almost full of them, with woollen socks stuffed on top to hide them. They had left everything in place, and Tony, the constable, was standing by to make the arrest and pick up the boots with the discs intact. He would ring for another policeman to stand guard with him, as Bullock had not yet returned from his train trip with Aaron Dunstan.

*   *   *

Later that day, there was a phone call from a London hospital. The caller said, 'My name is Nurse Joanne Sudbury. I am trying to identify a patient, a woman, who has been assaulted. A passer-by found her unconscious on a park bench. He thought for a moment that he was looking at a drunk, until he realised there was blood flowing from her head. He called an ambulance, and she was transported to our emergency ward. She is still alive but unconscious. She was lucky the man who found her covered her with his coat and called the ambulance, or she could have died from hypothermia. There was no identification on her and no handbag, but found in the pocket of her jacket was a small piece of paper with this phone number written on it. Do you have any idea who this woman could be?'

It was Alicia who had taken the call. She immediately thought of Sandra Dunstan but asked for a description of the person before saying her name. When the description was given, she knew she had it right and asked, 'What is her condition? She is a client of ours. You are calling the Gray and Armstrong Private Investigations office. From your description, I think you will find that she is Sandra Dunstan, née Jenson. She called into this office a week ago to tell us she was going to a rehabilitation clinic for drug addiction.'

The nurse on the other end of the line said, 'Yes, we think she is a drug addict, but she does not deserve this. She has been hit on the head at least twice with a garden edging brick, obviously picked up in the park. The ambulance drivers looked around for a weapon before they brought her in, and they found the brick with blood on it. We have handled the brick carefully in case fingerprints can be taken from it.'

Alicia asked, 'What will happen to her now?'

'She will be here with us for some time. When she comes around, we will need to have the police talk to her. They have been notified, of course, but she has not woken up yet. We will keep her in an induced coma until we see a change in her condition. At the moment, it is critical. Do you have any details of her next of kin?'

'I am afraid that her next of kin is most likely the perpetrator of the bashing, according to what Sandra said when we saw her in this office. Advise me at this number if there is any change in her condition. My name is Alicia Armstrong, and I will try and hunt down any relatives she has. I would like to know when she comes around, as I have had dealings with her, and both my husband and I have an interest in her case. Perhaps she will be able to give us an idea of who bashed her, and we can follow it up from this end, as we are aware of who her husband is and where we can find him.'

'Yes, certainly. I will put your name down on my form. It sounds like we should give the husband a miss in this case.'

'I am sure Sandra will appreciate that, thank you. I look forward to hearing from you again soon.'

When Alicia told the others in the office of the call, they were all appalled, with Percy saying, 'I wish now we had followed Aaron and Bullock on to the train. We might have been able to stop all this from happening.'

James shook his head. 'No, it is not your fault, Percy. It is possible they would have twigged us following them if we got on the train, and we did not know where they were heading at the time.'

'I am aware of that, James, but we knew they were a threat to Sandra. And why did they take off together? It was probably to get to her to try and shut her up. She must have defied them, so one of them hit her. I bet it was Bull, because he has the most to lose. He has tried prison once and would not want to go back, but if Sandra dies, he will be locked up for a long time. His paedophilia will not be popular with the other prisoners. He will not have a pleasant time during his stay in a prison. I am sure he is aware of that from his earlier time there.'

'What do you think we should do, Percy? Do we need to talk to the policeman in London who has been called to check the situation out?'

'Yes, James, it is a courtesy to speak to them and get their permission to follow Bullock up and interrogate him. I imagine he has been picked up by our police force by now for the things we found in his flat. I will make a few phone calls to see how far they have got with him. While I am on the phone, I will also follow up on the police report made at the hospital. They must be waiting to interview her if she is still unconscious.'

'Thanks, Percy, I appreciate that. I have quite a lot here to keep me busy. Seeing as I was away for several days, I need to catch up on things. We will wait to see what you can get from the phone calls before we act further.'

Percy made the local phone call and went back into James's office. 'Bullock has *done a runner*. He spotted the policemen waiting for him and ran off, and by the time they came downstairs, he had disappeared. They are still looking for him but think he has left the area. One of the policemen stayed behind to watch his flat in case he returns. I have requested that we search his possessions to see if we can pick up where he has gone. He cannot stay away indefinitely, and we may be able to find something.'

'Good man, Percy, let's go. This is one man I would like to see convicted. He is a nasty fellow, but when I look at his photo, he looks like the innocent party in this story. Somehow I cannot see Aaron Dunstan bashing his wife. He has not got reason enough, but Bullock does.

'His attempt to kill Sandra went wrong when the man walking his dog found her. He would not have expected her to be found so soon. He does not know that she is unconscious, as no news has gone out about it that we know about, and he is not aware that we have already searched his flat and found the backup discs. He may think that we have found Sandra and that she has spoken to us about him.

'He must be very confused at the moment, and his first inclination will be to lie low until the policeman moves off. We can stand down the policeman and watch the flat from a distance in a parked car. He will probably phone a neighbour to see if the police are still waiting. What do you suggest, Percy?'

'I agree that he must be confused and may also ring a neighbour to see if the coast is clear, but I do not think we can wait around before going into his flat to try and find a place he could hide out in. I think you should go to his flat, James.

'Ring me when you have finished, and I will move into position in the car to wait for him. When you leave, the neighbour can advise that the coast is clear but he will not notice me moving up to park the car. You can walk around the block and join me in the vehicle. I will bring some sandwiches and a flask of tea in case things get delayed. I will take the camera to photograph anything suspicious, and you should take one also to photograph anything you find inside.'

'That is a good plan, Percy. I will tell Alicia that we may be a little late home.'

*   *   *

When James arrived at the block of flats where Bullock lived, he knocked on the neighbour's door when he saw a light on there. The man who opened the door had obviously just arrived home from work, as he was still in his work overalls. James introduced himself and told the man he was going into Bull's flat to search it. He said that the police wanted to talk to Bullock, and someone had reported stolen goods stored in his flat. James had a warrant and was going in to try and find out what it was all about. He handed the warrant to the man to read to prove his point.

He went on to say, 'The police had a watch on the flat since early morning yesterday, and when Bullock arrived back from wherever he had been, he ran away when he saw the policemen. To the team looking for him, it indicated a guilty conscience, so I am here to see what it is all about. I will only be here about half an hour, and if I do not find anything, I will leave and come back when Bullock is available to talk in the morning.'

The man introduced himself as Tom Patchett, and he nodded the whole time James was speaking. James asked, 'Are you aware that Bull has spent time in jail previously?'

Tom Patchett nodded again. 'Yes, he told me about it. He was sprung for stealing a camera at the beach. Six months inside for that seemed a long sentence, and he hated his time in jail. He hated it so much and is so bitter about it, saying it was not deserved, he would not do anything to make him eligible for another sentence, so I do not think you have the right man here.'

'I was not aware that he had stolen a camera. I am not so sure if that was the reason for his prison sentence, because such a crime is normally given a fine. Okay, thanks for the tip, Tom. I will go and look for myself. That should sort it out. I will give you a knock when I leave so you will not have to think a burglar is present.'

Feeling he had the man onside, he went into Bullock's flat, using skeleton keys to get inside. He timed his half hour while looking through the paperwork he found in drawers. Everything was neatly labelled in files. He looked at the photos on the desk and saw a picture of Bull with a younger girl who appeared to be his sister; they both had red hair. The back of the photo was signed by Kirsty Bullock, saying 'happier days'. Kirsty was slim and neat, and her hair was long and wavy; she was quite a pretty girl next to her chubby brother, Andrew. There were no other photos displayed in the flat, so James believed that Kirsty must be special. He decided this was about all he was going to find. Bullock obviously cleaned up after himself and left nothing lying around. If something else was required to find the man, he would have to look up Kirsty Bullock for information.

James left the flat, locking the door after he exited, and knocked on Tom Patchett's door. When he answered, James said, 'I did not find any stolen goods, Tom. I will be off to report to my police companions that we will have to catch up with Bull himself for an explanation. Thanks for your help, Tom.'

He went down the stairs and left the area, walking around the block, as Percy suggested. He found him ensconced in his car; parked under a tree so that it was in shadow, but with a good view of the road and the footpath and the entry to Bullock's flat.

As he climbed into the car, James said, 'We should not have too long a wait. I talked to the neighbour, who thinks Bullock was jailed for stealing a camera, and told him we will be back tomorrow, so I think he is on the phone now, talking to Bull, saying the coast is clear.'

They ate the sandwiches Percy purchased and drank the tea and waited ten more minutes before James said, 'Here is Bull now. That did not take long. He must have been close by. We will have to look into that. We may find some more pornographic or paedophilic personalities where he has been hiding.'

Percy turned to watch Bullock striding along, confident in his belief that he was not being watched. 'I think it is time to ring our police friends for an arrest and pick up those discs Bullock has hidden in the wardrobe.' He waited until Bullock had gone into his flat so that he would not hear the call, and Percy spoke to the police department, who said they would send two men right away.

Fifteen minutes later, a police van pulled up behind them, with two policemen, and the four men quietly went up the stairs to the flat.

James was right when he said Bullock would be confused about his charges. When the policeman handcuffed him, he said, spluttering, 'I did not hit the bitch very hard. If she has recovered enough to report me, she asked for it, the slut. You cannot believe a word she says. She is a druggy and is always *ten sheets to the wind*, so you can never take her word for anything.'

James and Percy looked at each other and gave a thumbs up.

Percy said to the policemen, 'You have just heard him confess to hitting Sandra Dunstan with a brick. She is in intensive care in a London hospital, and if she does not recover, it will be a murder sentence this man will be looking at.'

James suggested to the policemen, 'Look in the wardrobe for the wellington boots, behind a suitcase, and bring the boots and the packages inside with you to the station for the charge of possession of paedophilic Internet discs. This, together with the assault charge on Sandra Dunstan, should send Andrew Bullock away for a very long time.'

While the policemen took Bullock away in the police van, James knocked on Tom Patchett's door. He explained to Tom why they were arresting Bull. Tom was astounded and said, 'He is such a quiet man and so fastidious. It is unbelievable. Was his previous jail sentence for the same thing?'

'Yes, he was caught taking photos of small children in a park toilet block. I do not know if the camera was his or a stolen one, but the sentence was for taking photos of small children in a state of undress.'

'Well, you do not know who you are talking to any more. I believed him when he told me his story, and I felt sorry for him. He was so angry at going to jail, saying it was undeserved, but from what you tell me now, I think it should have been for life!' Bull's neighbour was amazed at the revelations and angry that he had been fooled by him.

Percy and James made their way to the police station to explain the assault on Sandra Dunstan, reporting what the London policemen had told them of the case. They would leave the case with the police from now on. They had done their bit and would submit a report with a detailed account to the police department the next day.

James rang Alicia to tell her what had happened. She suggested he bring Percy back to their apartment for a top-up of their sandwich supper, as she had a nice bowl of home-made soup which should go down well. She was so pleased that Bull had been arrested, and asked, 'What was Aaron Dunstan's role in the bashing of Sandra?'

'We will have to pay Aaron a visit tomorrow to ask that question. There was no mention of Aaron from Bull. Perhaps they parted company somewhere along the way. Bullock seemed to think that because he did not hit Sandra hard enough, she recovered to tell the story about his assault on her. But there was no mention of whether Aaron was present when he did it or where Aaron went later. This is a mystery we will have to explore in the morning. It has been a long day today.'

6

J ames assigned Percy and Kate to visit Aaron Dunstan the next
morning. He felt he did not want Aaron to recognise him, in case
anything came up with Jody in the future.

When they came back to the office, they said Aaron's explanation
was that he went to the clinic where Sandra was receiving rehabilitation.
He knew about it because Sandra had been applying to various places for
some time, and on Wednesday of that week, Sandra had disappeared.
There had been a phone message to Sandra, and she had written down
the details: name and address, the time the place was open to visitors,
and a deadline of Friday of that week, at two o'clock in the afternoon,
for her to take a place, or else it would go to someone else.

He explained that Sandra always said she was going to try
rehabilitation but always somehow dropped it at the last minute. This
time she seemed to believe she could do it. The reason she dropped
out the other times was that she did not know what to do with her
daughter. This time she did not take Jody with her, so she must have
found someone to look after her. He did not know where Jody was. He
had asked their friends if anyone knew, but no one had any idea. Aaron
thought she may have taken Jody to her brother in London before going
to the clinic.

He went with Bull to the rehab place and asked permission to see
Sandra. 'We were told she was not allowed out or to have visitors, but
when we explained that it was about Jody, her daughter, they let Sandra
out, saying she had half an hour before she had to be back. We went

to a park and tried to talk Sandra into withdrawing her comments about Bull in the statement she had given to you at your office, but she refused. We tried for the half hour the clinic gave us, and then we walked away, leaving Sandra sitting on the park bench.

'Bull said to me, 'There is one more argument I can use with Sandra. Don't wait for me, I will go straight to the railway station and go home." I told him I was going to see Sandra's brother about Jody before going home, so I walked off.

'Sandra's brother, Paul, had no idea what I was talking about. We have not seen him in two years, and I could tell by his apartment that Sandra would not have left Jody with him. He is not married, and his unit looks as if he has a cleaner to make it shiny and clean. He spends several days a week working on an oil platform, so there would be no one to look after a child. I am still at a loss as to where Jody has gone.'

Percy said, 'We believed Aaron's story. He is not aware of Sandra being in hospital. We decided not to tell him yet until we are sure Bullock has been charged. He seems believable in his worry about Jody. But he does not deserve a beautiful little girl to give away to a paedophile, so we did not enlighten him.'

'What do you think, Kate?'

'I was surprised to find a nice, homely flat with three bedrooms—a real family home, nicely furnished, decorated, and clean. I expected a muddle, but there was no sign of it. I have been in other drug addicts' homes and usually found a mess, but this was surprisingly neat and clean. I asked for a look into Jody's bedroom and saw that it was neat, with a small refrigerator and a table and chairs.'

Kate continued, 'I would say Jody has many meals there that she has got for herself, as little as she is. It was like any other child's bedroom except for the fridge and the table and the chairs and the food on the shelves. I would say she was locked in to fend for herself. When I closed the door as we were leaving the room, I noticed that there was a small lock on the outside of the door, so she must have been locked in her room while the grown-ups were doing their own thing.'

James looked horrified. 'How terrible it must have been for her, alone and unable to get out! No wonder she is a passive child. She has not been allowed to live a normal life till now. I think that Aaron's quest to find her is to stop her from talking about her life with them, more than out of any fatherly feeling.'

Alicia had been listening with a look of disgust on her face. 'Poor child. I do not think we should tell Granny about this. She is likely to go and hit Aaron with her umbrella for his behaviour. I feel like taking my umbrella to him as well. What a disgusting man.'

The team laughed at Alicia, and Percy said, 'I can just imagine you and your granny taking to Aaron with umbrellas. Let me know when you are going to do it, and I will come and watch.'

Alicia laughed with them. 'I know it sounds silly, but what else could we do? It is so frustrating to hear these stories, and we are not able to do anything about them. In the olden days, we would have stoned Aaron out of town.'

'I will hunt down the details of their home. It does not look like a rental property. If Sandra survives, we may be able to get an injunction to sell the unit to pay for surgery on her back. To me, it sounds like she is the person keeping the house clean. When they had their car accident, they must have got some compensation for it. From all accounts, it was not their fault. A bus ran into them. The bus went through a green light at some speed, not realising that the traffic in front of it was backed up and not moving, and the bus hit the rear of Dunstan's vehicle. It was a five-car pile-up, and Dunstan's vehicle was the worst hit—it caught the bus in full flight, so to speak. I looked it up during the week,' James said, looking around at the others.

'Good for you, James. I agree that the place does not look like a rental. It is far too neat somehow. And with rentals, you are not allowed to hang paintings on the walls, and this one has some lovely paintings. It is very tastefully decorated. Someone has good taste,' observed Kate.

Alicia looked interested. 'Sandra was good at art at school, I remember. She was always beautifully dressed. We never saw those dresses in the shops, and we wondered if she made them herself. I was not in her group, but it never stopped us from commenting about her. Our group consensus was that she made the clothes herself, as they would have been very expensive in the shops. We were just out of school, so none of us could afford clothes like she wore. We all admired her style. She looked lovely in anything she wore.'

Kate looked unbelieving. 'We are talking about Sandra Dunstan, aren't we? The woman we spoke to looked dreadful and way older than you, Alicia.'

'Then she must have gone through a rough time in her life in the last five or six years. Truly, she was beautiful in her teens and early twenties. I did not see her again until recently and did not recognise her when she spoke to me. She is the same age as me, twenty-seven on the last birthday.'

Kate was at last believing. 'It must have been a terrific accident when the bus ran into them, to have caused so much damage to her. I suppose when you have constant pain and take multiple drugs to get relief, it has an effect on you. I am not sure how much Aaron had to do with the drugs. She said when she was here that he had bad headaches caused by the accident. It looks as if they spent money on the house instead of seeing a doctor to fix their pain.'

'It seems the prescription drugs for the pain were the cause of their addiction. They took those instead of surgery, which they probably both needed. They dropped out of the healthcare system too.' James sounded sympathetic. 'It is easy for us to criticise, but to be in daily pain, with a small child to bring up, can easily lead to taking pills to assuage the pain. I think we should take Jody to a hospital to see if she has absorbed any drugs from her mother's breast milk.'

'That is a good idea, James. I will make an appointment for her, although except for being a little passive, she shows no signs of it. The passivity could be put down to her lifestyle of being locked in her bedroom to fend for herself.' Alicia looked pensive. 'With Granny as her daily companion, she seems to be waking up and is much livelier now since being with us.'

Percy stood up. 'I have a backlog of work to do, so I need to get working.'

James looked guilty. 'Me too. Okay, folks, lunch is over. Duty calls.'

*   *   *

A week later, Alicia had another call from Nurse Sudbury. 'Sandra has at last woken up and remembers everything about her assault and has given a statement to the police. I sat in on the interview in case she needed anything, but she went through the interview as if it was something she had been going through over and over in her mind. She was so glad to get it out to someone else. It was someone named Bull who hit her with the brick from the garden edging. The policeman said they had picked up a print from the brick and identified it as that of Andrew Bullock from their files. So that mystery is solved.'

Alicia told the nurse that Bullock had been picked up a week ago on another charge, but this was good news for Sandra's husband; they would now notify him of Sandra's whereabouts. They had not told him yet, as they had been waiting for Sandra to identify her attacker.

Nurse Sudbury went on, 'Sandra is allowed visitors now. We have found that she cannot walk yet. We are not sure if it is because of the hit on the head or the back problem she has. She has had a scan, and there are several vertebrae in her back which appear to have crumbled. The doctors want to follow up on her medical history. She has told them of being in an accident four years ago. Poor girl, she must have been in considerable pain, from the look of her scan results. The doctors have not yet come up with a remedy for her, but at the moment, she can only get around in a wheelchair, I'm afraid.'

'We will bring her four-year-old daughter with us. We have been looking after her since Sandra went to the rehab clinic. Her husband does not know about us having the child, so we would appreciate if you do not mention it to him. Sandra may perk up from the visit, knowing Jody is safe with us,' Alicia explained.

'I am sure it will please her. She is still troubled by withdrawal symptoms, of course, and generally will be confined to bed until we have worked out how to help her. It is early days yet, but I think she will be with us for some time.' The nurse sounded sympathetic.

Alicia said, 'Thank you for explaining it all to me. We have been worried about her, but we have not mentioned it to her daughter. When Sandra left her with us to go to rehab, we told the little girl her mother was going to hospital, so it will not be a surprise for her to see Sandra in a hospital bed. Will you be on duty on Sunday?'

'No, I am in charge of the ward Monday through Friday, and I have the weekends off.'

'Then we will not be able to see you to thank you in person. We are very appreciative of your update. Perhaps another time. We have a business to run during the week, and Sunday is our only free day,' said Alicia.

'I understand. We will watch over Sandra for you and keep you in touch with what we are doing for her,' finished the nurse.

When Alicia told this to the team, they agreed that Aaron not be notified of his wife's place in a hospital until after Sunday, as he just might turn up at the same time as them and spoil Sandra's attempt to hide the girl from her father. They would ask Sandra first whether to allow Aaron to have access to Jody.

Percy said he would go and see Aaron on Sunday afternoon and tell him the story of Bull's betrayal and Sandra's hospitalisation. Aaron needed to know, and if Percy went at that time, it would be too late for Aaron to catch James and Alicia at Sandra's bedside with his daughter.

7

Alicia made an appointment for a Charles Chamberlain to see James at ten o'clock on Friday morning. There was no mention of what the appointment was for, just that James was recommended to him by the lawyer Alec Overington, who explained that James and his investigators often solved problems for him.

James met Mr Chamberlain at the door of the office and invited him to his private office, asking if his client would like a cup of tea or coffee. Chamberlain smiled and accepted the coffee offered and sat down facing James, laying his briefcase on the desk and opening it up.

James nodded to him, and he handed a bundle of photographs to James and started his story. 'A couple of weeks ago, I had reason to go to London for a business meeting. This particular day, I took the train, as the building I was attending the meeting in was a short walk from Waterloo Station. It made sense to use the train rather than to fuss around to find a parking spot, and it also gave me time to study the papers I would be presenting. I saw a man with a companion when I boarded the train here. On the return journey, I saw the same man. I want you to investigate him for me.

'I live on the other side of the city here, on a small holding which we find relaxing to potter around in on the weekends. However, my son and daughter find it inconvenient because all the fun takes place in town, and they need transport to attend. I denied them the use of a vehicle in case they would drink, and I would drive them instead. I would pick them up if they required transport when it was late. They went to schools in town, and I would take them in and drop them at their school on my way to work. They would catch a bus home after school. However, I have lived to regret that decision. My eighteen-year-old daughter disappeared in January, accepting a lift from a stranger.

'The night my daughter disappeared, she had travelled into the town on the bus to attend a get-together with her friends from school because the placings for university had been announced, and they wanted to share their news. They were all excited, and my daughter, Leanne, was happy to announce her placement for a medical degree. She was over the moon about it, as a lot of study had gone into her previous year's work at school. We were very happy for her. She was always a good student, and we were very proud of her achievements.

'Leanne went to the party with her friends against my wishes, and I was to pick her up when she phoned me. I got a call from her just before nine o'clock, saying not to worry about picking her up, as she was arranging with someone from close by our home to drop her off. I argued with her and said I was leaving to get her, and she said, "You have to let go of the apron strings sometime, Dad. I will be okay." Then she hung up. Those were the last words I heard from her. She never arrived home. I sat up waiting for her to come in. I was still awake when morning came, and she had still not arrived. I felt such a dread and still do. It is a hard thing to come to terms with—our beautiful daughter is missing and gone from our lives, and we do not know what happened to her.

'I called the police at eight o'clock in the morning and described what had happened. They were very sympathetic but asked me if she had maybe gone home with a friend or perhaps had slept in and would call later. Leanne would not have done that without telling us. It was the way she was brought up. She knew we loved her and worried if she was late, and after her call to me to say she was on her way, with someone giving her a lift, it did not sound as if she had left with a friend for a sleepover. We told this to the policemen, and they said they would go to where the party was held and make some enquiries.

'The arrangement for the meeting with the young group was the pub, the Jolly Green Frog, here near your office. The police got the security pictures for the evening from the manager of the pub. I have placed a copy in that group of photos on your desk. Leanne is there. She looks amazingly happy and beautiful, having a good time with the friends she had gone through school with. I cannot believe any of them would have harmed her, but somebody did, as she has not come home to us, nor have we heard from her. What has brought me to see you is this man.' He pointed to a man on the fringe of the group.

James looked at the photograph and let out a sigh. 'What was he doing there with a bunch of young people?' he asked. 'He is at least ten years older than most of them.'

'I asked the same thing of the police, and they said he is a journalist doing a column for the local paper on the placements for the young graduates. They checked up on him, and he admitted to being there. He has not had a car since a crash he had three years previously. He has access to his paper's vehicle when he has to travel for a job, but no vehicle was booked out for that occasion because it was a town job he was working on.'

'So what is it you want me to do about him?' asked James.

'As I said, I travelled by train to a meeting in London, and I noticed that man with a companion on the same train that morning. He was also on the journey home later in the afternoon. I was already seated, and the carriage was quite crowded. The only seat available was in front of me, across the aisle. This man came into the carriage and sat in that particular seat. I sat looking at the man for the length of the journey home and could see his head pulsing as if he was about to collapse. He was squirming as if he was uncomfortable. I know that is a strange description, but it is an accurate one. As soon as another seat became available, the passenger sitting beside him moved away, obviously annoyed.

'I found it a strange experience. I felt the man had been following me and had entered that carriage because the train was full. He could not hide anywhere else, and he was squirming because he was uncomfortable sitting in front of me. The feeling is so strong, and I cannot shake it. I know he is a journalist and do not want him writing anything about me in the press. I want to know if you are willing to hunt this man down and check him out. I can afford the fees your lovely secretary quoted to me over the phone.

'I want to be able to face my wife and say we have found out what happened to our daughter, to set her mind at rest, but I particularly do not want stories written about our family in the newspapers. This man was the person conducting interviews on the night of my daughter's disappearance. Perhaps he knows more about it than he has said so far.

'Alec Overington is my lawyer and a friend, and when I spoke to him about my train experience, he suggested I speak to you and ask you to investigate this man for me to lay my demons to rest. Someone must know something. I have been relying on the police, but they have not come up with any answers.'

James said, 'Firstly, tell me about all these pictures and papers you have here. I need to put myself in the picture to get a feel of the evening in question.'

Chamberlain leaned over and pulled a photo out of the group on the desk. 'This is a picture of Leanne at her school break-up night, just one month before her disappearance.'

James took the photo, looking at a young woman with long blonde hair. He called Alicia into the office and introduced her to the client. He held up the picture and asked her, 'Who does this remind you of?'

Alicia looked at the picture for a long time. 'This person looks very similar to Sandra Jenson at the same age.'

James looked at his client. 'I believe you have picked out the right man. Sandra Jenson is his wife, who was a beautiful girl, very similar to your daughter at the same age. I will be very happy to check into what happened that night in January for you. It is too much of a coincidence that Leanne and Sandra look so much alike, and I am sure that Aaron Dunstan did not miss the likeness.'

'That is a good start,' Chamberlain said. 'The rest of these papers are the police reports, which include statements from most of the young people at the party. Alas, it has all led to nothing of any interest so far. I know it is what they call a cold case now. I get the impression from my police contacts that they have no more leads and that me trying to do my own investigative work on the case is not helpful. However, if they lost a daughter in the same circumstances, I am sure they would want answers too.'

'Yes, I agree with you. It is a dreadful circumstance, and we will do our best to find out the truth. If Aaron Dunstan is involved, we will find out how he did it and how he stayed out of the limelight. My first move will be to visit the police station and advise them of what I intend to do. It is only a courtesy to inform them, but it may shine a light on the investigation in some way.

'I will read through all these reports before tackling Aaron Dunstan so that I have a better sense of things as they happened, and I may be able to pick something small but important from them. I will keep you informed on my investigation. It is important that you are kept in the loop, as it is your money I will be spending. I thank you for your faith in me to do this job.'

'Alec Overington seemed to think well of you. After meeting you and your wife, I also have faith in you. Thank you for listening to me. I find that most people will not discuss it and will change the conversation quickly if Leanne's name is mentioned. It is as if she never existed to anyone else. I find that very hard to take, as she was such a beautiful, intelligent person, and she very much existed for my wife and me. Our son is three years younger than Leanne and misses her in his life. They were great friends. We can never forget her.'

'If you think of anything else, please give us a call at any time of the day or night. This is my card, and my private number is on the back. It is better to keep the momentum up on the case, as even the smallest thing can be important and may bring a solution. I will do a thorough check on Dunstan because, like you, I believe he is the man to look at. I know a little about him, but only surface stuff, so I will look deeper into him.'

Chamberlain stood up. 'I feel as if we may get somewhere, even if it is only to clear my mind about this man. He has entered my head, and I find it hard to concentrate on anything else until I learn more about him and his presence at the party that evening in January.'

'I will ring you on Sunday evening. I have Saturdays off to help in Alicia's grandmother's bookshop. We both help out that day, as it is too much for Granny to do it all herself. But I will be back on the job on Sunday, and that should be a good day to catch Aaron at home.'

'Thank you, James. I appreciate your kindness in listening to me.' He smiled at Alicia as he went out of the office, saying, 'Good morning, Mrs Armstrong.'

'What a nice man. What a terrible shame to lose a loving child in the prime of her life. I do feel sorry for him and his wife,' said Alicia to James after the office door closed on Charles Chamberlain.

James raised his eyebrows. 'And what an almighty coincidence that Dunstan is on our radar at the moment. This afternoon, I will ask at the newspaper he works for to check on the cars on the evening in question. I will also visit the police station for background on the case, but it looks as if they have kept the father well informed anyway.

'I will go over the friends' statements this evening. Perhaps you could read them over first this morning so we can compare notes this evening. When we see Sandra in hospital on Sunday, we can ask her about that period in January to see if she noticed any changes in her husband at the time, if she is okay to answer questions.'

'That all sounds good, James. I do not have much at the moment, so give me the statements and I will read them now.'

'Thanks, Alicia. This seems to have fallen into our laps just when we have Aaron in our sights. I can hardly believe it. Quite honestly, he seemed a silly surface type of man to me. I could not believe he hit Sandra with a brick, but now we are talking about him committing a crime against a young girl. That is a big change in our thinking. I will have to try and clear my mind and sort out my thoughts carefully. I have been dodging him because of Jody, but I will have to forget her relation to him and approach him as a suspect.'

'Have lunch before you go to the newspaper office, James. You always think clearer when you do not have your tummy rumbling for something to eat.'

James laughed. 'Good thinking, Alicia. It will save me from embarrassment.'

*　　*　　*

He set off for the newspaper office straight after lunch and asked for the manager. He was directed to an office with papers loaded on chairs and benches and with a big desk with a tall middle-aged man behind it.

'Come in, Mr Armstrong. I am pleased to meet you at last. Your name has been mentioned in many conversations around town as the new man on the block, but you keep a low profile.'

'I am here, sir, to ask a few questions about Aaron Dunstan. I believe he works for you.'

'No longer. I let him go in January. He suffered headaches and was a hard man to work with. He could not stand noise and would get angry at everyone talking at once, as they do in an office like ours. I respected the fact that he had had an accident that caused the headaches. I gave him some leeway and an office of his own and allowed him to work at home also, but his work became very erratic, sometimes hard to understand. They were not articles for newspapers, so we used his submissions less and less. We actually sent him off in January because we had a misunderstanding about him using our executive vehicle for his own use.'

'That is the question I wanted to ask you, sir. Did he take one of your vehicles on the evening of the fifteenth of January?'

'Yes, I think that was the date. The police asked the same question, but we told them no cars were signed out for that date. It was only a week later when one of the staff wanted to use the car to pick up a VIP at the airport for an interview that we found out the car had been used by someone, and the petrol was at so low a level that it had to be filled up before it could be used again. We asked around the office, and no one volunteered any information, until Dunstan came in and said casually that he had been the one who borrowed it to visit a friend whom he wanted to impress. The date he mentioned was not the one the police were asking about, so we did not inform them. I was so angry about this transgression. I told Dunstan to remove himself from our office. He was dismissed, and he handed back the office keys, including the garage key. I felt he could no longer be trusted.

'I had bent over backwards for this man. He had worked for us for ten years, and when he had the car accident, we covered for him, paying him for several weeks until he returned to work. He was a difficult man after the accident. He could not stand noise, so we gave him an office of his own. He was always complaining about something. This caused dissension in the offices. Most of the others walked around him, trying to keep out of his way, and it became awkward when he was here.'

'Would you mind giving a statement of what you have told me, sir? I have been asked by the father of a missing girl to follow the information the police had, and this is my first port of call.'

'By all means, James. I no longer feel as if I have to cover for an employee. If Dunstan was at fault in any way, I no longer feel I can give him a reference as I might have done a few years ago. He was a good worker in his earlier days in this office and submitted some interesting articles, but he lost his touch in later years. I no longer think of him as an employee. I will write out a statement and send it to your office.'

'Thank you, sir. I greatly appreciate your time and willingness to help.'

'Call me Eric, James. Eric Hendy. We may meet again sometime.'

'I will look forward to that, Eric.'

James walked away, saying to himself, '*Yes*, that went down well.' He decided to leave going to the police until after Sunday. By then he would have more information for them. He decided that he and Alicia, with Jody, would go to the London hospital to visit Sandra on Sunday morning and that he would go with Alicia to confront Aaron on Sunday afternoon. He looked forward to confronting Dunstan, with the car issue confirmed and the photo of Leanne in his briefcase. He decided that he needed to make an appointment with Aaron Dunstan to make sure he was able to meet him. He did not want the man to leave town just when he wanted to question him.

When he returned to the office, he asked Alicia to ring him and make an appointment to have a pint at the Jolly Green Frog pub on Sunday, at four in the afternoon, as an old friend wanting to introduce her husband. She looked up the number and rang, speaking to Aaron in a friendly manner. It worked. He agreed to meet them at the pub as Alicia had stated. She looked triumphant. 'I have not lost my touch,' she said. 'Am I to meet him at the pub with you?'

'Yes, I think if you and Jody come along, it will interest him, and he might open up to you. Bring Jody's little bag with her toys in it for her to sit and play quietly. Granny may be interested in coming along as well, and after the initial questioning, she might be able to take Jody for a walk, away from the conversation. We will need to ask Sandra about all this. She may still want Jody's whereabouts kept from her husband. Being in a public place may quiet Aaron down, especially in that particular pub. They do have private rooms at the pub, so I will go and speak to my friend, the publican, and request one of them. I think being back at the pub, and with a photo of Leanne, may loosen Aaron's tongue about the evening in question. Once we get him talking, I think it will be hard to stop him. He has kept it bottled up for some time now, and it must play on his mind.'

'Will you ask for a policeman to listen in?'

'Not this time, Alicia. Perhaps we could arrange some sound equipment in the room to record the conversation. If we are able to get a confession from Aaron, we can record it for the police. I will think about it. Sandra may be able to clear him, so it is better not to jump to conclusions before we speak with her.'

'What about the newspaper man's statement, James?'

'I should get that this afternoon. Eric Hendy seemed to be on the ball, and he said he would have it delivered here today. It does not really matter at this time if it is late. My knowledge of it should trip Aaron's confession, I hope. I will go now to the pub and ask the publican about the private rooms and if they have any sound equipment in case we need it.'

'It is hard to believe that Sandra and Aaron featured way back in my past, and they now seem to have taken over our lives. The only plus I can see in the whole thing is, we are saving little Jody from all sorts of terrors. She is such a sweet little girl and so adaptable. I do not really want to take her to see her father and bring back all her bad memories.'

'Okay, Alicia, we will not include Jody in our pub conversation after all. We will leave her with Granny until Sandra gives us permission. You are right, she should not see him and revive bad memories. I thought seeing her would get Aaron more relaxed, but we have enough evidence to get him talking without Jody having to be exposed to him. If we are unable to get a confession, it means he would once again be free and will know where to find her. That would not be a good thing. It is better if we keep that information from him until we find out more about him.'

'That is true. We will think more about our strategy over the weekend. We may come up with something else after talking to Sandra. Everything is up in the air until that time, James. We are jumping to conclusions a little at the moment, second-guessing Aaron and listening to other people's prejudice against him. We may have it all wrong.'

'I have been thinking that too, Alicia. We do not know this man, only what we have heard second-hand. Sometimes you can be swayed by other people's opinions when they do not know the full story. We have to keep in mind that Aaron was in a dreadful car accident which has made him a bit abnormal. Sandra was angry with him when she made her statement, and that also can skew our thoughts on him. I think we will start our conversation trying to find out where he came from, to put him in a relaxed mood before charging in on him.'

Alicia smiled. 'I think that is a good strategy to get him onside. The alacrity with which he consented to meeting us must mean he is feeling lonely and isolated. He does not know about his wife being in hospital and anything about his daughter's disappearance. It is probably weighing on his mind, the way things are happening. He does not know us. When I knew them previously, it was a vague friendship, more with Sandra than with him. I am not sure he recognised my name. I did introduce myself as Alicia Newton Armstrong, but I am still not sure he knew me.'

'Whatever you said to him worked, Alicia, or he is so curious he is willing to talk to strangers.'

'Sandra may have changed her mind by now. She is being looked after as she should have been four years ago, and probably now she does not have to think of how to get through the day. Her worries have gone away. She will know her daughter is safe with us, and the nurse has probably told her we will be coming to see her on Sunday. So she will be more relaxed and in a better frame of mind to tell us her story, and we can ask about Aaron without getting her upset.'

'True. It will be interesting to find out more about Aaron from her. She is the closest person to him and must know the real man.'

Alicia thought for a minute. 'We must remember to ask Sandra if she wants us to notify her brother, Paul, that she is in hospital. I knew of him at school, but as he was a year or two older, I had no contact with him.'

'Yes, we can do that. Percy got his address from Aaron when he saw him. We will ask Sandra in case she does not want him to know what happened to her.'

'There is a possibility of that. Didn't Aaron tell Percy he had not seen Paul for some years?'

'Families drift apart, Alicia. I have not seen my sister for at least three years since she went to live in Australia. I do not even see my parents so much since they went to live in Spain. Mother always gets a cold when she comes back to the UK, and that puts her off. We will need to have a holiday soon and visit my parents in Spain. Perhaps we can go for Christmas and close the shop and take Granny with us.'

'What will we do with Jody? We will have to get her a passport to travel with us.'

'We will work that out a bit further down the track after we have sorted Sandra and Aaron out.'

8

Sunday was a clear, sunny day, and James and Alicia set off with Jody holding their hands to catch the London train. They caught a cab from the station to the hospital, thinking this would save them time if they were to be home again at four for their appointment with Aaron Dunstan.

They were allowed to see Sandra immediately, as they had advised Nurse Sudbury that they would visit; she had noted it down for them to go straight to Sandra's bedside.

Sandra was lying flat on her back, with only a soft pillow for her head support, but she looked cheerful. Jody ran straight to her side and clung to her arm, as that was all she was able to reach. James lifted her up beside Sandra on the bed, and the two lay for a while, hugging each other and not talking.

After a little while, Jody went to sleep, and Sandra spoke softly. 'Thank you for bringing Jody in to see me. I did not believe Nurse Sudbury when she told me, but I was wrong. Everyone here has been so kind to me, and they are going to operate on my back to see if they can fix it. They say I must not get my hopes up, as the damage has been done over such a long a period that it may not be a success, but they will try their best for me. The alternative is that I will spend the rest of my days in a wheelchair. I will not be able to walk far in the future, whichever way it goes.

'They are angry here that my previous doctor only gave me prescription drugs instead of an operation at the time of the accident.

The doctor says that if something had been done when the damage was fresh, it may have worked better for me, and it may be too late now, as the damage has worsened over the past four years.

'It is partly my fault because I put up with the pain so that I could look after Jody when she was born. She was so beautiful and was such a wonder to me. If I had been operated on, I would have had to spend so much time flat on my back, unable to do anything, and Jody would have had to go into care. I did not want that. So I can only blame myself.

'But truly, when you are young, you cannot see into the future. If I had a choice again, it would be different, so I have agreed to surgery and will pray for success, although I know in my heart that it is too late and that a wheelchair is my fate now.'

Alicia was wiping tears from her eyes. 'I am so sorry, Sandra, but you will not have to worry about Jody. She has settled down with us, and Granny looks after her while I am at work. They get on like a house on fire, and they love each other. She is very happy with us. She is going to start at preschool soon and will love being with the other children her own age.'

James said, 'Sandra, I am sorry, but we have to ask you a few questions about Aaron. However, first, we want to let you know that Bull, or Andrew Bullock, has been arrested and has confessed to us and the police officers that he hit you with the garden edging brick. We also searched his flat and found quite a lot of computer backup discs which we presume will show him to be a paedophile and will send him to jail for a very long time.

'He has exonerated Aaron from your assault, as they parted company soon after they left you and Bull went back to you for the assault. Aaron went to see your brother, Paul, to see if you had left Jody with him, but of course, we know the answer to that. We want to know if you would like Paul to be advised that you are here in hospital and if you wish for any one of your other relatives to be advised.'

Sandra looked thankful. 'Thank you, James, for the thought. Yes, I think Paul would want to know. You do not have to tell him the circumstances. Just say I am here for a back operation. Perhaps I will tell him the rest of it in time, but I would like him to remember me as I was.

'My parents are in care in a nursing home. They aged quickly from their drinking addiction, and I believe my father is heading for Alzheimer's and probably would not know me now. I will visit them when I recover from my operation. We were never a close family. When we got together, it was always a battlefield rather than a family gathering as most people know it. What is it you want to know about Aaron?'

'You said in your statement that Aaron was talking about selling you for sex. Is that correct?'

Sandra looked apologetic and uncomfortable. 'Not quite. I was very angry with him for bargaining with Bull about taking photos of Jody. He had joked about selling me for sex when our money got low. He had lost his permanent job at the newspaper in town in January this year and worked part-time for another paper, but they were not good payers. Sometimes we were flat broke. I knew it was only a joke, but to have it mentioned to me made me simmer with discontent. I would get angry each time I thought about it, and resentment built up in me. He only said it once. I knew it was a joke, but all the same, I took umbrage at it.'

'You are saying it did not happen?'

'No. I am sorry, James, but by the time I got to your office, I was so angry and stressed that I said it even though I was lying, just as I lied to your grandmother, Alicia. I am sorry, I have no real excuse. It is just that I wanted you to believe that I had to go into rehab.

'When I saw you in the shopping centre, Alicia, I knew you were the one I could safely leave Jody with, and when I went to the bookshop that Thursday, I went to pieces when you were not there. I had been very fragile for some time, quick to tears because the pain in my back would get me down. The drugs were wearing off quicker each time I took them, and I was at my wits' end. I knew it was only a matter of time before I collapsed altogether and would not be able to walk.

'In a way, Bull did me a favour by hitting me with the brick. It brought me here to this hospital, with the wonderful nurses and doctors to care for me. You have made me so happy to see Jody and how well-cared-for she is and how comfortable she is with you.'

'The other thing we want to know about Aaron, Sandra, is whether he is capable of murdering someone,' said James.

Sandra looked shocked. 'Certainly not. He is so soft-hearted he will not even growl at Jody when she plays up. He has never hit me. He has nursed me through many days and nights when I was off my head with the pain in my back, and he has never said a cross word about having to clean up after I had vomited all over the bed—this has happened several times with the drugs I have been taking.'

'Can you remember January fifteenth, Sandra? The evening when he went to a pub to interview some schoolies playing merry?'

'Yes, I remember. The police made it memorable. They came around asking questions about what time Aaron arrived home and if he had gone out again. The answer was, he came home at nine o'clock with a roaring headache. He insisted on sitting at his desk and typing up the report and emailing it to the newspaper before going to bed. You can check with the newspaper what time the email arrived, with pictures as an attachment. He went to bed after taking his medicine, which helps him sleep, about eleven o'clock and was in no shape to go and break into a garage to borrow a car and take a young woman for a drive to murder her.

'The loud music and voices at the bar had given him the headache. He had asked that he not be given that particular job, because of the noise factor, but Eric Hendy had been away for that weekend. The next in charge was a beast of a bloke and had insisted that Aaron take it on, calling him a time-waster and a lame duck. Aaron did the job, knowing the consequence would be a huge headache which would make him feel ill for hours.'

'What about Aaron taking an executive car from the garage and taking a long drive later?'

'He was so bitter about the comments at the newspaper office like "Are you sure you did not take the car out?" that two days later, he went to an interview in Bournemouth for a job he had seen advertised and took the executive car. He was so angry at the retorts from the people he had worked with for ten years that he did it in defiance. He knew they would end his job. He said they were not worth working for any more.

'Eric Hendy was the only one he appreciated. He had helped Aaron out when he came out of hospital after the car accident, and he was very helpful in getting us compensation at that time. The other journalists always compete for the good jobs, and this causes bad blood. Aaron was a good journalist before the accident. Eric kept him on despite the decline in his abilities, but Aaron always knew it was only a matter of time before he was dismissed.'

James said sympathetically, 'It certainly seems to have been a hard four years for you, Sandra. You have cleared up a few questions for me. I have been asked by the father of the girl who disappeared that night, the fifteenth of January, to find out what happened. The fact that Aaron had been questioned came up, so I thought I would confirm it with you.'

'Have you seen a photo of that girl, James?' said Sandra pointedly. 'Aaron said she looked similar to me when I was that age, but her personality was all venom. She hated her father for pushing her to study night and day and for never allowing her any freedom. She hated the farm where the family lived, and she never wanted to go back to it.

'She had graduated and won a place in medical school to study to be a doctor, but she was not going to commit to another five years of study. She had enough of study. She now wanted only to have fun. Aaron has all that on tape. I listened to it and could not believe how much she hated her life with a good family who loved her and only wanted the best for her.'

'Does Aaron have all the interviews recorded?' James was excited. This will make his enquiries easier. It sounded as if Aaron was in the clear if Sandra was telling the truth.

'Yes, he keeps all his interview tapes. He says it makes things easier if he has to interview a person again, because he can check up on what questions he asked the first time, so he does not repeat himself,' Sandra confirmed.

'The next thing we want to know, Sandra, is if you want us to tell Aaron where you are and why, so he can visit you.' Both Alicia and James looked anxious for the answer.

'Yes, I am steadier now. I have been so well-looked-after by the hospital staff here, and I am ready to see him. It is not his fault that Bull hit me. Before you came and told me that Bull has been arrested, I did wonder about Aaron's place in it, but I knew in my heart that Aaron would not be a party to it. It is not in his make-up to hurt anyone, especially me. I am the love of his life. We get on well generally, and he does look after me. It was just that I was working up to a breakdown that got me all het up. They say you take your temper out on the person closest to you, and that was true for me.'

'And are you ready for Aaron to know where Jody is living?' asked Alicia.

'I will leave it up to you. I have been thinking about things since I have been lying here. I presume you went to the child welfare people after I left Jody with you, because I am a drug addict *por favour* of the doctor handing out prescriptions willy-nilly to me. They would not look kindly at me having Jody in my care for a while. I can understand that, especially after I signed that dreadful statement, which I presume you showed to the police. Am I right?'

'I am afraid so,' said Alicia. 'You did not give us a good description of your life, and I am sorry to say, you did not look as if you could look after a young child.'

'I can understand that. As I have said, I was close to a breakdown. Also, I am sure it is going to be a while until I can move properly again, if ever, going on what the doctors have said to me in the last few days after they gave me scans of all sorts. I did not know all this when I left Jody with you. I am sorry if I have caused you any distress, leaving Jody like that. Now that I have come through the breakdown period, I feel very guilty about what I have done to you. What would you like to do?'

Alicia looked nervous. 'We would like to keep Jody with us. We— all three of us, Granny, James, and me—love her. She is a delightful child and no trouble to us at all. She fits in with us, loves the thought of school, loves spending time in the bookshop, and is generally happy, but she was delighted when we told her we were visiting you today.'

James thought Alicia looked nervous, so he decided to take over the explanation. 'The welfare people have granted our wish for Jody to live with us. You will have to prove you are able to look after her when you are rehabilitated. We may have to work out a solution when you recover enough to come home.'

Jody, who had been sitting up beside her mother for some time, said, 'I call Alicia mummy now because she looks after me, and Granny looks after me too. But you are my real mummy. Until you come home, I want to stay with them in the bookshop. I love it there. There are always lots of people to talk to me, and they all say hello to me.'

Sandra was weeping silently and, hugging the little girl, said, 'I want you to have a happy life, Jody. If you want to stay with Alicia and James and they are willing to look after you, then you can stay. When I am able to come home, we will have to share you.

'I think it is all right to tell Aaron where she is, James. He will like to know that she is safe. He is not a bad man. It is just unfortunate that he also has a problem after the bang on his head and the vertebrae fractured in his neck. When there is quietness around us, he is a delightful companion.'

A nurse had noticed Sandra crying and came over to them and said it was time for Sandra's medication and rest. It was time for them to go. The little girl climbed down from the bed after kissing and hugging her mother one more time and waved to her as they left the room. James had called a cab, and it was waiting for them as they left the hospital.

9

Alicia said to James that Aaron seemed to be discriminated against by quite a lot of people, all because he had a problem with noise, which had been caused by the car accident. She suggested they take Jody with them after all to meet her father and explain the situation to him. It was time to explain where Sandra was and what they were doing with Jody.

James had to agree. After the conversation with Sandra, he had to admit that the prejudice he previously felt was all because of other people's observations of the man and Sandra's statement, which had been taken while she was distraught. She had spoken so lovingly about Aaron at the hospital that he could not be as bad as others were making him out to be.

*   *   *

When they arrived at the Jolly Green Frog, they found Aaron sitting at the bar, talking to the publican, Benny Goodman, whom James had met the previous year when he had spent time at the pub. Benny showed the group into the private room that James had requested.

When Aaron saw Jody, a look of disbelief came over his face, and he picked the little girl up and said, 'I have been looking for you all over the place, Jody, and you have been here within a few yards the whole time. How I have missed your sunny smiles. Are you all right?'

'Yes, Daddy. I live with my new mummy and daddy in the bookshop now. My real mummy says I can stay there with them if I want to.'

Aaron looked at Alicia and James and said, 'How did this come about?'

Alicia answered, saying, 'Do you remember me from school days, Aaron? I was not part of your group because I did not drink alcohol. Sandra met me in the shopping mall a while ago and left your little girl with us when she decided to go into rehabilitation for her drug addiction. James and I were on a trip to the Isle of Wight at that time, so we could not speak to Sandra when she left Jody with my grandmother. It was quite a surprise to come home and find that our family had grown while we were away.'

James continued. 'I am James Armstrong, Alicia's husband. Sandra went to my office after leaving Jody with Alicia's grandmother and made a statement there. The statement was very degrading for you, I am afraid, and we decided to take it to the police to look at, which is why you were picked up for questioning. Since then, several things have happened to clear things up.

'We followed you from the police station and saw you meet up with Andrew Bullock and leave on the London train. We searched Bullock's flat with a warrant for entry and found a number of backup discs hidden in the wardrobe. It was presumed they were of a paedophilic nature. We had the police waiting to arrest him when he returned from London, but when he saw them waiting outside of his flat, he ran away.

'We waited, my partner and I, until he returned, and called the police to come back to arrest him. When he was arrested, he seemed to think we did not know about his computer disc stash hidden in his wardrobe, and he shouted, "I could not have hit her hard enough if she has accused me of hitting her." He continued in that vein until I pointed out that he was confessing to the assault on Sandra in the park in London.'

Aaron was dismayed. 'Is this true? He left me and went back to assault Sandra?'

'All true, I am afraid. Luckily, soon after, a man walking his dog found Sandra on the park bench, bleeding from the head. He called an ambulance. The drivers picked up the brick which was the weapon used, for evidence for the police, and Andrew Bullock's fingerprints were identified on it by the police from their records on his earlier conviction. Sandra is in a London hospital. The hospital rang our office because a small piece of paper in her jacket pocket had our office number on it. She had no other means of identification on her at the time.'

Aaron looked horrified. 'What hospital is she in? Is she all right?'

'She was kept in an induced coma for two weeks but has now come around. We went to see her this morning, and we took Jody with us. Sandra is unable to walk and must use a wheelchair to move around, and that may be necessary for the rest of her life. We did not notify you because we were uncertain until this morning of your part in the whole affair. We had that dreadful statement that Sandra gave to us to go by. We saw you go on the London train with Bull, so until we could speak to Sandra, we did not know what to do. I am sorry. This is such a mess.'

Aaron looked very distressed. 'This is all my fault. I knew Sandra was close to a breakdown. She was getting very fragile and could hardly walk any more. It is only because of her strength of mind that she continued. I tried to get her care long ago, but she refused because she was afraid they would take Jody away from her.'

'How did Bull come into the equation, Aaron?' asked James.

'He saw Sandra and Jody in the shopping mall and followed them home. He had been a follower in our happy earlier days but had always been on the edge of the crowd. He recognised Sandra—he had a crush on her in our earlier life—but it was not Sandra he wanted this time. It was Jody. We did not realise for a while what he was after, but we still did not encourage him on his visits. He became a nuisance, turning up at our home any time of day and in the evening.

'I heard, through the courts, of his earlier jailing and decided he would be a good story for the newspaper. I now do part-time work for a Bournemouth group. I tried to draw him out to find out more about his predilection for children, to write an article about it, and it was during one of these times that he asked for Jody, to photograph her, and said he would pay me £500. I saw the look on Sandra's face after this conversation and knew she had got the wrong end of the stick.

'There is no way I would have allowed him to have a minute with my little girl. In fact, I put a lock on Jody's door, and whenever Bull turned up, I would put her in her room and lock the door so he would not even get a glimpse of her. Jody has always been an intelligent little girl and understood that I did not want that man to see her, and she would play happily in her room until he had gone and we unlocked the door again. We put the lock on the door to stop her from accidentally walking out of her room while Bull was there, as we could not take the chance of him seeing her again.'

'What about the refrigerator and the food in the child's bedroom, Aaron? What was the reason for that?' asked James.

Aaron looked very distressed. 'When Sandra would feel very bad, she would take a painkiller, and it would make her sleepy. She would lie down on Jody's bed and watch her play and sometimes go off to sleep. That was the side effect of the painkillers. If Jody got hungry, she would help herself to some cheese from the refrigerator and some cracker biscuits off the shelves or fruit, poor little mite. If I was at work, she had to look after her mother and play very quietly by herself. She is a very thoughtful child being brought up under difficult conditions, but she has the love of both parents.

'I have the disadvantage of not being able to manage with a lot of noise. She knew this and was always quiet in her play. I am getting a bit better now. It has been four years of torture for both Sandra and me, and at last I find I can manage a bit better. Hopefully, it will improve. Since I do not have the worry of turning up to the newspaper office every day, it has taken the tension out of me. I have two cracked vertebrae in my neck. The doctors did not have a way to fix them, I understand. The headaches have lessened over time, but I still wake up with a painful neck each morning and get tired. I still do not like loud noise. It makes my head throb. I try to avoid such things as train rides because of the noise they make, as it makes my head throb dreadfully, especially if I am tired.

'I am better off than Sandra. Her back has got worse over the four years, as she has done things she should not be doing, like walking to the shopping centre, but she is very determined and said she could not sit at home all day. She has gone downhill and has been in pain the whole time, but she refused to go to the doctor, as she believed they would only give her more morphine. She refused to take it, saying she had an addiction already and did not want to get worse.

'Sandra's capabilities have been dreadfully affected by her back, and she knew it was only a matter of time before it gave up on her permanently. Hopefully, they are helping her at the hospital. I will go and visit tomorrow. Thank you for all you have told me and for looking after Jody. What are your plans for Jody now? Have you discussed it with Sandra?'

'Yes, Sandra has agreed that we continue to look after her until further notice. Jody is very happy with us. She loves my grandmother and the bookshop. We have enrolled her in a preschool playgroup for the new school year, which she will enjoy immensely, and she is getting on fine with her life. You are welcome to come and visit her at any time now that we know that you are not going to sell her,' Alicia said with a smile to take off any insult.

'I am just so happy to see her safe and happy. She is obviously comfortable with you,' said Aaron. Jody was already asleep on Alicia's lap, as it had been a long day for her.

'There is one more thing, Aaron,' said James, looking a little anxious. 'Sandra told us that you keep your interviews on tape. Do you still have the tape on the January fifteenth party here at this pub?'

'Yes, I do keep all the interviews I have. It is amazing how often I have to listen to them again by request. Do you want that particular one, James?'

'I have been asked by Charles Chamberlain to help find out what happened to his daughter. The police have not come up with any answers. Sandra told us that you keep tapes of interviews, so I would appreciate if I could borrow it and listen to what happened that night to make a young woman disappear.'

'Do you want to come home with me now to pick it up, or shall I drop it off to you in the morning?'

'We can walk back to the bookshop. I will carry Jody, and then I can go on with you and pick up the tape. I promised Chamberlain that

I would call him this evening to tell him how far I have got, so it would be good to tell him of the tape. Perhaps he will want to hear it too, if that is all right with you.'

'It will give you an idea of where Jody is living now also, Aaron,' Alicia added. 'It will reassure you that she is happy and well-cared-for.'

'That sounds good. I really appreciate all you have done for us. I should have realised earlier how low Sandra was getting and organised for a nurse to call on her. I feel terribly guilty about everything that has happened.'

'Perhaps it has turned out for the best, Aaron. Sandra is getting the help she needs now. The nurses are looking after her, and she is much happier and settled in her thinking. She misses Jody, but perhaps you can take Jody on Saturdays to visit her. It is a very busy day for us in the bookshop, and Sunday is the only free day we have, usually.'

'It is good to have such care taken of us all, thank you. I will call again on Saturday, and Jody and I shall have a day together, visiting Sandra. We will all appreciate that.'

*   *   *

They called into the house next to the bookshop to introduce Granny to Aaron, and Alicia and Jody stayed there while James continued with Aaron to his home to pick up the tapes. Like Kate before him, James admired the decor of the place and asked who organised it. Aaron proudly said, 'It is all Sandra's work. She paints when she cannot move around because of her back. Sometimes she gets up during the night to paint, because she cannot get comfortable in bed, and paints half the night. It takes her mind off her pain. She is very artistic. The only part I play in it is to get the paintings framed and hung. She has the third bedroom as a studio and spends a lot of time there, while I work on the dining table with my computer.'

'Would you show me the studio, Aaron?'

'Sure, James. It is just as she left it when she went off to rehab,' he said as he opened the door. 'She uses oil paints with water now instead of turpentine, because of the smell, for Jody's sake. Sandra seems to think it is safer.'

Inside the room, James saw other paintings stacked along a wall, an easel set at sitting height to suit Sandra, and a large box of paints and brushes in jars. It was all very neat and packed up, ready to be used again any time it was needed. Beside the easel was a small table and a chair, with puzzles and books and coloured pencils and paper stacked neatly on the edge of the table, ready for Jody any time she was in the room. On another table, under the window, was a sewing machine, with a shelf for fabrics and drawers under the table for cotton.

James pointed to the sewing machine and said, 'Alicia said that Sandra used to make her own clothes. Does she still do that?'

'It has got a little difficult for her in the last year or two. She often nags at herself that she should be making things for Jody, but her back will not allow her many things she would like to do. So Jody goes on wearing jeans and tees. I noticed she had a dress on today. Whose work was that?'

'That would be Alicia's granny. She loves dressing Jody up, and the little girl parades around like a model when she gets a new dress. It is fun for both of them,' said James.

Aaron pulled a wry face. 'Unfortunately, she does not have any grandmothers of her own interested or able to look after her. It would have solved our problems if we did have someone interested, but no one has come forward. Sandra is so possessive of the child. I am surprised she left Jody with you, to be honest. It is not as if Alicia was a great friend from our past. She wasn't more than an acquaintance, really.'

James was sympathetic. 'It shows how desperate she was getting, I suppose. Alicia was surprised as well. That is why we took Sandra's statement to the police. We had no idea what was going on, and reading through the statement, we all agreed—my office staff and us—that it was the best thing to do. Also, the child welfare people were disturbed to read the statement. You may have trouble getting her back.'

'I had not got that far in my thinking,' Aaron said. 'I have been totally amazed the turn of affairs and have been trying to work it out in my head whether to report Jody missing. The only thing that stopped me was that Sandra had been so calm about it all when we met her at the rehabilitation centre that day. Jody is her baby, and if she was not worried, the child must be safe.'

'Jody is fine, Aaron, and accepts that her mother is sick and in hospital. Now that she has seen you as well, she will be even more accepting of the situation. We will keep her with us until Sandra is able to cope.'

'I too will be more accepting now that I know what is going on. I have been going over and over in my mind where Jody could be, and I am happy now that I have the answer. Thank you again, James.'

'I had better be off. I have to ring Chamberlain before dinner. You are not doing a newspaper story on Chamberlain or the missing girl by any chance, are you, Aaron?'

'No, I did not like the girl, and the evening still rankles with me. No, I do not want to revisit it.'

'I will listen to the tapes I have in my hand as soon as possible to see if I can pick up any indication of what happened to his daughter. Good night for now, Aaron. Wait, I meant to ask you. Do you have any memories of what Leanne Chamberlain said that night?'

'I remember she looked very much like Sandra at that time in her life, but I also remember being disgusted with her comments on her family. She may have looked like Sandra, but you never heard Sandra speak about her parents in a derisory way, even though she had good reason to.

'This Leanne was no patch on Sandra. I cannot remember all she said at that time of night in a noisy pub. I was feeling very low and had a roaring headache. I came back here and wrote up my story, leaving the bad parts out, and sent it off. I have not revisited that night at all, but if you let her father hear her story, he may get disgusted with her also. Perhaps you should let sleeping dogs lie. You listen, but not him.'

'Okay, Aaron, I will think about that and listen first. I will see you again. Bye for now.'

* * *

After Jody fell asleep that evening, James rang Chamberlain, as he had promised, and told him he did not believe that Aaron Dunstan had anything to do with the disappearance of Leanne, nor was he following him; James told him the story as Sandra had told him. He did not mention the tapes. He would take Aaron's advice and listen to it first with Alicia to see if he could pick up anything and decide whether he should bring it up with Chamberlain.

He set the tape recorder up, and he and Alicia listened to the noisy pub conversations. Alicia said, 'With the affliction Aaron has, it is no wonder he felt ill with a headache. The throb of the music alone is enough to give someone a headache, even if they did not have the problem that Aaron has. We can barely hear the voices through the music, and they all seem to be talking at once.'

They listened to Leanne Chamberlain talking directly into the tape. What they heard was as Sandra had described. A little time later, they heard a male voice, someone called Mel, say he was going to London that night on the late train. He had an appointment to start work first thing on Monday morning; he had applied for a position with an ambulance trust as a student paramedic so he could study while working, and he had been accepted. He thought this was a better way of getting a job than doing a diploma course.

Leanne's voice was heard asking, 'What time are you leaving, Mel?' At this stage, he seemed to have turned away from the tape recorder, and they did not hear his answer. They listened to the end of the tape, much of it about the New Year and the courses some were going to do. Several said they were going to look for a job. Two said they had jobs to go to. One was going to work in the customs office and sounded excited about starting in two weeks, after she had a holiday. She said she was so happy she did not have to go back to school. The other was a male named Gerald. He was going to work in the family business. He was not too happy about that, but his father had agreed he could have a month's holiday first. So he was going on a train trip around Europe, stopping off when he thought it looked interesting and just pleasing himself for a change.

That was when they heard Aaron speaking to the publican, saying that was all for him and he was going home. He switched the tape recorder off.

Alicia said, 'The notes I read said much the same, although Leanne's diatribe about her family home was not mentioned. Mel going to study as a paramedic was mentioned, but not when he was to leave. The remainder mentioned was as much as they said on the tape. I suppose Aaron was using some discretion in his interpretations of the tape and, in Leanne's case, merely said she had earned a place in medical school when she topped her classmates in her last year at school.'

'Thanks for that, Alicia. We have had a long day, so I will read the notes over when I go to the office in the morning. So much has happened today that I must admit that my mind is in a whirl, trying to work through it all. I will take the tape recorder to work tomorrow and let Percy and Kate listen to the recording and see if they come up with any ideas. My immediate thought is that we will have to follow up on this Mel person. Did you catch his surname?'

'It wasn't mentioned on the tape, but in Aaron's notes, he is Melvin Morrisey.'

'Thank you, Alicia. Could you look up the one who was going to have a train trip around Europe?'

'Yes, that one is Gerald Stone. His father owns that big hardware store on the highway as you go out on the road to Winchester.'

'Good, I think both of those lads could do with an interview from us. Both were moving away, and perhaps Leanne decided to go with them.'

'That sounds like a possibility, James.'

'Okay, we will leave it for tomorrow. Right now I need to go to sleep to rest my mind. I feel as if I have been wrung out.' James gave a yawn.

'I feel the same, James. Taking on someone else's problems is hard work. I feel so sorry for Sandra and Aaron and what they have been through. At least it has not seemed to have affected Jody very much. She is such a lovely child.'

'We must ask Aaron to invite you over to see Sandra's paintings. I am sure you will be impressed.' James knew Alicia was interested in paintings, because of her mother's collection on the walls of Granny's house.

'Yes, I would like to see them. Perhaps we can talk Sandra into a public exhibition of them for sale when she comes out of hospital. It could be a means to pick up a bit of money to cover their expenses.'

10

James took the tapes and papers to his office next morning and spread it all out on the meeting room table, including the photos and police reports for the missing Leanne Chamberlain. Percy and Kate inspected them with James. After James's explanation of the Sunday visits he made to Sandra and Aaron, he voiced his opinion that he now felt Aaron was innocent of the things Sandra had made a statement about.

Percy had also been thinking over the weekend and said he and Kate had changed their minds about Aaron as well. Sandra was obviously not well and had been venting her spleen with the stories she told, as you do with your nearest and dearest.

Next on the list, James said he believed that Leanne Chamberlain had managed her own disappearance because she was bored with the farm experience and the small town and wanted the bright lights of London. He left them to listen to the tapes and look through the reports and photos to see if they could work out what he was thinking.

Percy was the first to talk. 'It is possible that she either left with Mel or went travelling with Gerald, or perhaps both. Mel was leaving that night because he had a job to start. Gerald had not yet finalised his trip. It was in the "to do" basket. She could have gone to London with Mel and met up with Gerald. But Gerald would be back working for his father by now, so what happened to Leanne?'

'Your thinking is the same as mine, Percy. Why don't we go and visit the Stones' hardware store and ask Gerald these questions?'

'We will take my car, James. I need to get fuel on the way.'

'Kate, can you look up Mel Morrisey's parents' address and send it to me? We will call there on the way back and leave them a note if necessary. We should not be gone long.'

*   *   *

Stone's Hardware was on the edge of town, in a commercial area. It stood clear of the other properties around it because of the timber and other goods stored down both sides of the building; however, it presented a neat appearance. They entered and were immediately taken notice of by a young man with a large apron over his clothes. James guessed the young man was Gerald Stone, because of his age group, and when he asked for Gerald, the boy grinned and said, 'That is me. How can I help you?'

James handed the young man his business card and introduced himself and Percy. 'We want to ask you a few questions about the party on the fifteenth of January, when Leanne Chamberlain disappeared.'

Gerald Stone did not waver in any way. 'Yes, it was a good party, but nothing out of the ordinary. What do you want to know?'

'You spoke about travelling around Europe at the time before having to start work here with your father. Did you go on that trip?'

'Yes, I did, two weeks later. I stayed until my mother's birthday party was over and left the next day.'

'Did you meet up with Leanne Chamberlain on your trip?'

'No, I went with my cousin, Jim Stone. He is a year older than me, but we get on well together. We had a great time.'

'Do you know where Leanne Chamberlain is, or is there anything about her you can tell us?'

'Sorry, no, I can't. I have not heard anything about her since her disappearance. As far as I know, no one has heard from her at all. We often talk about her when anyone from school meets up, but it is a mystery.'

'What was your opinion of her, Gerald? Did you like her? Was she friendly with anyone in particular? Did she have a boyfriend?'

'She was all right. A bit stand-offish. She would sit and study during the lunch breaks when the rest of us would kick a ball around, whereas some of the girls would join in. She seemed to like her own company better than ours generally, and I do not think she had a boyfriend—none of us, anyway. She talked to the other girls a bit but did not seem to hang out with anyone special. I always thought she was a bit shy.' He shrugged. 'When I think about her, I realise that although she was in my class through senior school, I never got to know her very well at all. I am sorry I cannot be of more help.'

'Can you suggest any girls she may have talked to at the party?'

He shrugged again. 'Not really. She was the type of girl who was good to look at but somehow never seemed willing to make conversation, and that is why I thought she was shy. You could try Bettine Smith. She was one of the happy groups. I do not know how well she knew Leanne, but she was at the party that night. She has gone into nursing training. She may be closer to Leanne, because Leanne was going to do medicine.'

'Do you know where I could find Bettine?'

'Yes, she works at the coffee shop in the mall near your office, from 4 p.m. till 8 p.m. most days of the week.'

'Thank you, Gerald, for your cooperation. We will have a cup of coffee in the mall tonight.'

James's phone rang as they went back to the car, with Kate sending in the Morriseys' address and telephone number. The address was at a small village several miles away, so James decided to ring the phone number Kate had sent. The phone rang out, and James concluded there was no one at home and said he would ring this evening; perhaps the family was at work. 'What do you think of the situation, Percy?'

'Like you, I am sure Leanne did a runner to get out of town and away from her parents. But how is it that the father does not know this? Is he blind and deaf?'

James shrugged. 'It sounds as if he is somewhat of a helicopter parent, someone who hovers over their children and does not allow them any freedom. We will have coffee with Bettine Smith this afternoon. Girls sometimes have a better understanding of the other pupils at the school than boys do. They spent five years in each other's company for several hours a day. Therefore, someone must have some ideas.'

'I agree. Alicia is a good example of that. She understands people much better than I ever will. Perhaps you should take Alicia for coffee instead of me.'

James looked sideways at Percy. 'You could be right. If anyone can get something out of someone, Alicia can do it. I will ask her. She has listened to the tapes and read the reports, so she is well up on everything. It will be right up her alley. We might close the case this afternoon,' he said with a laugh.

*   *   *

James and Alicia went to the coffee shop to talk to Bettine, who turned out to be a jolly girl, slim and pretty. She whipped around the tables quickly. After James ordered coffee for two, he asked her if she would sit with them for a few moments; the shop was quiet so late in the day. When he explained that he wanted information on Leanne Chamberlain from Bettine's point of view, she became quite animated.

She said, 'It has always been my belief that Leanne and Mel Morrisey went to London together. Both went to primary school in the village near where they both lived, and they came to our senior school because they were good students and wanted to do courses their local school did not have available. They travelled home on the bus together each day. He seemed to be the only person she was really friendly with. She was not interested in any other boy, and she was a quiet person who was not outgoing enough to make friends, even with other girls.

'Most of the other students had gone through primary school together, so they had already made friends by the time they went to senior school. I suppose it was the same for those two. Mel mixed with the other boys, playing football with them and, of course, doing some projects. Leanne was a loner. She joined in doing projects with other students but otherwise kept to herself, usually studying at break times. It was no wonder she was dux of the school.'

Alicia asked her, 'Did she confide in any way to anyone about her home life?'

'She said once that she would not come to a school ball because her father would bring her in and stand around waiting for her, and she could not bear the embarrassment. I admit I felt sorry for her. Her father dropped her at school each morning, although she took the bus home, usually with Mel, in the afternoons. My impression of her was that she was unhappy with her family life. I heard her say at the party on the fifteenth of January that she hated the farm where she lived. I think she felt like a prisoner of her father. I do not know much about her mother, although she once described her mother as a mouse. She had a younger brother. She said he was the only one she loved and that he felt the same about the farm as she did and that when she finished school, she would get as far away from her parents as possible.

'Because she did not speak of her home life very much, the comments seemed to stay in my mind. These are fragments of things she has said over the years, not just one conversation, and it is all I learnt about her over the years. The only time I ever saw her animated was at that party. She had a drink, and I do not think she had ever had alcohol before, because she lit up as soon as she finished it. I saw Mel take a second glass away from her and say something to her, and she laughed at him. I do not know if she had another drink that evening, although it is possible she did when I was not looking. I think I watched her because she was acting so vivacious, and it was not her usual manner at all.'

'Do you know anything about the Morrisey family, Bettine?'

'Not very much, I am afraid. Being from out of town, Mel did not attend any social occasions either where we got together as a group and chatted.'

'You have been very helpful, Bettine, thank you.'

'Will you let me know if you find her, please? We were not close, but I would like to know if she is all right.'

'Yes, we will do that if we find her. In case you are no longer employed here at the coffee shop, can we have your telephone number? Can you remember what time you left the party that evening and if Leanne was still there?'

'I think Leanne left with Mel. It was as soon as the interviews were over. She said she was going to the station with him to see him off.'

'What time was that?'

'The party broke up about nine, maybe a little later. Leanne and Mel left first. I was home before ten. I remember watching a show on TV before going to bed.' She wrote her number on the back of the card James had given her.

Alicia wrote the number in her notebook and gave her back the card, saying, 'If you think of anything else that could be important, give us a ring or pop into our office, just outside the mall.'

'Yes, I will. I have noticed your office there.'

They went back to the office, even more convinced that they would find Leanne with Mel in London. James had another try at ringing the Morrisey family. This time, a younger voice answered the phone, identifying himself politely as Adrian Morrisey. He called his mother to the phone when requested, announcing them to her correctly. James was impressed by his phone manners.

James once again gave his name to Mrs Morrisey and asked her if she would advise him of her son Melvin's address in London. She immediately gave him an address and a cell phone number, saying, 'He works odd hours. He is studying to be a paramedic and lives in a unit supplied. What is your interest in him?'

'It is nothing to do with Mel specifically. I am searching for Leanne Chamberlain and wondered if he knows where she has gone. Would you know anything about that?'

'I know of Leanne Chamberlain through Mel, but I have had nothing to do with her. I heard on the news in January that she went missing after the party Mel went to with her, but I have not heard anything else. Mel went to London after that party to start a job. He was taken on, and he started work and study the same week. He rings me periodically but has had no time to come home for a visit. He says that between studying and working and doing his washing, he is kept very busy, and he will come if they give him a break. He has never mentioned Leanne in any of his calls.'

'Thank you, Mrs Morrisey, for your time. I will contact Mel directly to see if he can shed any light on our problem. It sounds as if he is progressing well if they have not sent him home already. Goodbye for now.'

As he put the phone down, he sat looking very pensive. Percy asked what he had come up with. James said, 'I am starting to have new thoughts about Leanne Chamberlain, and they are quite dark.'

'What is it, James, that is worrying you?'

'We have only Charles Chamberlain's word that Leanne rang him that evening. Everybody else we have spoken to has said Leanne hated her father and did not want to go home. What if he rang Leanne during the evening, and she said to him she was not coming home again? What would you expect this helicopter father to do?'

'Hop in his car and go and fetch her.'

'That is my thought too. No one saw where she went. She had had a drink and probably felt brave. Let's look at the pub's security footage again and see if we can spot him.'

They set up the film on a wider screen to see the whole bar area, with the young people standing and sitting around. They watched as the youngsters arrived and Aaron interviewed people on the sidelines. They watched as Aaron spoke to Leanne, and they saw the look of defiance on her face and Aaron's disgust with her before he turned to Mel and spoke to him. They watched through the rest of the film and watched as the crowd dispersed slowly. Then in the doorway, they saw Chamberlain scowling and looking at his daughter. It was a momentary appearance and could have been missed if they had not been carefully watching for him. It appeared as if he had been listening and watching while his daughter was interviewed, and he had been walking out of the room when the camera caught him.

Percy said, 'I think it is about now that we contact the police and give them all we have.'

'Yes, I am afraid so. I first want to ring Melvin Morrisey. Even if he is at work, he must be able to take a call. I want to confirm that Leanne did not go off to London with him, before we go any further. I do not want to have egg on my face if we are wrong about Chamberlain.'

He made the call, and it was picked up immediately. 'I apologise for ringing about things, Mel, if you are busy. Are you free to talk?'

'Yes, sir, you have caught me at lunch, the only free time I really have between work and study.'

'I am ringing about Leanne Chamberlain, Mel. When was the last time you saw her?'

'It was ten o'clock that evening of the party. I left to catch the train, and she walked to the station with me to say goodbye. I was to catch the ten o'clock train but got a lift by car instead. She went to the bus station to get a bus home, and I did not hear from her again. I wrote to her to ask her how she is doing in her course, but I never got an answer. Then I received a message from my mother saying that it had been reported that Leanne disappeared that night.

'I am afraid I have no ideas on that. I know she was unhappy at home and was threatening to leave, but she had been saying that forever. I did not really expect her to disappear and not say anything to me. I was about her only friend. Her father kept a close watch on her but missed the fact that we travelled each day from school by bus together. She used to laugh about that, pleased to have one over on him.

'She hated her parents for not allowing her more freedom, although she did not say much about them. I think she was embarrassed for them, more than anything. They were living the rural life, and she would laugh about it. I am sorry I cannot help you in the search for her, but I would appreciate if you would let me know if you find her. I do care about her and did not think she would leave me in the dark for so long and not answer my calls and emails.'

'Thank you, Mel. If I am still looking in a month's time, would I be able to come up to London and chat with you some more?'

'Sure. I suggest you ring before you come. They keep me very busy here, but we can work out a date and time.'

After this session of talking to Mel Morrisey, James asked for Kate, Percy, and Alicia to discuss 'the case of the missing chamberlain girl' he called it with the information he now held. After he told the others of the interviews and phone calls he had made and after he showed everyone the glimpse of Charles Chamberlain exiting the doorway of the pub, he asked for their input and opinions.

Alicia spoke first. 'The appearance of Chamberlain in the doorway compels me to believe he has hidden his daughter, but if so, why is he asking you to find her?'

Kate spoke next. 'I think the same as Alicia. There is something sinister about him asking you to find her. Or was he trying to point his finger at Aaron, making us suspicious and thinking to cause Aaron harm?'

'Well, I am with the girls,' said Percy. 'There is something suspicious about him asking you to find Leanne. He turned up to the party and saw Leanne and Mel walk to the train station together. Perhaps they kissed, and the father went berserk and grabbed Leanne. But what then? Did he take her home? Was he so angry at her defiance that he strangled her? We need a warrant to search their home and interview the wife and son, but at this stage, I think we have to talk to the officers who have been dealing with the story.'

'It seems we all think it was Chamberlain, but why and how is still not clear. Yes, Percy, I think you and I will take a trip to the police station and see what their ideas on it are, and yes, we need to get a warrant and interview the wife.'

Alicia said, 'Before you go off to the police station, James, what about a background check on Charles Chamberlain? How long has he lived on his farm? Where did he come from? I thought I detected a slight northern accent when he spoke to us here.'

'Good thinking, Alicia. Also, I will ring our lawyer friend who recommended me to him. He may have a bit of background to tell us. Okay, Percy, let's do these checks. I will start with the lawyer, Alec Overington.'

He dialled the lawyer's number and the call was picked up immediately. 'Hello, James, this is a change. It is usually me ringing you. What can I help you with?'

'Hi, Alec. You recommended me to Charles Chamberlain, and I have started the search for his daughter. What we need at the moment is a little information about the gentleman himself. Can you give us any background on him?'

'Not very much, I am afraid. He came to us several years ago to write a will, and we have done a few business things for him. He is an importer and exporter of luxury goods, and he has had a few customs problems from time to time, but nothing significant. He was here last fortnight for one of those dealings, and he was rambling on about seeing Aaron Dunstan on the train. He was the reporter doing the schoolies report for the press when Charles's daughter disappeared. Chamberlain said he seemed weird and said perhaps Aaron was the one who may know something about his daughter, or he may be wanting to write about the family and Charles did not want that. To stop him going on and on about it, because at this stage I was thinking he was the weird one, I suggested you could check Aaron out for him. Did he go to you?'

'Yes, he did. I thought he seemed a loving father in pain because his daughter disappeared, but after talking to a few people and following the sequence up, we now think here in our office that he was the one who did his daughter in. Do you know anything of his background—where he came from, how long he has been here—anything at all to get an insight into the man?'

'Yes, he does have a northern accent, very slight. It sounds like Manchester. If he came from wealthy parents, he would have gone to a good school, and that lessens the accent. So that may be why it is slight. I think he came from money, because there has been a big outlay for luxury goods. I am sorry, I cannot discuss his will. I made that up some ten years ago and do not remember the details anyway.'

'In your opinion, did he sound a bit demented talking about Aaron Dunstan?'

'You are sounding like a lawyer now, James. You must have learnt something along the way in your studies.' He laughed. 'Yes, he did sound demented and sat here with me, droning on, really talking to himself. He seemed to be off in another world, which is when I suggested he contact you.'

'We cannot understand why he would ask me to follow up leads if he is the perpetrator, which, to all of us here, seems possible now that we have so many facts uncovered. Is it a guilt wish, do you think? To me, it sounds as if he should lay low. No one so far has suggested he did the deed, and the police have not come up with anything. In fact, they missed the biggest lead of all. Why has he stirred up the hornet's nest?'

'That is why you are the detective, and I am only the lowly lawyer, James. You will work it out. You are good at what you do. All your staff are brilliant, including your wife. If I can think of anything else, I will give you a call. May I suggest you get your fee from Chamberlain before you rush in and say the wrong thing.'

'We always take a large part of the fee when taking on a job, so we are covered with that.'

'Good man.' Alec laughed. 'I may have a new job for you soon. I will give you a call when I work it out.'

'Thanks, Alec. I feel better after all those compliments you paid us. I will see you soon. Bye.'

Kate came in to see him, bringing in a list of properties around town that Chamberlain owned, including the farm, each of them with a high valuation. Percy had been working on the timing of Chamberlain arriving in the area, and they realised that all the properties were bought within one month, as if he had arrived with a lot of money and had a spending spree. The documents showed that a British bank was used for the payments, all cash deals. It was in March, fifteen years ago.

There was no mention of where he came from. Leanne must have been three or four years old at the time, and her brother a small baby. Alicia traced births to see where Leanne was born and when. Eventually, she found a Manchester birth record. Leanne had been born to a Lorraine Chamberlain and a Francis Chamberlain. There was no birth in that period registered to a Charles Chamberlain. The mystery was growing. There was no record for a son born to Charles Chamberlain so who was the boy Leanne called her brother?

With all this information, James decided to go and visit the policeman in charge at the local police station, who had been investigating the missing girl. There were missing links in Chamberlain's story, and he felt he needed authority to look further. He made an appointment so that he caught the right person, not someone down the chain of command. The appointment was made for nine o'clock the following morning.

*　　*　　*

Percy asked if he could go with James. He was intrigued by all the anomalies in the case and wanted to hear the policeman's point of view. They set off with all the evidence they had in a briefcase, to show if necessary.

They were not kept waiting, and shook hands with the burly policeman, who looked as if he had a desk job that kept him from exercising. When James laid out the story for him, the policeman held up his hand. 'James and Percy, I am amazed and very impressed at all the information you have here in such a short period since Chamberlain came to see you. The crunch in the story is that the family is in protective custody—hiding in plain sight, as it were.

'Fifteen years ago, Lorraine and Francis Chamberlain were doctors, with their own practice in a suburb of Manchester. There was an incorrect diagnosis of a sick young boy, who eventually died, and his family took it badly. The doctor—it was Francis— sent the boy home, diagnosing his condition as flu and a rash from an allergy. In fact, the child died of meningococcal disease two days later. That disease has very difficult symptoms to identify initially, and it quickly takes over the body, often of a young child, and causes death within a few days.

'The father of the child went crazy and stalked the two doctors. Lorraine and Frances left Leanne with her Chamberlain grandparents for a weekend and went to a restaurant to celebrate their fifth wedding anniversary. As they came out of the restaurant at the end of the meal, the father of the deceased child was waiting with a gun and shot both of the doctors. He was yelling at the time, "I will hunt down all of your family and kill them! Then you will know how it is to lose a child!" It was too late for them to know how it was to lose a child. He had killed them both.

'The families of the dead couple were absolutely devastated by their loss. The man was diagnosed as insane at the prison hospital he was sent to. He was a leader of a religious sect, and others of the sect started stalking Chamberlain family members. It seemed as if they were concentrating on Leanne, because they appeared at her preschool several days in a row, waiting outside for her to appear. The family became frantic, too afraid to take Leanne out of the house. It was a shot from one of the crazy man's brothers at Charles—who was Dr Francis Chamberlain's elder brother—as he walked out of his house, that made them decide they had to leave the area and take Leanne away for her safety. The Chamberlains are a well-to-do family, they asked for protective custody, and it was approved. They put their property into the hands of their lawyer to sell for them and moved here.

'Charles Chamberlain has been very protective of Leanne over the years, and she did not know the story behind it all, until Charles told her on her eighteenth birthday. She did not take the story well, ranting at her "father" for keeping the truth from her for so many years. It took her some time to accept that Charles had done it all for her protection.'

'Charles has knowledge of where Leanne is now, I presume,' said James.

'Yes,' said the policeman. 'The whole idea of the disappearance of Leanne was to alert the crazy people looking for her so they would think she is dead.'

'Am I right to presume that she went to London with Melvin Morrisey?'

The policeman smiled. 'You are good, James. Yes, they went together that evening. In fact, Charles took them in his large car with their luggage. They are now to be married. That was the reason Charles went to London last month, for his "business meeting". He will set the couple up in their own apartment, and both will be attending university, with Leanne Chamberlain—who will now be Leanne Morrisey—to study medicine and Melvin to study to be a paramedic.'

'We assumed most of these things, but we still cannot see why he came to our office for us to arrange to give a breakdown of Aaron Dunstan. It is illogical. Besides doing a quick story on the party and the guests, Aaron is completely out of the picture, as far as we can see.'

'I think he was a little afraid that Aaron would do a further story on Leanne and spoil his story. He wanted confirmation that Aaron was not concerned. That is all I can see. We checked Aaron's story out in January and did not believe he had any further interest in Leanne.'

'When were you informed about where Leanne had disappeared to, sir?' asked Percy.

'A week after the presumed disappearance. We were getting too close to the truth, so Charles decided to let me into the picture. None of the rest of our people are aware. They were surprised they were pulled off the job and are probably still wondering.'

'We have put quite a lot of time into this story, so we will send him quite a large bill for our time,' James said, sounding bitter.

'Rightly so. He asked you to do it for his own peace of mind, I presume. He is well able to pay your account, so do not be stingy on the bill.'

Percy said, 'One more question. Who are the woman and the boy at the farm with Chamberlain?'

The policeman looked admiringly at both men. 'You do get to the nitty-gritty, don't you? The woman was a police officer who volunteered to accompany the family to watch over Leanne while Charles was working. She was involved in a sexual harassment and rape case where she was the victim. The boy was the result of that rape. She was to leave the police force, and Charles asked her, with the assistance of the squad up in Manchester, to accompany him to look after Leanne. She agreed to the move, with the stipulation that the boy never be told the true story of his father and the rape. That is why Charles claims him as his own son. They married a few years later, and Charles adopted the boy.'

'Well, all I can say is, it is just as well we did not get the warrant to search the farm for bodies, as we were thinking at one stage when everything pointed to Chamberlain. The only thing that stopped us was the question of why he had asked us to check out Aaron Dunstan. It was confusing us.'

'When I saw the appointment with you in my diary for this morning, I rang Chamberlain last night to get permission to tell you everything, and when I asked him that same question about Aaron Dunstan, his answer was that he thought Dunstan had been following him when he saw him that day on the train. He did not want Aaron writing any more about the family or stirring up the old story of his brother and his wife being murdered and starting the trouble all over again. That is the only answer I have for that.'

James looked sceptical. 'I will ring him today and assure him once again that Dunstan is not interested in him. He has too many problems of his own to worry about.'

The policeman looked interested. 'What worries has Aaron got? He used to be a familiar figure around here in his heyday of reporting. I haven't seen him or heard from him for a while.'

'He had a car accident four years ago which injured both his wife and himself, and they are both in a poor state of health. His wife is in a London hospital, awaiting surgery, and will probably be in a wheelchair when she comes out. Aaron is improving slowly but still has some difficulties. The job he did at the party of schoolies was his last job for the local newspaper. The couple have had a very difficult four years since the accident. They also have a beautiful daughter, born the day of the accident. My wife and her grandmother are looking after her while her mother has her surgery.'

'I am sorry to hear about that, James. Aaron was always a jolly chap and always had a joke to tell us.'

'We will be off to our next job. Thank you, sir, for trusting us with the Chamberlain story.'

'Any time you are looking for an answer, we will be happy to help out if we can. It was good to see you both.'

Percy and James shook his hand and left the office. Percy said, 'I think Chamberlain was trying us out to see how watertight his daughter's disappearance is.'

'I think you are right, Percy. Why else would he come to us? He knew the answers already. I presume he wants to keep up the disappearance story. Well, as long as he pays for our time, we haven't lost anything. I will ring him when we get back to the office and sign the deal off.'

11

Kate came into the office on Friday morning, looking excited. She said to the rest of the team, 'I think I have found a new job for us.' They looked up, and she said, 'I have a friend who runs a successful restaurant in town, and he rang me last night because he knows I am working in the private investigations field.'

'Sounds interesting, Kate,' said Percy. 'What did he have to say?'

'In the past few months, his restaurant and several others that he knows of have had a man come into their dining room and eat his way through the menu and then get up and walk out the door without paying. The first time he did it, they thought he had forgotten to pay his bill and would come back later and pay, but this never happened. They gave up on him, but a few months later, he was back in a disguise, with a wig and wearing glasses and a different type of clothes. So until he walked out without paying, they fed him, and they were disgusted with themselves for not recognising him. Once, he came in with a female companion, acting lovey-dovey with her at the table, and then they both went out the door without paying.

'My friend, Paddy, said that after the first time it happened, he put in some security cameras, but this guy always set himself up facing away from the cameras and sitting close to the door for a quick getaway. Paddy rang some other restaurant owners he knows, and they too have had visits from this man and sometimes the lady as well.'

'What has he done about it so far, Kate?' asked James.

'He installed another camera over the door, facing the direction of the seat the visitor usually chooses. The man turned up at lunchtime yesterday, and Paddy has a nice photo of him coming in and sitting down at the table he likes at the restaurant and again leaving. It is the first time they have been able to get a picture of the offender.

'Paddy employs university students to wait on the tables. He says he was once at university and was always broke and hungry, so he likes to help those who help themselves and are willing to work. But this gives him a big turnover in staff. Therefore, the man has been able to get away with not being recognised.

'He rang me yesterday and explained all this to me and said he and two other restaurant owners are willing to put their funds together to pay our bill if we find this man for them. They realise we may not be able to get their bills paid, but they want the man's actions closed down. What do you say, folks? Is this a job for us?'

Percy said, 'Make an appointment with Paddy, Kate, and you and I will go and look at the camera and his restaurant. I presume that if the chap went to Paddy's place yesterday, he will be turning his attention to one of the others next. We will have to look on the street directory at the distances and the dates he visited each, and see if there is a pattern.

'We can get copies of the photo Paddy has and we will post them in every restaurant around his pattern. Someone should recognise him from the photo and call us or the police when they see him walk in. We can put a stop to this quickly. We will take the photo to the police and see if they know him or can identify him.'

'Great, Percy! I am glad I am able to add to our jobs.'

'This should not take us very long, Kate, but it will be interesting visiting the restaurants in the area. I am always looking for a different place to eat rather than cooking for myself.' Percy asked James if he rang Charles Chamberlain yesterday evening.

'Yes, he was very polite and thanked us for our time and said the cheque for the final account was in the mail. No other explanations, really. I did not like to push him into saying why he felt it necessary for us to prove things to him, so that is that. It is not up to us to wonder, so it is into the archives with that one.'

'A good place for it. At least we now know the answer. There must be a few people around town worrying, in case we have a predator in our community.'

'Well, I am going to ask Alicia to go to the coffee shop this afternoon to tell Bettine Smith that Leanne is safe and well, so she will pass the news around. No more details for her, but to leave those young people unknowing is almost criminal in my view. They will be wondering all their lives about what happened to Leanne. We need to close the story down.'

Percy nodded. 'That is good, James. I agree with you. They do not have to be told any more details, just that she is safe.'

Kate came back to Percy to say, 'Paddy is going to the restaurant now to get ready for the lunch trade. He should be there in fifteen minutes.'

'Good, Kate. Do you know where to go? We will go in my car. Okay, James, we are off. See you later.'

'Good luck. This sounds like a tasty bit of work for you both.'

'I hope so, James. That is why I volunteered for it,' said Percy with a grin as he went out the door.

James turned to Alicia. 'It's Friday again. The week seems to fly. Do you plan to visit Sandra again this Sunday and take Jody to see her? I guess we both believe all that Sandra and Aaron have told us.'

Alicia sighed. 'We know now that the drugs were all prescription ones for the pain they both had. It is a completely different story than what we initially believed. We did jump to conclusions about them, I am sorry to say.'

'What do you think their future will be, Alicia?'

'If Sandra is confined to a wheelchair but Aaron is able to care for her, there is no reason they cannot manage a four-year-old child between them. The hardest part of handling a child is over. Jody is well able to dress herself with just a little help.' Alicia stopped to think and continued, 'Perhaps the doctors can arrange for Aaron to be Sandra's carer and be paid for it. Others seem to be able to get that title and seem to do all right. They would both get a pension then—Sandra, a disabled pension, and Aaron, a carer's pension—and with child payments, they should manage okay. Maybe some of Sandra's paintings can be sold to give them a bonus from time to time.'

'I am sure they would be eligible for all that. It should have been offered to them after the accident. I suppose the compensation money they were given would have stopped any payments, but as they have set up their home with it, it should be no problem now. I will look into it. Maybe if I have a session with Alec Overington, we could work something out—pro bono, of course.' James grinned. 'I did not squander all my time getting a law degree for nothing. We should come up with an answer between us.'

Alicia smiled. 'I believe you, James. I see the lawyer in you come out quite often, although I am sure you are unaware of it.'

'Is that right, Alicia? You are correct, I am unaware of it, but I suppose even if you are not actually working at being a lawyer, something must rub off on you.'

'I am proud of you, James. You work things out so quickly, so logically, much quicker than the average person.'

He hugged her. 'Thank you, Alicia. Now are we going to visit Sandra?'

'I think we should all go—Aaron and Jody too—to have a chat about the future. I thought it might be a bit early for it, but Sandra needs to be reassured about having Jody back. I could see the pain she felt when she thought she might lose Jody altogether, and I put myself in her place and knew what she might have been feeling.' She sniffed, close to tears. 'I cannot bear to cause her any more pain. She has had so much in her lifetime. We will keep in touch with her when she does come home, and we will give her as much help as we can.'

'Yes, Alicia, I felt her pain also. They can manage as a family with the doctor's help. It may be difficult for them, but other people manage from a wheelchair and Aaron does seem to care for her and Jody. He could still work part-time as a journalist. It is something he is already doing, and there would be no reason not to continue. Okay, will you contact Aaron and tell him what we think and organise for the four of us to visit Sandra on Sunday if he thinks it is a good idea? You can put it so much better than me.'

'Yes, James, I will do it now while the office is quiet,' she said, dialling the phone number.

After speaking with Aaron for some time, Alicia put the phone down and turned to James. 'Aaron would be happy to go with us to talk to Sandra. Each time he has visited, she got very emotional, and he is worried that it is because she thinks she has lost Jody to us. His belief is that she will pick up if she knows what we are thinking. He could not reassure her, because he did not know our thoughts and what the outcome of her surgery would be.

'He said he spoke to the doctor of the ward about Sandra's operation, and they think that unless a miracle happens when they operate, Sandra will be in a wheelchair for the rest of her days. He said the doctor was very matter-of-fact, so he believes that will be her destiny now. The doctor said they are saying this now for Sandra to get used to the idea and to not be overwhelmed after the operation when they disclose the truth to her. If a miracle does happen, she will be uplifted, but they are not confident it will be a positive result.'

'Did you mention the coming-home bit of our conversation?' asked James.

'No, I thought we would leave that for Sunday. Perhaps you could discuss it with your lawyer friend this afternoon to get an idea of if we are thinking correctly. I would hate to get their hopes up only to have them dashed after the operation.'

'Okay, I will ring him now and give him the low-down. I will also have a word with him about the Dunstans joining a class action against the airbags that exploded in the car. Sandra saved her own life and also Jody's by leaning forward before the airbag on her side of the car exploded. It was the airbag that damaged her back. He can have a think about it for the afternoon and get back to us before we go to the hospital. He may not have enough time to get a positive on it, but he will have an idea. This has not been my expertise up till now.'

'It is good to add to your expertise, James. It all counts.'

'Yes, I can see it could come in handy in the future, especially as there is a worldwide class action now against the manufacturers of airbags. Many people have been injured by them, and some have been killed when the expiry dates of the airbags passed. It is up to the manufacturers or the car salespeople to have them looked at before things happen, like what the Dunstan's experienced.'

He rang Alec Overington's number and asked if he had a moment to talk.

'I am free for ten minutes, James, go ahead' was the answer.

'Alec, I have a family problem. It is not my family, but some acquaintances that are in a bit of trouble. Sandra and Aaron Dunstan were injured in a car accident four years ago. Sandra was eight months pregnant at the time, and their car was hit by a bus hurrying to get through the green light, not realising that the traffic up ahead had come to a standstill. The bus hit the back of the Dunstans' vehicle at some speed, and the airbags exploded when the Dunstans' car was pushed into another car ahead. When I say *exploded* that is exactly what happened. They disintegrated, showering the occupants.

'Sandra had seen the bus coming in the rear-vision mirror and leaned over to protect her baby. Luckily, the baby came out perfect after Sandra was cut out of the car, and a beautiful little girl was delivered when she got to the hospital. Sandra had several vertebrae crumble in her back. Aaron was injured as well, fracturing two vertebrae in his neck and suffering whiplash. These injuries have given them both a hard time over the years. Aaron has suffered from neck pain and headaches, even some backaches at times, and cannot bear to have loud noises in his vicinity, which has caused him to be dismissed from his job as a newspaper reporter. Sandra is in a poor state. She is now in a London hospital, where they are going to do surgery to try and alleviate her pain. Unfortunately, she has worsened so much there is not much chance of her ever walking again, and she will probably be confined to a wheelchair.

'Both Dunstans have become addicted to prescription drugs for the pain. Sandra became so bad that she was heading for a breakdown and left her little girl with Alicia and her grandmother so she could try rehabilitation for the drug-taking. But as the hospital told us, because of her constant pain, she is not likely to kick the habit on her own. She needed the drugs to look after her baby, now a beautiful four-year-old.

'The reason I am ringing you is to enquire if you have any ideas about welfare payments now that Aaron is unemployed. I believe they should both be eligible for welfare. Sandra at least will not be able to do much in the future and should be eligible for a disability pension and perhaps some care. Aaron is improving. He is recovering but is still not able to stand noise, which will stop him from fully entering the workforce. I can see him being Sandra's carer, and between them, they will manage with the child. The class action for the airbag explosion is the main purpose of my enquiry. Do you have any ideas on all this?'

'Whew, that was a full ten minutes, James. I am having a recording made of the conversation and will read it back to myself later to make sure I understand all the issues. It sounds as if your friends have had a tough time of it. The welfare issue is a matter for the government. We could submit a recommendation to them, but it is for them to look at it and decide. A doctor's report will do the most good for both of them, so if Sandra is already in hospital, make sure you get a full report from them.

'Aaron should be examined as well. He sounds as if he should have been getting help already if he cannot work. I have read about the airbag problem and that some vehicles have been recalled, but I will have to look it up to get more details. So do not promise them anything from that yet. It could be years before it is completed, but it is a good idea for them to join the action for it. I will have to let you know when I have time to look up what is required. Do you have a copy of the initial report on the accident?'

'Yes, I will send you a copy. I looked it up after Sandra left Jody with us. Sandra looked as if she was in pain and could not stand straight. She is the same age as Alicia but looks ten years older. Alicia and Sandra were in the same class at school, and Sandra looked so bad that Alicia did not recognise her at first. Alicia and I will pay the bill for your time, Alec. They are down and out now because they have both become addicted to prescription painkillers. We feel so sorry for them and want to help if we can.'

'This will be pro bono, James. They have not brought anything on themselves, and it does us good to do something to help our friends.

Good luck with it all, James, and I will get back to you with the airbag class action information.

'One more thing, James. I am aware that you have a law degree and have never practised. Would you like the odd case to keep your hand in? It is not that I think you would be rusty on it. I have seen you in action and know you can do it. We can try the easy cases at first, and you can work up to harder ones as you go along. We can register you for our office as an assistant initially, and if you want to go on with it, we can discuss it further down the track. What do you think?'

'You have taken me completely by surprise, Alec. Let me think about it for a while and talk it over with Alicia, and I will get back to you. I must say, I have not given anything like this a thought, as we have been busy building up the private investigations business. It actually sounds like a good idea, but I need to think it over. Thank you for the thought, Alec.'

After he ended the call, James sat and thought over the conversation. It had taken him completely by surprise, but it actually did sound like a good idea. It would be a shame to waste the years of study he had put into gaining his law degree.

Percy and Kate had not yet returned to the office, so he went and told Alicia what Alec had said about the problems facing the Dunstans. Then he went on to tell her what Alec had said about giving him some work in his office.

Alicia was not surprised. She knew what James was capable of and had every confidence in his being able to do it. She hugged him. 'That sounds wonderful, James! Even if it is only the easy cases he gives to you, it is good for your experience. Percy should be told early that you are contemplating it—that is, if you are. It need not interfere with your work here. We have been busy, but we do get quiet periods, which is when you can do something for Alec.'

'Mmm! It needs a bit of thought, and yes, I will tell Percy straight away that an offer has been made. I do not want Percy wondering if I am stabbing him in the back.'

Percy and Kate returned and reported that they had put photographs of the man they were trying to trap in all the restaurants they could find.

Many of the waiters said they recognised him; however, he sometimes wore a wig, they said after examining the photo. 'This man has been operating for some time, it seems. He works one area and then moves on to another area. There is hardly any restaurant he has not hit. He must be putting on weight by now. He likes to eat well.' Percy laughed as he said this. 'His latest itinerary seems to be the area where Paddy's restaurant is situated, so we should get a call any evening. Kate and I will be right on to him.'

12

Just as Percy finished his report, a young woman pushing a pram and holding a toddler by the hand walked into the office. Alicia greeted them, and the woman asked if she could speak to a private investigator. Alicia smiled and turned to the group gathered near the desk and said, 'Take your pick. This is our entire staff.' She pointed to each in turn, introducing Percy, James, and Kate.

James took pity on her, as she looked very uncertain. 'Perhaps I can help. Come into my office. Alicia will look after the children for you while you tell me your story.'

She followed him into his office, giving Alicia an apologetic smile as she went and waved to the children.

'Please take a seat. To start, can you give me your name and a bit of background?'

She gave a tentative smile and said, 'I am Anne Mahmoud. My husband, Jarish, is a Muslim, and I am uncertain about what is happening. He is a good man and was born in the UK to Pakistani parents. Recently, he has been going out in the evening for about two hours, twice a week, Monday and Wednesday. He comes home from work, has dinner, changes into black trousers and a shirt and a black beanie, and leaves the house. I ask him where he is going, and he laughs and says, "Man's time off. I am going out for a bit of exercise. It is better than dozing in front of the television." That is his answer each time I ask. He comes home dusty and sweaty and very tired. I am afraid he is doing something illegal. It may only be my imagination, of course, but

I want you to follow him for me and find out where he goes and what he does while he is missing from our home.'

'Are you afraid he is training to be a terrorist, Anne?'

'That has crossed my mind, but I do not feel ready to accept that. However, I suppose asking you to follow him means that, in my mind, it is what I am afraid of. He has never expressed any sentiments about admiring terrorists, so I cannot see him suddenly becoming one. He has always been a happy family man, happy in his work and with his friends. To me, he is not terrorist material. However, I want to put my mind at ease and find out where he regularly goes twice a week.'

'That seems an easy enough surveillance job. If you give me your address, I can start on Monday. What time does he come home from work?'

'Six o'clock, usually. He has dinner and is gone again by seven. He comes home again about nine. He goes in our car, and I have not been able to follow him because of the children.'

'I will ask Alicia to come into this office, and I will watch the children where they are now. Alicia will tell you our fees, and you will have to sign a form requesting the surveillance. Depending on what I find out on Monday, I may have to follow him again on Wednesday. That should be enough. But if anything more is required, I will let you know before we carry on, for you to decide on whether you want us to continue.'

'Thank you, Mr Armstrong. It will put my mind at rest, just knowing. It is a terrible thing to suspect my loving husband, who has never done anything for me to doubt him before. I think it is the talk about terrorism wherever you go or when you pick up a newspaper or watch the news. It makes you doubt everyone.

'It has been on everyone's mind since the raids in London and Manchester. The world is turning sinister, and you don't know who to trust any more. Luckily, we have been away from it here in our town, but it seems to be spreading. Whoever would have thought that they would bomb a place where children and teenagers gathered to have a concert? It is the worst sort of story to hear.

'That is why I have to know what my husband is up to. We love him, and he returns our love. I cannot understand why home-grown young people are doing all these terrible things, and it preys on my mind each time my husband goes out. Someone must be getting to them and teaching them all those terrible things. I must know what he is doing.'

'Relax, Anne, for the next few days. Rather than have me call you, if you can come in here to see me on Tuesday next week, there will be no record on your phone.'

'That is why I came into your office. I thought of that. I do not want to turn my husband against me.'

'That is good thinking, Anne. We will get on with things and set your mind at rest.'

* * *

On Sunday, the Armstrongs went with Jody and Aaron Dunstan to see Sandra in hospital and came away saddened that they would lose Jody to her parents but happy that they had made the decision. Sandra could go through her surgery with the thought of uniting with her husband and daughter when she recovered.

* * *

On Monday evening, James took Alicia home from the office, had a quick meal, changed into casual wear, and then set off to the Mahmoud's house to wait in a secluded spot. He saw Jarish Mahmoud set off in his car, and James followed him. He drove steadily to a barn on the edge of town and parked amongst other cars already there.

James looked around at the area. It was quite isolated and obviously used to be a farm. There were two houses close together, and this barn where he stood had been the machinery shed when the farm had been worked.

He followed Jarish and two other young men into the barn and found a table with a notebook for registering the men entering the large area they walked into. He signed his name underneath the others on the dated page and added up the number of others. There were eighteen signatures. Next to the book was a bowl with £1 coins, almost filled up, so he added his donation on top. He turned to see what was going on in the huge barn area.

The eighteen men were standing in rows an arm's length apart, as he had done in his physical education classes at school and university. Standing in front of the men was a young man, perhaps thirty or thirty-five years old, dressed in shorts and a T-shirt, who looked very fit, despite his artificial right leg. He was chatting with a couple of the men while the others lined up. He looked at his watch and said, 'Okay, chaps, it's time to start.'

He led the group through warm-up exercises and then broke off to have the men pair up and to show them how to evade weapons, such as knives, aimed at them. The men followed his example, some better than others, some struggling to stay upright.

James had no problem keeping up with the many moves. He had done most of these exercises during his university days, and although it had been some time since then, he was still able to keep up, as the man he was tackling was not as fit. The leader moved amongst the group, showing ways to better their positions.

They had a ten-minute break, and then the leader asked them to run around the inside perimeter of the barn for ten minutes. James looked at his watch; the time had passed so quickly, and he realised the group would be stopping soon to go home, if Anne Mahmoud's husband was to arrive at his house at nine o'clock. He was right; the group was called together, and they did some cool-down exercises and then were dismissed, each chatting as they made their way out to their vehicles.

James stayed back, watching the men disperse. The leader had said little to the men, other than to tell them how each move was done; there had been no idle chatting. When the last man had gone out the door, James turned around to see the leader looking at him curiously as he said, 'Well, matey, what did you think of that? It is your first time here, isn't it?'

'Yes. I am James Armstrong. Do you mind having a word with me? I have a few questions about what you are doing here.'

'Go ahead, James. I am curious as well. You do not look like one of the workmates I usually get. I noticed as well that you seem to have done all this before. You swung into it like a pro.'

'Certainly not a pro. It is the same routine used to get fit at university if you played a sport. I used to be a cricketer, and being fit was a necessity to chase balls. I am a little out of practice. It has been a while. I am curious as to how you got this outfit going. I looked back at the pages of your book on the table and noticed that you are building up your numbers quite quickly, obviously by word of mouth, as most of the chaps seem to know each other.'

'Yes, it is a bit of a wonder to me as well. I was having a drink at one of the local pubs and was sitting at the bar. There were several men sitting at a table in a group, and they asked me over. My artificial leg is like a magnet, and everybody wants to know how I got it. I was a soldier in Afghanistan. I had just got out of the army and arrived home feeling a bit sorry for myself, so I had gone for a beer and some company to jolly myself up.

'After telling them about the army, we started to talk about the knife attacks on innocent people in the marketplace in London. It was showing for the tenth time on the television above the counter in the pub, and we watched as people were running away because the attackers looked like they had suicide belts on. I opened my big mouth and said that suicide bombers rarely have knives to slash out at all and sundry, because they are wearing their weapon. You do not see suicide bombers running around, trying to hurt and kill people. They just detonate their bombs. The men attacking looked like hoodlums to me. Therefore, those men with the knives needed someone to take their knives off them, and if you knew how to do it, you could have had three men to take to trial to find out their motive, instead of three men lying dead as martyrs.'

James said, 'And you were asked how to do it?'

'Pretty much so. It started with those eight men in the bar on my front lawn next door, and it gradually got bigger and bigger. My father gave me the use of this machinery shed and cleaned it out for me. If it keeps growing, I will have to move outside. That will be fine in summer, but a bit cold in winter.'

'I am sorry, I do not know your name.'

'Sorry, mate, I should have introduced myself. I am ex–army sergeant Harold Burton, generally called Harry. You are here for a reason, aren't you, James?'

'I am a private investigator with Gray and Armstrong Private Investigations in the city. I was retained by one of the wives to find out what is going on. Her husband leaves the house two evenings a week and does not tell her where he is going, and he comes home sweaty and dusty. She wanted to confirm that he was not doing terrorist training.'

'I wondered when the enquiries would come. It has not been clandestine and started off small, but it has grown so quickly even I am surprised. I am also surprised that all the men turn up for both sessions each week, and none have dropped by the wayside yet. I thought the neighbours were the ones who would be complaining, but I have had a word with a few of them. They seem to think it is something needed in the community. As one old dear said, "It will get them away from their games and phones and put a little life into the young 'uns." I had to laugh, but she is right. We have grown a little slothful in later years.'

James laughed. 'She sounds like my wife's grandmother, whom we live with. She started a book club for youngsters to learn about books instead of phones.'

'Good for her. Now we can learn a thing or two from the older generation. It was my idea to train them as anti-terrorists, so you can put Jarish's wife at ease.'

'You spotted my client then?'

'He is the only Pakistani in the group, but like me, he is an ex too. He is an ex-Pakistani now. His heart is all British. When I was getting to know the first group, I interrogated him about his sympathies. I wanted to know where he stood if a fight began. If someone tried to cut his wife and children, he will defend them very quickly. They are his life, and this country is his home.'

'Well, Harry, you have put my mind at rest, but what are you going to do about all the other enquiries which may surely come? The barn seems dark, looking at it from outside, and black-clothed men marching in and out will arouse most people's curiosity. These are getting to be terrible times with terrorists, and surely other people will be wondering what you are about.'

'It was not my idea to wear the dark clothes. That is something that has evolved by itself. What do you suggest, James?'

'I think you need a sign describing what you are doing. As an example—I have never had to think of something like this before— what about "Harry's keep-fit classes. Everyone welcome. £5 entrance fee for two hours of exercise overseen personally by Harry, ex–army sergeant"?'

'Wow, that actually sounds pretty good off the cuff, so to speak. I notice you put the price up. I was only asking for a small amount to pay the electricity.'

'Have you got another job, Harry?'

'Not now. I am on a disability pension until I find a proper job. The prosthetic is still new to me. I do have a little trouble with it, as it can get very uncomfortable with all the exercise I do.'

'I should think that is an understatement. But just think of the aches and pains you are giving to most of those young men using muscles they forgot they had.'

Harry roared with laughter. 'I did not think of that. I was too busy feeling sorry for myself. But you are right, it all gets better in time, or so my doctor says.'

'Why not make this your permanent job, Harry? Until you build up some more numbers, you are allowed to earn a certain amount before your pension is cut off. That will give you some time to build your business. You are very good at making the message clear and watching for mistakes so they can be dealt with. Your army training is clear. If necessary, give your initial blokes a discount—not the whole eighteen that turned up tonight, just the first ones. The other thing that comes to mind is that you should include a little CPR lesson in your act, in case someone needs it after all the work they do. For someone completely unfit, it could cause a problem.'

'It has all taken me by surprise, the way it has happened. Yes, I can see the CPR lesson could be a bonus to my program. I will put some thought into it. What else will I need besides the sign, do you think?'

'I think if the authorities came to visit, they would say you need more toilets for this many people, and if you take females, they will also require separate toilets.'

'I have thought of that, with the numbers growing, but I am not sure how long we are going to maintain the numbers and if they are going to increase any more. It is a big expense for a disabled pensioner.'

'Work out a business plan, Harry, and take it to the Small Business Council. They may give you a grant, seeing as you are teaching our lads to get fit. You also require mats for the floor to stop the kick-up of dust. It is not bad in here, but it may not pass the health department regulations.

'If you have heating, you may need some ventilation and also cooling in summer. If you add these items to your business plan and get some prices to go with it, they may include them in the grant. This is all supposition, Harry. I have never tried for a grant, but I do know they are willing to listen. And if you can put a good story over, they can be very generous. Perhaps I could add my voice to the story to give to the right people to help you out.

'I must be off for now, or my wife will be wondering what is going on. Here is my business card. Give me a call when you get a few ideas together, and I will see what I can do. Meanwhile, if I am free next Monday or Wednesday, I will come back for more exercise. I did enjoy it.'

'I appreciate all you have said, James. I presume you are in touch with the police in your job?'

'Yes, it goes with the job. Have they been to see you?'

'No, but I expect them to arrive sooner or later.'

'I will contact the main man and tell him about you and what you are doing. You can expect a call from them, but they will be friendly, in my opinion.'

'You are a marvel, James. Thank you for everything.'

'Goodnight, Harry,' said James as he waved on his way out of the barn.

* * *

James was able to put Anne Mahmoud's mind at rest the next day when she called in at his office. He waived the fee, saying that he had enjoyed himself joining with the other men in doing exercises to keep his fitness up and that Jarish was enjoying himself and keeping fit at the same time.

* * *

Percy came into the office the next day, after his day off, to report that the restaurant food thief had been captured on Saturday evening by Kate and himself. Kate did not usually do evening work, but because this one had been at her instigation, she had wanted to finish it. Percy and Kate had booked for dinner at the restaurant they marked out as the next possible one on the man's list, and they were very pleased with themselves when they saw their quarry arrive and take up a seat near the door.

They waited until he reached his dessert dish and saw him stand up when the waiter turned away from him to prepare his order. They watched him walk out the door, all done very casually and without any rush, as if he was fully aware he had escaped notice.

Percy and Kate had prepaid their account when they ordered, so they could leave at any moment necessary. They followed the man out the door and down the road till he stopped at a car parked at a car bay and pressed the car key button to open the doors. Then they made their move, making a citizen's arrest and taking him to the police station to book him in. They returned to the restaurant to report that they had picked the thief up and that he was now being interviewed at the local police station.

Kate had gone to Paddy's restaurant on their way to the office to report the charge.

13

Alicia made coffee and brought out a cake she made that morning. She said this was to celebrate all the cases they had successfully concluded in the last couple of weeks. She asked James if he wanted her to go and see Bettine Smith this week to report on Leanne Chamberlain. She had gone to see her last Friday, but Bettine had been off work for an exam at the university that day.

James turned to her and said, 'Hold on to that one for a few days, Alicia. I am still not happy with the Chamberlains' explanation. It has been going over and over in my mind, and I have not been comfortable with it. Something is missing. Give me a couple more days to think it through. I might take all the bits and pieces we have on the case home with me tonight and go through all the conversations again. Sometimes by going over things something pops up that you have overlooked. There is something not quite right with the Chamberlain story. I just want to make sure what we did was all that was needed.'

'The police were happy with closing the case, James,' said Percy, looking at James enquiringly.

'Yes, they were, Percy, but they had the entire history of the family, which may have clouded their minds about the disappearance. Chamberlain has made his way successfully through the local business community, and that may have diverted them as well. We are looking at the story with fresh minds, and I want to make sure my gut feeling is not playing up on me. I want to do a bit more checking first.'

'Well, if you find something that does not sit well with you, let's talk it over before you act, James. I do not want to put us on the outer with our police connections.'

'I can understand that, Percy. I will let you know if anything comes to mind about the case.'

'Thanks, James. I am sure you understand the politics of the case.'

'Yes, but that should not interfere with any findings we come up with. There is a young woman who is missing, and we only have Chamberlain's word on where she has gone. I would like to confirm it. I know we will not be paid to continue, so I will do all the extra work in my own time. I just have to make sure I can live with myself and not ignore it because I am not being paid to do it.'

Percy looked a little affronted. 'That is not what I meant, James. I just did not want to step on the police chief's toes. We get a lot of work from them. All the interesting jobs come through them. We do not want to miss out because we made the police chief cross.'

James grinned. 'I was thinking of going over his head to my friend in the London police, seeing as that is where Leanne has supposedly gone to hide. Perhaps I should go see the local police chief again to make him happy before I ring Jack Whistler in London. "Keep him in the picture" type of thing. Will that be better, Percy?'

Percy grinned too. 'Okay, I got the message, James. Do you want me to come with you?'

'If you have the time, Percy. I have to see the local fellow anyway to tell him about Harold Burton's keep-fit classes, so I could just insinuate that I have a friend in the London police and that I was going to ask them to give me help in locating Leanne and Melvin Morrisey just to clear the case.'

'I would like to come along and watch the play, James. I like the way you get around people and get them to tell you what you want to know. It is a real art.'

'I will make the appointment, Percy, and you are welcome to come for the lesson. I mean to take Alicia with me to London on Sunday, and we will possibly stay over until Tuesday morning, when we will be back here for work. Alicia will be a good companion for the interrogations with Leanne and Melvin, just in case there are breakdowns. She can patch them up—that is her forte.'

'What a couple. You are made for each other. I really admire the way you work so well together.'

'Thanks, Percy,' said Alicia and James together, looking at each other and laughing.

Kate came through the door, smiling. 'Hi, everyone, I have just got word from the policeman on duty that the guy we picked up is a well-to-do businessman. He lost his wife to cancer about the time he started cheating the restaurants, and the first time he went off without paying was a mistake. He had not meant to go without paying, but he had just received a call saying his wife, who was in care, was dying. He had rushed out of the restaurant to go and see her. It was not until he was in a restaurant the next time that it occurred to him that he had walked out without paying, so he tried it again. The habit grew on him. He is willing to pay back all he owes and will not do it again. He knew he was doing wrong.'

'Congratulations, Kate! A job well done.' Alicia gave her a kiss on the cheek, and Percy and James shook her hand.

'Now, James, tell us all about your Monday night adventure,' said Percy.

James described what and who he had seen at Harry Burton's barn. He went on to tell Percy and Kate about Alec Overington's offer to him about doing some law work to keep his hand in, saying that he had made no decisions on it yet, as he had been too busy over the weekend to think about it. Whatever decision he made would not mean him working less for the investigation team.

Percy looked very thoughtful. 'I was waiting for that. Alec looked very guilty when I saw him the last time. I wondered about it, but now I know what it was all about. You certainly attract job offers, James. What do you think of this last one?'

'As I said, I have not had time to think about it so far, and with the Chamberlain case in mind, I will have no time for a day or two. I should be able to work on the thought before the next weekend. We shall see what comes of it. I would like to keep my hand in. After all, I did years of study to get the degree, but quite honestly, I have not approached Alec. It is all his doing so far.'

'I believe you, James. I could see he had something on his mind, but he did not say what it was. I thought that it was a new job for us and that he would get around to it in his own time.'

'If I do decide that I want to do it, Percy, that fellow Ken Johnson, who we met on the Isle of Wight, seemed interested in a job. If I decide to go to London to chase up Leanne, I might meet up with him again. He works in my mate's department. Anyway, leave it to me for a while. There is no hurry, and it may all be talk on Alec's side. I will wait until he gets back to me before I do anything, and that will give me time to get used to the idea.'

'We are doing well so far, James. I would not like to stop or slow the flow of work.'

'I do not envisage abandoning our work here, Percy. I am amazed at how well we have done in such a short time. There is no need to go elsewhere. It is just a means of keeping my mind busy and my hand in on the law, so to speak—to keep me up to date with the way things happen.'

'Okay, James, I will leave that one to you. When do you propose going to see the police chief here?'

'I will ring now to see if we can go today. That will give me time to organise with my London friends to get permission to look through university lists to find Leanne Chamberlain—or Morrisey, if she has changed her name.'

James was able to go to the police headquarters straight away, so he and Percy put Kate in charge of the office and left.

* * *

The police chief was quite affronted that James wanted to continue looking for Leanne Chamberlain, but he said he would not interfere if James wanted to include his London police contacts. He also thanked him for letting him know and said he would be interested in seeing the results.

The police chief was also interested in Harry Burton's keep-fit classes and thought it sounded like a good idea. He said he would send someone along to see what was happening there, and if it looked good, he would speak to the council to allow it to go ahead. He would also speak to someone in the Small Business Grant Council to help the young man. He said it sounded like just the thing to keep young people off the streets, as there was not much around these days to hold their attention to keeping fit and healthy. This was the kind of thing needed, and this Harry seemed likely to keep it going if he had some help. He would see what he could do.

James and Percy came away feeling as if they had achieved something. They called next at Council House to get some names they could pass on to Harry, and they came away with several pamphlets and the name of the person to contact regarding a grant. They called at the post office next to post the information off to Harry, with a note from James telling him about his visit to the police chief that morning and wishing him luck.

*   *   *

Back at the office, James arranged for Alicia to ring Jack Whistler's office in London while he arranged his thoughts. Within a few minutes, Jack Whistler was on the line. 'Hello, James, what can I do for you?'

James told him of the Chamberlain details and ended by saying, 'My gut feeling is that there is more to this story. I want your permission and an authority to look at university lists to see if Leanne is registered with them, and also lists of paramedics registered, to check for Melvin Morrisey. I would like to be wrong in this case, but I cannot let it go without checking on the young people. I have a bad feeling about the whole thing and will be very happy to be proved wrong.'

Jack Whistler said, 'I remember that case in Manchester when the two doctors were gunned down because of the wrong diagnosis of a child. It made news all around the country. I was a young bloke just in the job at the time, here in London, and it had us all looking out for those people, even down here. They were a religious sect waiting for the end of the world millennium, but the only end was that of the headman's only son. The man went berserk after that. He died in prison by his own hand. No one knew how he managed it, but he died of strychnine poisoning. The same night he died, his wife also took strychnine. We presumed they had pills to carry them off if the world came to an end.

'Their followers vowed to carry on their pursuit of the doctors' three-year-old daughter. Newspapers were full of it. After several attacks by gunshot, the Chamberlains' older son decided to leave town and take the child with him. The news reports were on to the next subject by then, so I never heard what happened to them.

'This is an interesting subject, James. Yes, I will give you identity papers to present around London. You have me interested now, and I will help in any way I can. I presume your funding by Chamberlain has come to an end? I will arrange finance here for you to carry on so you are not out of pocket. Put down your train fares. If you stay overnight, go to the hotel where you stayed last year, and I will tee up an overnight stay for you and your wife and take care of any other expenses.

'Good luck with this. If nothing else, you will feel better after investigating the young people. After hearing the tale, I also see holes in it. It needs investigating to prove the case, one way or the other. I will be pleased to hear the end of the story. It is one that you cannot forget, and it needs a happy ending. When do you plan this operation, James?'

'Sunday is my day off, and I thought Alicia and I could go to London that morning so we can be ready to pounce first thing on Monday morning. We can go back home Monday evening if we do not find anything, or we can stay over till Tuesday if we find something, going home Tuesday evening.'

'That sounds feasible. I will book the hotel for Sunday evening, with another night if necessary.'

'Thank you, Jack. As I said earlier, I will be happy to be proved wrong. It is necessary for my peace of mind that I did not let go of the story too soon. Thank you for your help.'

'The paperwork will be left at the hotel, James, for when you arrive here.'

After he put the phone down, James went to tell Percy and Alicia the outcome of the call.

Percy was jubilant. 'It proves it is good to have friends in the right places. At least we will be able to close the case on a disappearance which we are all still thinking of. It is hard to leave it unsolved or at least unchecked. If you find Leanne in London, we can readily say to her school friends here that she is okay.'

Alicia said, 'I will go over all the details with you on what we have again this evening so it will be fresh in our minds.'

'Good thinking, Alicia. Two minds are better than one, and if you come with me, we may see different sides of the story. It is always good to have backup on the details. Sometimes the smallest detail can make all the difference.'

'I will arrange for Aaron to have Jody on Sunday so Granny can have a rest day. Aaron could take Jody to see Sandra. They will all like that. Granny needs a rest.'

*　　*　　*

That evening, James laid all the paperwork out on the table in the apartment, and both he and Alicia studied it. James brought out a notebook to write down the sequence of the events as they knew it. When the security footage showed Chamberlain, Alicia pointed out that the timing was when Leanne was loudly saying into Aaron's tape recorder that she hated her life. 'Charles Chamberlain must have heard her saying that. It seems pointe that Leanne had seen him and that the loudness of her voice was for his benefit. The look on his face shows he had heard her.'

James also looked disgusted. 'Aaron had said he was disgusted with what she had said and that she did not care who heard her, but looking again now at Chamberlain, I think the comments were directed at him, not for the general public.'

Alicia said, 'Yes, he does have a stricken look on his face, as anyone would with those words spoken in public about them, especially him. He gave up his whole adult life to protect her, and she did that in return.

She certainly took the story of the death of her parents badly. What she said is enough to make anyone angry, and for a man who gave up his own life for her protection, to be treated like that is awful.'

'It would be enough to make anyone angry with her. As Aaron had said, he was disgusted, and he is not her father. You know, I cannot believe that Melvin Morrisey would want anything to do with her after that diatribe about her family. I got the impression from his mother that he is a loving son and would not have liked Leanne talking like that about her family.'

'I agree with that, James, especially in public. It may have been the alcohol talking. Bettine said Leanne was not used to drinking. Drink does bring out the worst in some people. Perhaps Leanne is one of them.'

'That is a possibility, Alicia. It certainly loosens most people's tongues. If drink was the problem, do you think Chamberlain would have excused it?'

'We will have to ask him that question. I personally think that her words would have caused him pain and made him cross with her. You know, I think Melvin will have many of the answers to these questions. It seems to me as if Leanne is putting on an act for someone. Melvin seems to be the obvious person to know the answers. She opens up to him and seems to be distanced from the others in the group.' Alicia was thinking ahead to the interview with Melvin.

James started to pack up the papers and tapes into his briefcase, still with it all on his mind. He turned to Alicia again. 'I cannot get the conversation I had with Melvin out of my mind. He said he had tried to contact Leanne by phone and email, with no result. Something happened between them to make her not answer. Would it have been because he left her or refused to take her with him?'

'That would have upset her for sure. Young girls get very upset at being refused, especially as she had burned her bridges by vilifying her parents in public. She could be lying low somewhere, licking her wounds. She is at an age where her peer group means more to her rather than her parents—and these are not even her real parents—so I cannot see her not answering his calls,' returned Alicia.

'Well, we will try to find out if Leanne went to London, to medical school with Melvin, as Chamberlain said. That should be easy enough to find out. I will ring Melvin and make an appointment with him first, to get his point of view and the real story if we can get it, not Chamberlain's story as he tells it. To me, it is too pat, as if he made it up to stop the search for her.'

Alicia helped with folding papers to put into the briefcase, still thinking of what they would be doing during their time in London. 'I will check the universities in the morning to see which ones have the medical courses and get the address of the paramedic place Melvin said he is studying at. It will all be easier if we have that information before we go. Perhaps I can draw up a mud map so we do not waste too much time travelling between each institution. Sunday seems a good time to have the talk with Melvin. Surely he will have some time off from his study and duties—that is, if he is still doing the paramedic course he originally signed up for.'

James put the last document in the briefcase, saying, 'I will try for that. He has been there six months and should be in some sort of routine by now. I will ring tomorrow.'

*   *   *

The next morning, he rang Morrisey as planned, and the young man agreed to meet them on Sunday for morning tea in his living quarters. He gave James the address. He did not ask the reason for the meeting, which surprised James, but it was good that they would meet at the place where Melvin lived, to see the picture clearly.

Alicia and James set off with Aaron and Jody for the train to London and separated from them on arrival in the big city—Aaron and the little girl to go and visit Sandra, and the other two to wend their way to the hotel to book in and leave their luggage before catching a cab to meet Melvin Morrisey at the building where he lived.

At first sight, both James and Alicia were impressed by Melvin; he was a tall good-looking young man who greeted them with his hand out for them to shake. He invited them into a study, obviously his to use, with a small table set up with teacups and biscuits, ready for morning tea. His first words were 'Have you heard from Leanne?'

James was reluctant to tell the young man that there had been no word from his friend. However, that was what he was there for. He replied, 'No, Mel, there has been nothing yet. We are here to clear up a few clues to her whereabouts. So far, the waters have been a bit muddied by Charles Chamberlain, who told us Leanne is here with you. Can you give us any proof that this is not the case?'

Melvin looked astonished at what James said. 'She is not here with me, James. There is no accommodation for partners here in this centre. As you can see, this is my study, and the bedroom and bathroom are attached, not much bigger than a closet really. You are welcome to look. This group does not believe in anything but work and study, and I am happy to go along with that. We do not have much time for socialising.' He held the door to his bedroom open for James to inspect. There was a single bed and a wardrobe and a bedside table, and as he said, it was made for one person only.

The next question James asked was 'Did you take the train here, or did you accept a lift in a car after the party on the fifteenth of January? And if so, whose?'

'Mr Chamberlain offered to drive me here after the party. I accepted, as after I had a long conversation with both him and Leanne, it looked like I was going to miss my train and fail to get here before I was locked out.'

'Did Leanne come too?'

'No, she was angry at me and her father and refused to come, and we left her at the bus station.'

'Do you mind telling us about it, Melvin? The story Chamberlain told us is that Leanne is here in London with you and he was going to set up an apartment for you both so that you could go to university.'

Melvin looked distressed. 'That is what Mr Chamberlain offered me while we were driving to London that night. It was a generous offer, but I turned it down. I am too young to take on the responsibility he was asking of me. I had organised this placing here on my own and was not willing to lose it. Leanne is like a sister to me, not a lover. We are both too young to settle down, and I feel like a brother towards her. We had spent time together at school between the ages of five and eighteen, five days a week, and we were good friends. But that is all it was—just friendship.'

'Leanne did not take it well, Melvin?' Alicia asked.

'No, she was quite angry with me for turning her down. We are both only eighteen, far too young to think of anything more than friendship. I have no money. I know she comes from a wealthy family, but I was not—am not—ready for anything more than the friendship we have. When I told her that, she got very angry and sulky. I think that in her mind, she thought I would agree to bring her with me, but looking around, I know she would not have been happy with this. This is what I have chosen to do with my life. I am independent and earning my own way. I did not want to be reliant on anyone else to pay my fees.'

Alicia said, 'I think that is the reason you have not heard anything from Leanne, Melvin. Girls of that age feel badly at being told "You are only a friend". She obviously had built up more in her mind and felt let down. She will get over it in time and may feel embarrassed about it, so you may have to wait a while to receive a message from her.'

'I suppose I know that, Mrs Armstrong. I think it was because I was taken by surprise by them both that evening. I think now that if I had had some warning beforehand of what was being offered, I would not have changed my mind, but I would have delivered the message more gently, so as not to humiliate Leanne. I do care for her, and I know she was going through a hard time after being told about what happened to her real parents.

'She chose the wrong moment to tell me what she had in mind about coming to London. I could see all my hard-won interviews and acceptance into this house going overboard, and I suppose I panicked a bit. They—both her father and Leanne—took me by surprise with their timing, and I did not realise what was going on between them until later, when Leanne was reported missing. I felt guilty—and still do—about what happened. It could have been done differently, and we would have remained friends.'

James touched the younger man's shoulder and said, 'It was not your fault at all, Melvin. There is no need for you to feel guilty. From what I gather of the story. Leanne has always felt that something in her life was not quite right, and she blamed her family for it. When she was told the truth, she blamed Charles for it. That is unfair, as Charles has done so much and given up so much to protect her. I think she will realise it in her own time and will apologise to everyone, including you.'

Alicia agreed. 'I think so too, Melvin. She is like a child who has lost everything and feels hurt. One day she will come to terms with it and will seek you out to say sorry that she placed you in this situation.'

'Then you both think that Leanne is out there somewhere, hiding from the world?'

James and Alicia both nodded, and James said, 'Yes, we have just to work out where she could have gone. Do you have any ideas?'

'There is her grandmother in Torquay. She lives in a villa overlooking the sea. She and her husband moved there when Charles and Leanne moved south, away from Manchester. I only learnt that recently, when she told me about her parents being killed.'

'We did not know about the grandparents. We have to do a bit more research. Thanks for that, Mel. Do you know of the relationship between Leanne and her so-called mother?'

'She got on well with her when she was growing up. She never complained about anyone's care, only that there was too much of it and that they were very protective of her, which made her feel smothered. As she got older, it made her annoyed that she was not allowed to do anything alone and that her parents were always there. I can understand it now, but I do not think Leanne can. She is embittered at being left in the dark about her history.'

'Her uncle gave up his own life to protect her,' said Alicia. 'She is angry at the moment, and when she gets over that, she will be filled with remorse. I hope she sees that soon. Leaving everyone in a vacuum like she has is terrible for all concerned. It must be very hurtful to Charles Chamberlain.'

'Thank you, Mel, for seeing us today. You have filled in some holes for us. As soon as we know where she is, we will let you know.'

'I would appreciate that, James,' said Melvin. 'I have been looking forward to you getting in touch with me again. It makes me feel a bit better, rather than going over things by myself, feeling sorry about it all.'

James shook Melvin's hand. 'I was retained by Charles Chamberlain originally. However, I think he is afraid of any news getting out to the people who were trying to do them harm, and he has made up a story of the disappearance of Leanne to stop any circulation. I cannot blame him. It must have been a worrying time for him. The responsibility of taking care of his brother's daughter must have been thrust on him in the prime of his life and career, and he had to give it all up to keep her safe. It is sad that Leanne does not realise how much he has done for her. I am sure that he did not explain things to her earlier to stop her from being afraid of life.'

Melvin agreed with him and said, 'I can see that, but I do not think Leanne appreciated it as she should have. It seems to have sent her off on a tangent. I will keep trying her email and phone, and perhaps one day soon, she will see that we are not all trying to hurt her and she will answer my call.'

'As I said, Melvin, if we find her, we will let you know. Cheerio for now.'

'Thank you, James and Mrs Armstrong. I feel better about things. I may now be able to concentrate on my studies.'

*   *   *

As they walked to the cab they had called, Alicia said, 'He is a very nice young man, and I admire what he is trying to do to educate himself. It is a shame he is caught up in all this worry about Leanne.'

'It is because he is a nice young man. Leanne is lucky to have such a good friend. For both their sakes, I hope she reappears soon.'

'Amen to that,' said Alicia. 'What are we going to do for the rest of the day?'

'I thought we might go and have a nice romantic lunch together and meander along the Thames riverside at the Birdcage Walk. I found this little lunchtime restaurant when I was in lockdown here after the

Sahib incident last year. I missed you on Sunday and went for a walk to clear my head while I thought about joining Percy in the private investigations business. I saw this little lunch place and stored the memory for the next time we would come to London—and here we are.'

The cabby pulled over to the kerb and asked, 'Will this do?'

'I thought you knew where we were heading. You appeared to recognise where we were travelling and seemed to have a destination in mind. It does look interesting, James. I like the decor, with these old photographs of the area on the walls. It gives you something to look at while you are waiting for your meal.'

'The food is plain but good. I had a Cornish pasty along with a green salad last time I was here, and it was the best Cornish pasty I have ever had. I think I will have the same again.'

Alicia was reading the menu. 'Yes, I will have the same. I find bagels are a little heavy in the middle of the day. I am hungry. It has been a long time since breakfast.' She looked around. 'Is it late, or is it because this place is hidden away down a side street that it is not crowded?'

'It was much the same last time I came, so I think it is because it is down a side street. That makes us lucky to have found it. The coffee is good too.'

'What about the rest of the day, James? Have you any plans?'

'Do you want to play the tourist, Alicia, or would you prefer to go to our hotel for a rest? We can have dinner there this evening. It is quite good. Do you want to eat alone with me, or shall I invite my ex-boss, Harry Banning, to let him know how we are doing in the business? Or we could ask him for a drink?'

'He has done us such a good service, James, helping you along and advising you. It would be nice to ask him to dinner, along with his wife, to thank him.'

'Thank you, Alicia. I agree with that. I will ring him to come along to the hotel this evening for dinner if he is free.'

'I think I will enjoy a rest. We have done quite a lot of walking today, and I am a little tired. It will also give us an opportunity to go over the lists of places we need to visit tomorrow.'

'Okay, Alicia, the hotel it is. We will go ahead with looking for Leanne tomorrow at the medical colleges, but I think it is only a job that needs to be done. I do not think we will find her here. She would have tried to get as far away as she can, in my opinion. She would not have tried London institutions, in case she ran into Melvin.'

'Yes, James, that is going to make it harder to find her.'

'It will, Alicia, but she does not want to be found yet. We have to think wider. Maybe she has gone to her grandmother in Torquay. But I think that is the first place Charles Chamberlain would have looked for her. No, she will not be there.'

'What about her mother's relatives? They have not been mentioned yet by anyone.'

'No. I wonder why? We will have to check that out. What would you do, Alicia, if you wanted to get away from everybody you know?'

Alicia stopped for a minute, looking back to her youth and how she would have thought at eighteen. 'I think, under the circumstances, if I were in Leanne's shoes, I would want to go back to Manchester and find my parents' graves, for a start. I would look through all the newspapers from the time they were shot, to find the details. After that, I would try to hunt down any other relatives I have left behind, although not openly. I would try to stay away from them until I have researched them to see if it is safe to contact them.'

James looked at her and leaned over and took her hand. 'I think you are spot-on, Alicia. You are a marvel, as Percy often says. I think you have her in a nutshell. It makes so much sense, but how would she have got there? She is a young person who has never done anything for herself because of Charles's protective position over her. Remember, it was late at night, and she had not come prepared with more than a small backpack. Somehow she must have had help. She disappeared in the middle of the night. It sounds sinister, but was it? We will have to find out whether she had her own credit card or debit card. You cannot get from the south coast to Manchester without money. Did she go by train? By air? Or coach? For all those things, you have to pay. There must be a record somewhere.'

'Keep going, James. You sound enthusiastic—a new line to take and work out. Who could she count on to help her at that time of night? She did not have many friends, and those we know of say they did not help her. Melvin has been our best bet so far, but now we have to rule him out of the picture.'

'Yes, Melvin is out of it. She was too upset with him to go back to him for help. It really only leaves her stepmother and her younger brother, from the story everybody relates, unless she did research on the trains and coaches for that time of night beforehand. But she thought she would be going with Melvin, so I do not think that would have been looked at.'

'Your mention of the stepmother, James, fits in. Leanne would have needed money, and tickets are not cheap. She would have needed more clothes if she was thinking of leaving permanently or for a long period. She had burned her bridges with the insults she had publicly made about Charles, so she would not have wanted to stick around. I would say that if Charles had rung his wife and told her about those insults, the wife would have been happy to help Leanne disappear, one way or another. Leanne really did a job on her family, and they would have been cross with her. All they had ever done was care for and protect the girl. To have her lash out at them was not nice and very hurtful.'

'We are progressing here, Alicia. It must be the different atmosphere around us. We must do this type of thing more often.' James grinned at her.

'Your turn, James. I am out of ideas.'

'What if—yes, what if Charles had rung his wife and told her about the insults and he had sounded upset? He would have told her about driving Melvin to London and leaving Leanne at the coach station. If he was upset, it would have got the wife thinking about what to do about it. She would have paced around in Leanne's bedroom, pulled out a suitcase, packed some clothes for the girl, driven to the city bus station, and picked her up. Charles would have told her about leaving Leanne there. He would not have been able to just drop his protective attitude of the girl, even though she resented it. It has become a habit for him to protect her, so he would have told his wife. After that, I have run out of ideas. Let's have a break from this and continue later on.'

'As you said earlier, James, that was the nicest Cornish pasty I have ever had. They must make them here. It is not the one purchased from the supermarket. Also, as you said, the coffee was delicious. We will make this our little lunch place for whenever we come to London. Let us go to the hotel now and rest our brains, and we may come up with more ideas when we get into thinking mode again later.'

'Good thinking, Alicia. It has been a long time since I had a sleep in the day, but that is what I feel like at the moment.'

'It was the delicious food, James. It always makes me sleepy after a good meal.'

They had a very nice evening with James's former boss and his wife, who appreciated the call from James to join them. Harry Banning was interested to meet Alicia, who had been the focus in the passport scam and jewellery theft of Indian/British families who had been targeted by Sahib in his smuggling scam. Between them, Alicia and James had solved those thefts, and Sahib had been caught and charged. Alicia could see the friendship between James and his previous boss, and she was pleased to join the circle, feeling at home with the couple.

* * *

Next morning, James and Alicia set off to visit all the medical schools in the city, but as expected, Leanne Chamberlain was not enrolled in any of them. They decided that they were looking in the wrong area and rang Jack Whistler at police headquarters to bring him up to date with their thoughts of trying Manchester next to find the girl.

He seemed thoughtful when that was announced, and he said, 'Are you sure about that, James? It seems to be an improbable place for her to go now that she knows her history there.'

'This is my wife's idea Jack. You remember how good she is at solving crimes. We would have got nowhere with the passport and jewellery scam without her intuition last year. There is good reasoning behind her thoughts. She is thinking from a young woman's point of view. That is something we are unable to do, as men, so I am going with it. We may come back unsuccessful, but at least we tried. At the moment, our only other bet is to dig up the Chamberlains' backyard, and I do not want to go there yet. I have come to admire the man and do not believe he would hurt the girl. He has protected her for so many years now.'

'Even the worm can turn, James, if given enough incentive. It does sound as if the girl, Leanne, had been twisting the rope that held them before she disappeared. Teenagers can be maddening. I have one myself, so I know what I am speaking about.'

'Jack, why don't you ask your teenager what she would do in these circumstances? The only teenagers I know are those I questioned about Leanne, and I do not want to muddy their stories. Alicia's idea sounds like good sense to me, but ask your teenager. How old is she?'

'Just turned eighteen, as a matter of fact. Almost the same age as Leanne perhaps, or close to it. I will ask her this evening. She is at school at the moment. She will be intrigued by the story. I will ring you tomorrow with the result.'

'That would be great, Jack. I will look forward to her thoughts on it. We seem to be going around and around on it, but we have eliminated some of the prospects. Both Alicia and I like the idea that the girl returned to Manchester to hunt down the story of her parents, but maybe we are just running out of turns to take. I do not want to go back to Chamberlain until I am sure of my story. Do you remember the name of the woman with Charles? They married, by the way, and Charles adopted the boy she had from the rape.'

'I can have someone look it up, James, and give you the name tomorrow when I ring.'

'If you are going that far, Jack, find out who represented her at the enquiry. And does she have any siblings?'

'That should show up in the same group of papers. Well, now it is all on the computer. It was a closed enquiry because the accused were police officers, so you cannot check the newspapers about it. But it is in our records. I will get our best man on it.'

'I appreciate your help, Jack. It will save me so much time, and I cannot see the police records to find all this information anyway. I do not want to go through the local man. I think he thinks I am trying to block him out, so it is advantageous for me to keep away from him until I have some kind of proof that Leanne is alive and well and hiding from Charles.'

'I can understand your reasoning, James. Some blokes take umbrage at being overlooked on a case. I will do the best I can.'

'Thanks, Jack. I will hear from you tomorrow. Alicia and I are going home on the afternoon train. There is nothing more we can do here.'

14

They arrived home in time for James to check in at the office, go home for a quick meal, and set off to Harry Burton's exercise class. It was all a bit of a rush, but he arrived just as the first warm-up exercise had begun. At the end of the evening's session, Harry gave him a look, and James stayed behind as the rest of the men departed.

'I want to thank you, James, for the paperwork and note you sent me. I phoned your office to say thanks, but the lady I spoke to said you were out of town and would be back today or tomorrow.'

'That was Kate. Yes, I was in London, chasing up a few clues to find a missing girl. However, I was unsuccessful. A question for you, Harry. If you wanted to get out of town, you did not drive, and you missed the planes and coaches for the night, how would you go about it?'

'Depends on if I had the money, but I would hire my friend Freddy, the friendly flyer, to fly me out in his British Beagle Pup aircraft.'

'Freddy, the friendly flyer? What are we dealing with here?'

'His real name is Fred White, but no one ever calls him anything but Freddy. He flew fighter jets when we were based in Afghanistan, and he was a miracle man, in our opinion. He would come and help us when we were under attack. He would come out of the sun. With the noise of all the shelling, we did not hear him most of the time, but suddenly he would be there. We would all set up a cheer. He gave up flying and returned home after a miracle, as he called it, happened. A missile had been on his tail, and at the last minute, it was shot down.

Freddy reasoned that he had used up eight of his nine lives and that it was time he returned home. He now flies charter flights from the airfield here.'

'Wow, that is some history. Is it likely he could have helped a young woman fly to Manchester on short notice?'

'That is his thing nowadays. It is not cheap to hire an aircraft. Could your young woman afford it? It is not the usual way for young people to get around.'

'I do not know the young woman's financial status, but as her father is quite well-to-do, that is feasible. Her stepmother may have paid the account. Do you have Freddy's phone number so I can ask him a few questions?'

'Sure. It is stored in my phone. Copy it into yours. I ring him occasionally to have a drink. Would you like me to ring him and arrange that, and you can come along and meet him? He is a character well worth the trouble, and you could do your inquisition then.'

'That would be a great service, Harry. It will be my shout. I appreciate anything at the moment that will help me find this young woman.'

'I will ring him now. Any particular time, James?'

'Any time, Harry. The sooner, the better.'

Harry made the call and then said to James, 'Tomorrow at five. And you are near the Jolly Green Frog pub, aren't you?'

'Just around the corner. That would be great. Thanks, Harry.'

'One good turn deserves another, my mother used to say. It will be my pleasure, James. It is always good to have a laugh with Freddy.'

'Did you get any response from the police department, Harry? I thought the chief inspector seemed very interested and willing to help.'

'Not yet, James, but it has only been a few days. I did receive a note from the Small Business Grant Foundation, with a form for me to fill out. That was thanks to you, I believe?'

'I did call in and see them, and I enquired how it worked. They said they would contact you. That was the first contact, it seems to me. It is now up to you, Harry, whether you want to go on with it. Only you can make that decision. If there is anything else I can help you with, let me know, and I will follow it through for you.'

'I appreciate what you have done, James. I have been talking it over with my father, who owns this shed, and he said he will give me the shed to do what I like with it. I am still turning all that over in my mind, and I would like to visit my doctor to ask his opinion on it as well. Sometimes I get pain from the leg that is no longer there. They call it Phantom pain I believe. It keeps me awake after the exercises some nights, so I would like to ask if I am doing too much with it. That sounds like a real question. Can I do too much with a leg no longer there? It is possible that it is still new to me, I suppose. Anyway, I want his opinion before I do too much damage.'

'Okay, Harry, I will see you tomorrow at five at the Jolly Green Frog, and I look forward to meeting Freddy, your friendly flyer.'

When James arrived home and told Alicia about the Freddy story, she remarked, 'It sounds as if it could fit the bill. I am interested to hear what Freddy has to say.'

*   *   *

Next morning, Jack Whistler called. 'Your Alicia is well versed in what young women think and do. I told my daughter the story and asked her where Leanne could have disappeared to, and also why. Her answer was the same as your wife's. How about that?

'The next thing is the name of Mrs Chamberlain before she married Charles. Her maiden name was Meghan Clegg. She was helped by her brother, a young attorney at the time, named Ian Clegg. As far as we know, he is her only sibling. He did a good job for her. Both senior policemen resigned from their jobs before they were kicked off, and they were fined a very large amount of money, which was given to Meghan for her child. The stigma around the town was so disgraceful, blaming Meghan, who was the victim. She had to leave town to get away from the sneers and jeers, so Chamberlain came to her rescue. It was a disgraceful story and one a young woman should not have to face in this day and age.'

'It sounds like Meghan Clegg and Charles Chamberlain met at the right time for them both.'

'That is what I think also, but my daughter had a different view on it. She said, "It is no wonder Leanne felt left out of the story. All this was going on, and they waited fifteen years to tell her they were not her mother and father. She had been living a lie all those years, and she must have been terribly shocked to hear about it and that her real parents were murdered. My daughter could see why Leanne wanted to get away from them."'

'How twisted and awful for Charles Chamberlain, who was trying his best to help everyone,' said James, 'and now he is left in this vacuum, not knowing where Leanne has gone. Poor man, I do feel sorry for him. When I met him, I came away thinking what a nice man he is. Now that I know the full story, I feel even more sorry for him. All that he has done has been for others. What a shame.'

'What is your next move, James?'

'I am tossing up whether to face Meghan Clegg Chamberlain or go straight to Ian Clegg, lawyer, and ask him questions.'

'Lawyers can be tricky, James, but you know that.'

'Mmm, perhaps it is a good time to show what I have learnt and try the lawyer first.'

Jack Whistler laughed. 'Somehow I knew the answer before I asked it. Good luck, James. Keep me informed.'

James sat in his big office chair, a gift from the previous crew he had worked with, given when he had started up the business with Percy Gray. He thought over the story they had on Leanne Chamberlain's disappearance to date. He would wait until he had spoken to Fred White and then decide whether to ring Ian Clegg, but first he looked Ian up on his computer to see what type of man he would be dealing with. That done, he decided to write up a scenario of a conversation with the lawyer, to help him for when they meet.

Meanwhile, it was time to do some of the jobs that were outstanding; there were several insurance surveillances to get on with. He felt he had been dodging them for a while, and it was time he took a look at them. He was surprised to see that Kate had taken some of them while he had been away from the office. It had been a good decision to take her on;

she had proved to be conscientious about the job, getting on with things without having to be told.

Satisfied that things were up to date, he went back to his conversation with Ian Clegg, writing down all the pertinent points he wanted to make. He showed it to Alicia, asking her opinion. 'Do you think I should go and see Charles Chamberlain after I see Freddy the flyer tonight and he confirms that he flew Leanne to Manchester?'

'I think that would be a bit premature, James. Speaking with Ian Clegg first will confirm Leanne's presence in Manchester. However, I think we are getting a bit ahead of ourselves. Do you want to get in the middle of a family situation? It seemed to me when we last spoke to Charles that he wanted to go no further. Why would that be, do you suppose?'

James looked pensive and sat down beside her. 'He was hiding the fact that he did not want to find her. Remember, he had rung Meghan to pick the girl up and drove off. In his mind, Meghan was the last person to see Leanne. Meanwhile, she disappeared, and his wife was not saying anything. Do you think he thought Meghan killed her and had hidden her body?

While you were getting ready for bed last night, I stood looking out of the window over the Solent. It was at double high tide, which is what it is called when the level makes the water capable of taking large cruise boats at certain times of the day. I thought that the tide was running out fast and that anything thrown into the waterway while that was happening could be taken out to the North Sea and possibly never found. It was a macabre thought that made me think of how Leanne had disappeared just at that same time one night in January. It made me think that Chamberlain seemed reluctant to find Leanne. Perhaps he too had the same thought and is afraid to recognise it in case it is true. Meghan had not said where she took Leanne that night.

Now I am almost sure Freddy the flyer took her to Manchester and that Meghan swore to Leanne that she would not tell Charles where she had gone and she has been held by that vow. I am almost certain now too that there is trouble in the marriage. If Charles suspects his wife of getting rid of Leanne, he is covering up for her, and there must be some tension between them over it. What do you think of all that?'

'Wow, James, you have advanced in your thinking. You have brought up some real possibilities about the family. It is almost time for you to go and meet Fred White and find out if what you suspect is true. After that, depending on the answer, we will think further about it. It is only muddying the waters at the moment.'

'You are right, Alicia. At the moment, my mind will not let go of it all. Charles's story of Melvin and Leanne getting married shows that he was panicking that we would also come to the same conclusion as him regarding Meghan, and that is why he called a stop to us carrying on.'

'Poor man,' said Alicia. 'I really feel sorry for him, and all he was trying to do was protect Leanne.'

*　　*　　*

James arrived at the Jolly Green Frog pub just as he saw Harry and Freddy climbing the entrance steps, and then he joined them at a table. He was surprised to see a young man who looked more like a student than a fighter pilot. He wore jeans and a shirt and would not have turned a head in the street; this was a man adored and admired by his team in the army.

Harry introduced Freddy to James and said, 'I will get the drinks while you two have a chat about flying young women to Manchester in the dark of night.'

Freddy said, 'It was not the dark of night when we flew out. It was first light, and it is only an hour's trip by air despite it seeming like a long way to go.'

'What can you tell me about that young woman, Freddy? I am doing a piece for the police department to find that girl, Leanne Chamberlain, who seemed to have vanished into thin air on the evening of 15th of January has not done anything wrong except not tell her foster father, who is her uncle and guardian and who has brought her up as his own child. As she has turned eighteen, I presume she is allowed to travel wherever she likes without asking for permission. The police department is interested because she has been under its protection since the age of three, and to just disappear without signing out needs a follow-up.'

Freddy nodded. 'Yes, I remember her. Leanne Chamberlain turned up at the airport at ten o'clock that night, obviously distressed and accompanied by a woman she called her mother. She wanted to go to Manchester, but all the regular flights had gone for the day and the next one was not until ten or eleven the next morning. As I said, she was very distressed, so the airport staff suggested she ring me to see if I would take her.

'I met her and her mother in the flight lounge and talked it over with them, and they decided Leanne would go with me at first light, as it was a safer time to go and the weather report was good. The mother paid the bill. She left the girl sleeping in the lounge in the first-class division, as the girl did not want to go home and I woke her when it was time to leave. The mother left with a request that I hand the girl over to an Ian Clegg, a relative who would meet the flight at the Manchester airport. There was no conversation about why she had to go, and the girl was silent the whole way. Nothing else to report really, all cut and dried.'

'Thank you, Freddy. As you said, all cut and dried, but it has taken us six months to think of it. I casually asked Harry for any ideas, and he came up with you. I greatly appreciate your help.'

'Glad to be able to help, James. Any friend of Harry's is a friend of mine. He was a much-admired sergeant in the army and has come to terms with the loss of his leg without any whimpers of "Why me?" A great bloke.' Freddy spoke in a staccato style, as if giving a report, with a smile to keep the officious sound from coming through.

Harry joined them, with a barman carrying the drinks. As they were set down on the table, he said, 'I had to get Johnno here to help carry them. I am still a bit of a lurcher when carrying things. I still tend to slop drinks I definitely need more practice at it.'

'We can give you plenty of practice at carrying our drinks, Harry,' said Freddy with a big grin.

'I am sure you would appreciate it, Freddy. The only thing at the moment is that you would only get half a glass by the time I get here.'

'We cannot have that, old man. We will carry our own glasses or call in Johnno to help.'

'Did Freddy give a satisfactory report, James? Was it what you were looking for?'

'Exactly that, thanks, Harry. I will be off to Manchester in a day or so to check on the girl now that we know where she disappeared to.'

'Do you want a lift, James?' said Freddy. 'I have some packages to deliver on Wednesday to Manchester—"special government delivery". I could take you up, and your wife as well. I gather from Harry that she is your partner in this adventure. Unfortunately, the invitation does not extend to waiting time. I have to be back here the same day, so you would have to fly the regular airline on your return.'

James grinned at Freddy. 'That would be great. I have never had the experience of flying in a small aircraft. My education on flying is limited altogether, really. I have never been out of the country, although I do hold a passport. My last job made sure of it, but I never needed to use it. Trains have been my usual mode of travel, or coaches.'

'Wednesday then, James. I will be leaving at eight o'clock in the morning.'

'Alicia and I will be at the airport at seven thirty. We will not be carrying much luggage, as we will probably return on Thursday. Alicia is not like most women when flying. She was a flight attendant, so she packs only what is needed.'

'That will be a great change. I was mentally trying to work out where to put all the extra bags as I was offering you a lift. Every other party I have carried turned up with enough luggage to last them a year.' The laugh in Freddy's voice was contagious.

'Did you come from this part of the country before the army took you in, Freddy?' queried James.

'Yes, my family has been a part of this city for a very long time. I studied it before going overseas so that I could relate my history if needed. No one ever asked, but it gave me comfort to know where I came from and the type of people that came before me. When I was in a tight corner—which was every other day, really—I thought of home and family, and I would decide to come home after my time came up.

But somehow I would always get over that and extend my duties, until the last battle, when I thought my life would be over at any second. I could hear my heart pounding. It was so loud and painful in my chest. Suddenly the decision to come home became a reality. It was time.

I miss the life, the camaraderie of the other blokes, the endless card games. But the heat and dust, no, not that. I prefer green fields and daffodils and bluebells in spring. The lack of sunshine here at home sometimes gets me down, but at least it is not so hot in the cockpit of my little plane. No, I do not want to go back. It was like living in another time. The rest of the world was still here, waiting for me.

I feel lonely sometimes. I had lived with other groups of people for so long. But when I count up the differences, the answer was overwhelmingly to stay home. I will have to find a wife and have a dozen children to make up the people in my life.'

All this was said with a cheery voice, but one could feel the excitement of his life and the danger of it, putting his life on the line every day, and the relief that that was now in the past.

'I know you feel the same, Harry. Were you disappointed when they flew you out?'

'No, Freddy, much the same as you. When I was wounded, my first thought was relief. "Well, I can go home now. I have done my dash." It wasn't till some time later that I realised I would lose my leg.'

Half an hour later, James said farewell, glad he did not have to drive a vehicle home. He wondered how the other two would get home safely, but they assured him they would call a cab.

*   *   *

When James told Alicia what they had talked about and about the departure of Leanne Chamberlain to Manchester, she was very quiet. He asked her what she was thinking about.

'I am wondering why Meghan was anxious to help Leanne disappear, and to Manchester, of all places. I know we have concluded that Leanne would want to go to Manchester, but with the history of all that had happened there to both Charles and Meghan, it makes me curious as to why Meghan was prepared to send Leanne there. What did you come up with when you looked up Ian Clegg?'

'That he is an attorney and a successful one. He made his reputation working on Meghan's case. I got the impression that prosecuting two senior police officers and winning the case did a lot for him. He is married to Anne, a psychologist who works in the government sector and in private practice. They did not mention any children.'

'Have you contacted Ian Clegg yet, James?'

'It is only 8 p.m. now. I shall try to ring him and see if he will meet with us on Wednesday morning. We should be in Manchester before ten o'clock, easily. If necessary, we could wait a day for him to see us. I would like to speak to his wife also. They have had time to learn about Leanne by now.'

'Good. I agree. I still feel there is something wrong somewhere in the story. I cannot put my finger on it yet, but I am sure there is something else other than a mere disappearance. I am glad you have organised to take me with you. I would like to meet Leanne myself. So far, she has only appeared as a sulky child, but she has kept it up so long that it has made me think something else is going on.'

James made the phone call, and it was answered immediately by Ian. Ian Clegg recognised James's name, saying his sister told him that he had been investigating Leanne's disappearance for Charles Chamberlain but had been called off the job.

James apologised for the lateness of the business call and said he was arriving in Manchester at approximately ten in the morning on Wednesday, hoping to meet him or his wife to discuss Leanne. He asked if it would it be possible to have a meeting with them on Wednesday. 'We—my wife and I—would also like to meet with Leanne. So far, she has appeared as a phantom figure to us, just a short distance away but hard to get to.'

He explained that initially, Chamberlain had retained him to find Leanne, but when he signed off from that, the police department agreed for James's business to carry on with the search, as Leanne had been in protective custody with them.

The lawyer said, obviously looking at his diary, 'I can manage midday Wednesday. It is my lunch break, so I will see if my wife can meet with you also. If not, perhaps you can come for dinner at our house, and we will arrange for Leanne to be there. She has been working as a waitress in a lunch restaurant on a daily basis since being here and lives in a small flat close to the city. I would like to speak to you before you meet Leanne, so midday in my office. I will arrange for sandwiches and coffee to go for the three or four of us, if possible.'

'I appreciate your time, Ian. We have tried to keep everything secretive in case Leanne wants to return here. There is no need for the general public to know where she is. We will see you in your office at midday, Wednesday. Thank you. Goodnight.'

When James related this call to Alicia, she said, 'Yes, there is more to the story. I knew it.'

15

Wednesday turned out to be a beautiful late summer's day and was excellent for flying. Alicia was excited because she was allowed to sit in the Beagle Pup aircraft, next to the pilot, so she could see as far as the horizon. She remarked, 'I usually sat down the back of the aircraft so I could watch the passengers. This is a marvellously better way to travel.'

'A woman after my own heart,' joked Freddy. 'If you break up with James at any time, you must call me to rescue you.'

James intervened. 'No chance of that, Freddy. I am holding on to her. She is the best thing that has ever happened to me.'

'You are a lucky man, James Armstrong.'

'I am aware of it, Freddy.'

'To change the subject,' said Alicia with a laugh, 'what a lovely panorama for us to see, so lovely and green despite it being midsummer.'

'After Afghanistan, I appreciate the green.'

'I am sure you do,' said Alicia. 'I flew to Ireland once during my other working career and could not believe the colour there. It is aptly named the Emerald Isle. Freddy, when we get back home, would you and Harry come to dinner on Friday night? Unfortunately, there are steps to climb. Do you think Harry can manage them?'

'Harry is going out of his mind with boredom. I am sure he would climb a mountain for a good dinner. Like me, he misses the crowd around him. When you are in the army, you are hardly ever alone, and you get withdrawal symptoms when you pull out. It takes a while to overcome the experience.'

'So I will take that as a yes then?'

'Sorry, Alicia, I do like the sound of my own voice sometimes. That is a definite yes.'

'Do you have a lady friend to accompany you?'

'No, I haven't worked up to that yet. Neither has Harry.'

'We will be a jolly foursome then. Friday for dinner at the apartment above the bookshop at 8 p.m.'

It wasn't long before Manchester came into view and they were ready to land.

After they said thanks to Freddy and he pointed the way to go, they looked around for a train to take them to the city to find a hotel for the night. Midday came quickly; they had already searched for Ian Clegg's office so they would not be late for their meeting.

*　　*　　*

Both Ian and Anne met them in Ian's office. Ian was a sturdy-looking man with fair hair, and he wore dark-rimmed glasses. His wife was a surprise. She looked as if she had stepped out of a fashion magazine, with long blonde hair tied back into a chignon—a very attractive lady. They both stood and welcomed Alicia and James into the office and gestured to the sandwiches and coffee mugs on the desk. 'This is lunch most days,' stated Ian. 'I usually eat as I work.'

'Start eating first, and we will talk afterwards.'

'Thanks for this, Ian. It was an early breakfast for us this morning.'

After discussing the trip and eating the sandwiches, they stopped to examine each other. They were much the same age, maybe ten years between them, with the Cleggs being older, although Ian and his wife looked very prosperous. Alicia admired the dress Anne wore, and she asked if it was by a local maker.

Anne replied, 'It is a gown from Leanne's grandmother's shop. The shop is called Yvonne's. She is the designer and has the dresses made locally.'

'Is that the Chamberlain side or her mother's side of the family?'

'She is Lorraine Chamberlain's mother, newly discovered by Leanne and discarded when Leanne heard the excuses her grandmother Yvonne made for when her daughter and son-in-law were killed and for not taking in Leanne when she was three years old and allowing her to be taken out of Manchester by Charles Chamberlain.'

'We had assumed that none of Lorraine's relatives were available to take care of her,' said Alicia.

'Lorraine had a mother and a sister. Her father had left the family many years before she married Francis Chamberlain, and no one knows where he is.'

'What were the excuses that Leanne could not handle, for her grandmother and aunt not to look after her?'

'Yvonne was just establishing her shop—or salon, as she prefers to call it. Her dresses were selling, and she was very busy and had no time for a small child. The aunt lived in France and was modelling for one of the big agencies there, also with no time—or wish—to look after a small child. From what I have seen of Yvonne, she is not a naturally motherly person. She appears to me to be too tied up in herself and her business. I believe Lorraine had moved off to medical college accommodation early in her study period. Yvonne came out of her self-indulgence long enough to make the wedding dresses but did not welcome a grandchild, even early in Leanne's life.' Anne looked disgusted. 'Some people should never have children.'

'Lorraine must have spent quite a long time in the medical business with her husband. Who looked after Leanne for the pair while they were working?'

'I believe it was Leanne's other grandmother, Mrs Chamberlain. It was such a shock for the family when the murder took place. The father of Charles and Francis had been diagnosed with motor neurone disease a few months earlier, and the deaths of his clever son and daughter-in-law hastened his symptoms. He started to get worse quicker than he should have. The reason Mrs Chamberlain did not continue the care of Leanne was that her husband was in a bad state. Things were at a real low for the family.

'To evade more shootings, Charles purchased a house for his mother and a place in a nursing home for his father in Torquay, where they retired, and he disappeared with Leanne with the help of police officials. The thought behind it was that the people chasing them would not find the whole family together. Mrs Chamberlain accepted this after much discussion and agreed after my sister, Meghan, decided to go with Charles to help him out with Leanne.'

James intervened in the conversation. 'We want to make it clear that we are not chasing Leanne. She is free, as far as we are concerned, to keep any information from us. We are merely trying to find her to make sure she is safe and well. She is a private citizen and no longer a minor. The police want an assurance of her safety, as she has been under their care for fifteen years.'

Ian nodded and said, 'Thank you for the explanation, James. We wondered how much you wanted to know.'

'When Leanne left home,' James continued, 'she was very distressed, according to witnesses. We wanted to check that she was all right. Your sister was the last person who saw her before she disappeared, and she was not talking. It seemed like Leanne had disappeared altogether, and we wanted to check that no harm had come to her.

'It was a lucky chance that we were told of the flight at daylight that bore her away, and we followed it up. We want to see Leanne for ourselves to confirm her identity. We have a photograph to go by. We can call at the place she is working at, and that will be confirmation enough if you do not want to organise a dinner party tonight.'

'We have organised dinner tonight, James. Leanne has agreed to come and meet you. She realises how her quick exit from home must have worried some people, and she has calmed down enough now to discuss it. I do not think she is willing to go home yet, but you can ask her yourself this evening. I am sorry, I must leave you now. I am due in court in twenty minutes.'

'Thank you, Anne and Ian. You have lightened our load somewhat. We would love to come for dinner with you. We will see you this evening.'

They filed out of the office, all going in different directions. Alicia said she wanted to look in Yvonne's shop. She might pick up a dress for special occasions.

Wandering down the arcade, they noticed the shop just ahead of them. James said he would go inside with Alicia while she tried on dresses, and he would like to get a glimpse of Yvonne for his own analysis. Alicia was impressed by the clothes and chose two dresses to buy. She said one of them she could wear to dinner that night and the other one would do nicely for their Friday night dinner in the apartment. She was very pleased with her purchases. James agreed that they were nice and that she looked charming in them.

He was still trying to work out how a woman could ignore her grandchild for the sake of her shop. He did admit that the salon was impressive and obviously successful. The prices were high, but regardless of that, there seemed to be customers willing to pay for the quality. To him, it seemed a poor choice—a shop for a grandchild? What sort of woman would choose the shop?

*   *   *

They found the Clegg home by taking a cab. It was a lovely home set in a leafy street, furnished beautifully. Anne stated that her daughter, Sally, would also be joining them. She was the same age as Leanne, and the two were friends. The two young women arrived at the same time, and James and Alicia looked at each other with their mouths open. The reason for Leanne's arguments with Charles was suddenly clear to them. Leanne was at least eight months pregnant. Everything fell into place for them.

The housekeeper served the meal, leaving Anne to chat comfortably with her guests. After the meal, they adjourned to the lounge room for a coffee.

Leanne looked at James and said, 'I presume many of your questions have been answered since meeting me. The reason I left home so quickly was, that morning I told Uncle Charles that I was pregnant. He was shocked but immediately pinpointed who the father was—the young man who helped out as a handyman and the pool-cleaning at the house. Uncle Charles was very angry and sacked Jim on the spot and declared I would have an abortion straight away. When I refused to have an abortion, he announced that Jim would be made to marry me.

'My answer to that was, Jim was not to blame. I was locked away in that property every day, and I was bored. School had finished, and I was not free to come and go like other young people. So I seduced Jim in defiance, really—and curiosity, I must admit. I did not want to marry him. He is just a boy, and certainly the marriage would not have worked, as we are entirely different people with different interests. It was boredom that set me on the path to seducing Jim. He was not unwilling, but I did not expect to get pregnant so quickly.

Uncle was so disappointed in me. He imagined me following in my parents' footprints and becoming a doctor. I was not sure if that was what I wanted, and at least I wanted the choice to be mine, not his. I love my uncle Charles. Since I have been here, I realise what he gave up to protect me and everybody else. He is a good man, but so controlling about my education and what I should be doing. Maybe he was right. Maybe I would return to study and become a doctor. But I wanted it to be my decision, not his. He could not see this.

I realise that having a child will restrict what I decide to do. I inherited my parents' house here in Manchester on my eighteenth birthday. It was not sold during the shooting spree because it still held my parents' things, so it was left as it was for a year. Then Uncle arranged for an estate agent to clear the place out, with the things put into storage. It has been rented out all these years, and the money has accumulated. I have that to work with, and it will pay for my medical school fees and lifestyle until I am earning for myself. I still have these decisions to make about the baby while I am working. Other people manage, so why not me? I will manage too somehow.'

'It is a surprise to us, Leanne. None of this was admitted by Charles Chamberlain. The story of your disappearance kept growing, with all sorts of stories being made up, so we thought of the worst, until I found the person who flew you out, quite by chance. Otherwise, the story may still be snowballing. I will pass the message to Bettine Smith that you are safe and well, but I will not say where you are and why you left, I will leave that up to you. She expressed a wish to know you are safe. Others too wanted to know the same, so she will pass the message on.'

Alicia asked, 'When do you think you will be contacting your uncle Charles, Leanne?'

'I thought when the baby arrived may be appropriate.'

'That sounds good. He has tried to do the best for everyone. I think that is why he blew up when you announced your pregnancy. He blamed himself for not looking after you properly.' Alicia smiled at the girl. 'I can understand both of your positions, but he has been worried for you.'

'I am sorry. I know I have been very juvenile in my thinking. I thought Uncle Charles was trying to keep me a child. He did not realise that children grow into adults. He thought I still needed protecting, and I admit I did it all in defiance of him. I was very stupid to get myself in this predicament, but it has made me grow up. I have no one but myself to blame.'

'What of Jim, Leanne? Will you advise him of the baby's birth?'

'No. He does not know I am pregnant. He thought he was dismissed purely for seducing me, and it was very early in the pregnancy when I took off.'

'I presume your stepmother, Meghan, knew about the pregnancy. Why did she choose Manchester, where all the trouble started, to send you?'

'She trusted her brother to help me. She too has been locked away all these years, so she did not have many choices to resort to. I was adamant that I did not want to go back to the farm, and I wanted to go before Uncle Charles came home. He was driving Melvin to London, so we knew he would be gone about two hours.'

'We visited Melvin, and he also would like a word with you. He is worried about you.'

'Ah, Melvin, yes. I thought he would have helped me get away. It got so mixed up that night. It was Uncle Charles turning up at the pub that started the mess-up. I had started out meaning to tell Melvin that I wanted his help to move to London. He took it the wrong way, and panic set in. When Uncle Charles turned up before I had a chance explain properly, we were backing away from each other. I regret tha Melvin was my friend.'

Alicia took Leanne's hand and looked into her eyes. 'Melvin is still your friend, Leanne. He is still unsure of what happened that night, and he also feels as if he let you down. Ring him and let him know you are safe. We could tell him, but I think if you rang him yourself, it would mean so much more to him.'

'I am so glad it was you two who came to find me. You are both so thoughtful and helpful. I knew someone would turn up sooner or later and I could not hide forever, but I expected police officers.'

'We are representing the police department, Leanne. We need you to sign this form exiting yourself from your protection program. This would have come anyway, once you turned eighteen. However, your absence caused a problem.'

'I did mess up greatly, didn't I? I did not mean to cause all this mess. I am sorry.'

'Just as long as you are okay. You have caused a lot of worries, but everything is understandable now. Just remember, your family are the best friends you can have. Do not ignore them.' Alicia added.

'Not all your family members, I have found. Some could not care less what happens to you.'

'Have you tried to see your Chamberlain grandmother yet?' asked Alicia.

'No, not yet. I have been too busy working my way around here and looking up my other family.'

Alicia wanted to help 'Why not ring her, Leanne? She was your primary minder, I believe, before the shootings began. I am sure she would like to hear from you. The upheaval in her life was very traumatic at the time: She lost her son and daughter-in-law. She lost you, who had been very close to her—she looked after you while your own mother was working. And then her own husband's health took a turn for the worse. And in a way, she also lost Charles, her other son. It must have been a terrible time for her. I am sure she would overlook your little bump to

to see you again. Even having a great-grandchild to visit
nderful for her.'

looked sombre, sitting quietly, thinking of the world around
ow other people had been involved. 'That is a new thought for
s, I can see you are right. It is amazing how you can get carried
away with your own selfish feelings and not think of the older people
in your life. I do not remember my Chamberlain grandmother. I was
too young when we left her and went away. She lost her whole family in
a matter of weeks, as you say. How terrible it must have been for her. I
will ring her in the morning and see if I can go down to see her.'

James turned to Ian Clegg. 'I am curious to know what happened
to the sect that started all this shooting. Are the others still around?'

'The police watched them for some time after Charles and Leanne
disappeared from the city. The leader of the sect and his wife both killed
themselves before the trial was finished, and the other members hung
around for a year or two and gradually went their own ways, breaking
the sect up. The end of the world had not happened, the leaders were
gone, there was no more ranting in the parks to grow their numbers,
and they withered away. It is amazing that a charismatic person could
hold sway over people and convince them that wrong is right. There
is no mention of it at all these days. I think Leanne is safe here now.'

James looked happy at this announcement and said, 'We will advise
Charles that you are safe, Leanne. Also Melvin and Bettine Smith.
These people have been anxious about your whereabouts. We will file
this form that Leanne has signed, and as far we are concerned, there is
nothing more to add. Someone said to me that this long story needed
a happy ending, and I think we have it.'

James paused and thought for a minute. 'I need to add a word of
caution for you, Leanne. Your uncle Charles left this city with you under
desperate conditions. Someone was out to kill you. We do not have
specific names, and neither do we know if they are lying low because
they cannot find you or have given up the crusade. Your parents' deaths
created big news at the time, and they may surface and reignite the story
and the shootings if the word gets out that you are here and about to
have a baby of your own.

A newspaper reporter could do a spread on you if they find out by any means that you are back here and your baby could be in danger. There were many newspaper reports at the time, and your reappearance could cause a flutter of newspaper articles relating the original story and could bring out the people involved in the previous shooting attempts.

James added 'I do not mean to scare you, but be careful whom you speak with. If a young journalist hears about it, it could help their career. It was big news when it all happened, and to write about you now would be icing on the cake for them. Who knows what sort of person could creep out of the woodwork?' James's face showed how serious he felt about what he was saying.

'I would like to hear that you have found a good life with your Chamberlain grandmother in Torquay. However, I do not want to influence your decisions. I hope you have a happy life from now on, Leanne, and I am pleased to have found you alive and well,' Alicia said with a smile and a hug. She turned to the Clegg family. 'Thank you for making this so easy. Also for the delicious food. We will go first thing in the morning, to another story. Thank you, Sally, for being a friend to Leanne when she needed one.'

*   *   *

The next morning, they arrived home early and went straight to the office to report. James made a number of phone calls and was happy to announce the happy ending to Jack Whistler. To Melvin, he left a text message, as he did not answer his phone. Alicia went to the coffee shop in the afternoon and told Bettine that Leanne was safe and well.

There was only Charles Chamberlain left to contact; he had been in a meeting when James first rang, and he rang back later. The conversation was quite long, with Charles apologising for his attempts to put James off the story. James admitted that it was the story Charles invented that was the incentive to keep up the search. He advised Charles to talk to Meghan, who knew the whole story, and ended with 'Leanne is alive and well and healthy, and she will call you when the baby is born'.

The police department was happy with the result; the chief said it was a wonderful outcome to a sad history.

James was happy to complete all the calls. It was time to archive the story and get on to something else, but he was pleased he had followed his instincts to continue the search. *It always rankles in the back of your mind when you do not have an answer,* he thought.

16

Percy remarked that Alec Overington wanted to see them to discuss a new case and wanted James to ring him to set a time for an office meeting including all the staff.

'Hmm, that is unusual. It must be something big. Did he give you any idea what it is about?'

'No, only that it is an important case for us to tackle if we are interested.'

'Then I shall ring him straight away to set a time. Are you all free today or tomorrow?'

'Kate and I have been tidying up the outstanding cases while you were away. Nothing new has come in for a few days except the usual surveillance jobs, and we are quite well up on those for the moment. There is nothing urgent.'

'Good. Sorry to have left you with all the humdrum cases, Percy.'

'I did not mind, James. It is nice to have a break from running around. I suppose my age is telling on me.'

'Nonsense, Percy, you could run rings around half of the younger people we meet. It is because we have been busy. Everyone needs a break sometimes.'

'Thanks for those kind words, James. You have made me feel better about myself already and ready for what Alec has to offer.'

James made the phone call, and a meeting was set for midday the next day, with a sandwich lunch and coffee or tea to accompany it. For a change, Alec would come to Gray and Armstrong for the meeting, and that in itself was unusual and set them all wondering.

After the meeting, Alicia took a break to go home and prepare for the guests coming to the bookshop apartment for dinner, and she stopped by the coffee shop to order sandwiches for the meeting next day.

*   *   *

The sandwiches were delivered just as Alec came through the door. Kate had turned the coffee machine on and prepared the hot water jug for Percy, who preferred a cup of tea. They all gathered in the meeting room, and Alicia put a sign on the door saying 'Closed for lunch, back in one hour'. That would give them time to see what Alec had to say, even if they went a little overtime.

'Well, Alec, you have your quorum,' said Percy, after the sandwiches were eaten and they were sipping their preferred drinks. 'I must say, it looks as if you have set the cat amongst the pigeons. You do not always confer in our office. We are wondering what this is all about.'

Alec looked around the table. 'I have a new client who strikes at the heart of each and every one of us. My client is the daughter of a woman who died in a nursing home three weeks ago. Jane Lambert is the daughter of Winifred Lambert, who was a resident of a care unit for the aged. Jane states that her mother had been in good health and had been a resident of the care home temporarily for respite but had died suddenly one night.

'Winifred had been an outspoken woman who called a spade a spade, according to Jane, and Jane suspects her mother was "put away" by the nursing staff because they considered her to be a nuisance. She had been outspoken about some aspects of the place and, in particular, one of the male nurses, saying he was rude. This man had warned her to shut up or nasty things would happen to her. Winifred became afraid of this nurse and his attitude towards her and some of the other residents. She was a woman who had brought up three children alone. Her husband had died in an accident many years previously, and she had managed her life well without help.

'She had voiced her opinion that the care unit was taking away all her personal things, particularly her medication, which she liked to manage herself, as she had always done. This was ignored by the staff, who said it was mandatory that they manage any medication. She felt they were treating her like a child and insisted that there was nothing wrong with her mind and that the reason she was in care was that, at her age of eighty-seven, vertigo was slowing her down. She was sometimes very dizzy and had had several falls due to her dizziness, so her doctor had recommended she go into care to avoid having these falls.

'Jane had visited her the morning before her death and come away with the impression that her mother was healthy and feisty. She was shocked to receive a phone call from Valley Residential Care early next morning saying her mother had passed away during the night. Jane went to the care place and was told that her mother had been taken to a funeral chapel earlier. She felt that the staff were unhelpful and unwilling to talk about what had happened, just saying that Mrs Winifred Lambert had died during the night. Jane said she was taken up for the first two weeks settling affairs, but during this time, her mind was made up to have someone investigate the care home.

'She went to the police before the funeral and found them unwilling to investigate an older person's death, saying that old people die of all types of causes and that eighty-seven was a good innings. If she still thought something should be investigated, it was advisable for her to talk to a lawyer about her rights to an investigation, and they recommended me. She thought about it for a few days and decided to come to me to find out what she could do, very disappointed with the police's refusal to help.'

'What do you want us to do, Alec?' asked Percy.

'I think I am asking you to investigate the nursing home,' he replied. 'It is a bit vague. I do not know very much about those places, except that they take care of our aged relatives when they are unable to manage for themselves.'

Alicia said, 'We visit a nursing home to sit with an old friend who owned the bookshop that is now my grandmother's and who lived in our current apartment most of his life. He entered the care place because he has acute arthritis and can barely walk, and his hands are crippled due to the arthritis. We only stay an hour or two, so we do not know much about the operation of the place where he lives. He has been very happy with his placement, and I have never heard him complain.'

'He is very lucky then, I would say. You hear all sorts of complaints in the news about these places from time to time. There is talk of bullying and lackadaisical care.' commented Alec.

'I think it is because Rob is such a friendly, happy person by nature. People are attracted to him. He had spent his life in the bookshop until he was unable to go up and down the stairs because of the arthritis. He then bequeathed the bookshop and the apartment to my grandmother and to me.'

Percy said, 'I have forgotten about your Rob Gooding, Alicia. I said I would visit him sometime and never got around to it. We have been so busy.'

'Yes, we have been busy the last few weekends ourselves, and Granny has been going alone when she is free. I feel bad about that.'

James looked at the sadness on Alicia's face. 'We shall go this Sunday, Alicia. We have been neglecting him. It sounds like we can quiz Rob about what goes on in a care house. I am sure he will want to help.'

Percy looked at Alec. 'This sounds as if it will not be a five-minute job. How long do you envisage it going on, and who is paying?'

'The client, Jane Lambert, at first. If you find anything untoward, we may be given something by the police department. If the particular nurse is at fault, hastening deaths, it will become a police investigation. We only have to establish that there is a cause for concern in the first place. Jane went to the police without any proof at all, and even to me, it sounded a bit wild. But she was adamant that there was no reason for her mother to die so quickly. Of course, a heart attack can take someone quickly, but there are usually some indications.'

'How do you think we should approach it, Alec?' asked James.

'Because there is a possibility of a dangerous person giving drugs to the wrong people, I believe you should operate in pairs. I think the records have to be searched to see if other patients have died suddenly.

You need some type of walkie-talkie with which to speak with each other so you have backup all the time.

'Alicia would be good for talking to other residents to see if anything is wrong at their level. Percy too would go down well for chatting with other residents as a senior citizen. Kate could be good in the administration office. You too, James. Those positions will be safe enough, so you would only need to be there on your own for that purpose, and one of you could stay here to mind the show. You could take it in turns. Other than that, it is up to you to see if anything is out of order.'

'Do you have a deadline, Alec?' asked Alicia.

'It will be a hot issue in the care home once it is known what you are there for, so you will have to be in and out as fast as possible to see if there is just cause to continue. If so, the police department will come into it at that time. They may ask you to continue under their auspices at that stage.'

'Do you have the name of the nurse in question, Alec?'

Alec looked at his paperwork. 'His name is John Dewson. He has been there for several months, I believe, from Jane's explanations.'

Percy sat up straight. 'I know that name. I cannot remember from where, but I will check him out. I know him from somewhere. Do you have a description of him?'

'Jane said she only saw him a few times, as he normally worked the night shift. She described him as being of medium height, slim, with straight black hair and a thin face. He wore dark-rimmed glasses for reading slung around his neck on a cord when not using them.'

'That is a good description from an amateur. We should be able to recognise him,' said Percy. 'Even that description sounds familiar. I will probably wake up in the middle of the night and say I know where I have seen him before.'

'Alicia and I can go and see Rob Gooding at his nursing home on Sunday. Do you want to come along to meet Rob, Percy? We will start our investigations on Monday. We will need a warrant to examine the books and enter the property. Could you arrange that, Alec?'

'I have already put in an application, and it should be ready by Monday. You had better arrange your surveillance for Tuesday in case the paperwork does not arrive on Monday.'

'Good, that will give us a chance to tidy up any loose ends here. We will arrange the roster later today so we know where we stand for any other jobs that may come in.' James was making notes as he spoke. 'Do you have any more information on the nursing home staff, Alec?'

'Not at the moment. I could ask Jane Lambert to ring you and coordinate with you on the layout of the place so you can keep in touch with each other when this Dewson fellow is on duty. I do not like the idea of putting the ladies especially in any danger.'

Kate said, 'Forewarned is forearmed, Alec.'

'You have been trained for dangerous jobs, Kate, but Alicia is not, and she will be doing the ward duty.'

'Alicia is trained in watching the faces of people, Alec,' said James. 'She will do well talking to other residents. She will be able to pick up fear or ignorance easier than the rest of us, and one or the other of us will be close by to keep watch on her.'

Alicia laughed. 'I can speak for myself, everybody. I shall manage. This will be a different job than any I have done before, but it sounds interesting and I like talking to older people. I was brought up by my grandmother and Rob Gooding from the age of five when my parents died, so yes, I will manage.'

Alec looked at her with interest 'I did not know that, Alicia. I am sorry if I spoke out of place.'

'No problem, Alec. I do not take offence easily.'

'Okay, folks, I will leave it with you over the weekend, and I should be able to come up with the paperwork to go ahead on Monday. I will see you then. Thanks for the lunch.'

There was a buzz of excitement after Alec left. This would be the most dangerous job they had done so far and possibly the longest, depending on how things went.

*　*　*

Alicia left them talking about it to go home and prepare for dinner for the evening She was looking forward to having guests. They had not done any entertaining in the apartment since they had moved in. When she had told her grandmother about having friends for dinner and asked if she wanted to come too, her grandmother had declined and offered to have Jody sleep the night with her in her house. That would mean they would not have to keep their voices low in case they woke the little girl up.

Alicia had thought of asking Kate to come to dinner but decided to wait and see how the evening went before including any more people. So far, she had only cooked for James, Percy, and her grandmother. They all said they loved her cooking, but she was a little nervous with strangers, not knowing their likes and dislikes.

The evening turned out to be wonderful, and Harry and Freddy were the ideal persons to invite to dinner; they ate everything on their plates and entertained the group with stories of jaunts into the hamlets and hills of Afghanistan. It seemed it had not been all warfare; they had days when they could enjoy the countryside as well. They kept the war-type stories to themselves and only spoke of the fun times they had experienced.

Just before they left for the evening, Harry turned to James. 'Thank you, James, for your advice and help. I have put an application in for a small business grant, as you suggested. The police patrol called in on Wednesday evening and congratulated me on doing a good job for the community, so I submitted the grant form on Thursday. As that was only yesterday, I would say I will probably have to wait some time for an answer.'

James, Alicia, and Freddy all shook his hand and congratulated him. Freddy added, 'Well done, mate. I will have to come and see you at work. You are not letting your leg stop you, obviously.'

'It is only a leg, Freddy. You should see some of the other fellows who have lost both legs. It is admirable what they can do. It is a lesson in perseverance to see them getting used to having two prosthetic limbs. You have to admire them and the doctors and nurses who encourage them.'

After they left, James took Alicia into his arms and said, 'Congratulations to you, Alicia. That was a wonderful meal. You do not look hot and flustered, as you probably feel. We all appreciate what you have done here this evening.'

'Thanks, James. I admit I had a few moments of panic, but everything turned out great. And you are a good host.'

'With those two, it was easy. They kept the evening alight between them with their stories.'

'We should do this more often, James. It is a good feeling, knowing that all the trouble we went to was valued by our guests. They are really nice chaps.'

17

On Saturday, as usual, James and Alicia helped serve in the bookshop. James commented, 'I do not know how Granny managed Saturdays by herself. It is so busy.'

'I think she had help from some of the customers. They have been coming to the bookshop for so long that many have become friendly with Granny and are a bit more than customers when she is very busy, so they would pitch in and help out.'

'That is the only way she could have managed. She does have a lovely, friendly manner with all the customers, as if they are old friends, and it has paid off for her. Some of these people you see over and over, and even we are beginning to think of them as friends,' said James, laughing. 'We will go to the nursing home to visit Rob Gooding tomorrow in the office car. It will be much more comfortable for Granny, and we are going partially for work, to find out how a good nursing home is managed.'

'I am sure Granny will appreciate that, James. She has been struggling on the bus each time she has gone alone. Her right arm is still not working for her. Luckily, the bus driver realises that and helps her board.'

'It was certainly a bad break. I have noticed her arm is not straight anymore and seems shorter than her left one.'

'Yes, the doctors warned that because the shatter of her elbow was so severe, it may take a long time for it to heal straight—perhaps never.'

'What a shame. She is so stoic and does not complain and just gets on with the job. I have seen her cradling her arm. Does she still have pain?'

'She tries not to overwork it, as it does ache after a little work with it. She is still doing the exercises the physiotherapist in the hospital showed her, especially first thing in the morning. She tells me it seizes up overnight, and she can't lie on her right side for very long, as it hurts.'

'I am pleased that we can offer her a car ride this Sunday to go and see Rob.'

'I rang Rob yesterday to tell him we would be coming this Sunday. He said he has a surprise for me. I wonder what it is. He would not tell me, saying Sunday is soon enough.'

'We can drop Jody at her home to save time for both Aaron and ourselves. They are going to visit Sandra, I presume?'

'Yes, Sandra is going into surgery on Monday for investigative work. The doctors think her drug addiction has abated and she is strong enough now and has even put on a little weight, so she will manage the surgery.'

'Do you want to go in to visit her and wish her luck?'

'No, thanks, James. I am sure she understands how busy we are. But I will ring and leave a message tomorrow if I cannot speak to her, wishing her luck and telling her we will say a prayer for her. She knows now that Jody is happy with us and is being well looked after. Granny is doing most of the looking-after part with Jody, but she is loving it. And Jody is loving Granny right back.

'Aaron told me that he will go into the hospital very early on Monday and wait for Sandra to wake up after the anaesthetic wears off, to see how she feels and to find out the verdict as to whether she will be able to walk again or spend her days in a wheelchair. It will be too long a day for Jody. He will call in when he returns from London, to put us in the picture with Sandra's condition. I have asked him to have dinner with us in Granny's house so we all know what is going on.'

'That is fine, Alicia. We will set off about nine o'clock then. After we drop off Jody and drive to Winchester, it will be at least ten o'clock, so we will not be disturbing any of Rob's meals. It will give us time to wander around the nursing home and talk to a few people so we will have a clear idea of what we have to do on Tuesday.'

'It is good that we have Rob's nursing home to make a comparison, James. I know that when Granny was looking for a place for Rob, she visited most of the residential care places and thought that where Rob is now is the best of them all. I am really looking forward to going to see him.'

'Do not forget to pack a notebook in your handbag to write down what everyone tells you. We will particularly want to know if they keep note of residents coming in and out.'

'I am right on that, James. I have one for you and one for me. We will possibly be speaking to different people throughout the visit.'

*   *   *

Next day, they got up as if it were a normal workday, and they were ready to leave the house and bookshop at nine o'clock. They left Jody with her father and set off into the sunshine of a lovely autumn day for a happy jaunt. James said, 'We should get away from work more often. This is a lovely drive, and everything is fresh this morning. I love the look of the dew on the grass early in the morning, and there is not too much traffic yet, although it will probably be different on the way home again.'

Rob was at the doorway, sitting on a bench, waiting for them. He was pleased to see the three of them and gave them all hugs. He said, 'I have arranged for a tray of tea and biscuits for us. Someone will be out here with it shortly. You will see my surprise then, Alicia.'

Ten minutes later, the door opened, and a woman came out carrying the promised tray, which she placed on a table in front of the benches. Alicia looked curiously at the woman and said, delighted, 'It is Sharon Knight, isn't it?'

The woman laughed and grabbed Alicia and hugged her. 'It has been so long since I have seen you Alicia, at least seven years, and you have grown even more lovely in that time.'

'You haven't changed much, Sharon, although the glasses you are wearing are something I haven't seen before and made me uncertain of you. Your hair has changed to a shorter cut. Otherwise, you are the same as you were when I left to go flying.'

'I am told this is your husband,' Sharon said as she turned to James. 'I am pleased to meet you, James Armstrong. Rob has told me about you.'

Rob said, 'I recognised Sharon as soon as I saw her. More grown-up, of course, than when she visited the bookshop with Alicia. Sharon has been here a month now, Alicia, taking over the office. I did not tell you on the phone because I wanted to surprise you.'

'*Surprise* is the word for it. I am so happy to see you, Sharon. We have been back at Granny's place for several months now, and it looks like we're staying. I have not had much spare time to look up old friends, because I work with James in his business during the week and help in the bookshop on Saturdays. We only have Sundays free. What have you been doing, Sharon?'

'I went into residential care houses after I left school, and I was offered this posting for six months, relieving the lady who has been here for ten years or so. She has taken long service leave and is visiting her daughter in Australia and has gone for six months, extending her leave time, as I was available to take the job on. I must say, this is the nicest of the places I have worked at. I do relief work, so I have seen most of them.'

'Do you know the Valley Residential Care home, Sharon?' asked James.

She pulled a face and said, 'It does not have a good name, I am afraid. I was there a few months ago to work when the receptionist went on leave for several weeks. It was an unhappy place. One of the patients died while I was there. The nurse on duty at the time said she had fallen out of bed. I did not see her, but one of the day nurses saw her before she was taken to the funeral chapel. She said she had bruises on her cheek that did not look as if she had fallen out of bed. It was more as if she had been bashed. The night nurse was questioned, but he said he did not see her fall, just heard her cry out. There was no one else to say any different, so it was dropped. But everyone there was disturbed. It made the atmosphere gloomy.'

'The night nurse was John Dewson?' asked James.

'Yes, do you know him?' she asked.

'Not yet, but we will be making his acquaintance next week. Our business is private investigations, and we have been asked through a lawyer to investigate the death of another one of the residents from three weeks ago. Do you have time to show us around this house? We know it is good, because we have Rob positioned here, and he always tells us he is happy to be here and how everyone takes such good care of him. We would like to see how the house is run, records kept, et cetera so that we have a comparison with Valley Care. We start work there on Tuesday after we get the warrant to do so.'

Sharon sighed. 'I do know that everyone kept clear of Dewson. He is a permanent night-shift nurse, and I think most of the residents are frightened of him and will not say anything against him because of repercussions if they complain about him. The trouble with Valley Care is, because their reputation is poor, it has been hard for them to get proper staff. They are always short-staffed, so they turn a blind eye to lots of things. I was on day shift and only there for six weeks, but I was glad to get away from the place. Mainly because of the rumours going around, everyone was so despondent'

'Would you then show Alicia and me around?' asked James.

'Gladly, James. Follow me. We will start with my office—all the records are kept there—and then follow up with the sitting, TV, and dining rooms and then the bedrooms. We have separate sides for those that need more care, such as those with dementia, and then we have those like Rob, who are happy to wander around and can be trusted to sit outside like we are here. Those with dementia are locked in, poor souls. They have ample space to wander around here, but they have a habit of taking off and not knowing the way back. They disappear so quickly. Physically, many of them are fine, and they almost run away to try and get back to their previous homes. We are always sending out rescue teams. It is so sad.'

'Rob has told us that the staff are always very careful with the dementia patients and chat with them as if they can understand and that they are cared for in a special way, not ignored.' Alicia looked anxious. She had nothing to do with these types of people in her life and was not sure how to handle them.

'Yes, we have different stages of dementia cases here, but each of them is different. We try to treat them as if they are normal. It takes quite a lot of patience for the staff. We are lucky to have a good group of staff here.'

'I understand that the woman who died in Valley Care, whom we are investigating, was an outspoken person but very intelligent. Her daughter insists that she was not ill in any way and would be impatient if anyone spoke to her like a child instead of an adult.' James wanted to learn as much as he could from someone who had been there at the time of a death.

'From what I know about that nurse, he would not like an outspoken person. However, it is second-hand gossip I learnt after the other lady died. The staff spoke in whispers about it. I do not want to condemn him though, as nothing was proven at the time.'

James continued, 'We want to know if records are kept about the people who die there. I am sure that not everyone has a euthanasia death. We are aware that the majority of people are there because, like Rob, they are unable to look after themselves but certainly have the ability to know what is going on around them.'

'Yes, there are many like Rob, although nowadays many are helped in their own homes, so we are getting fewer here to look after. We are getting more and more dementia patients. Rob has been here several years now, but if he were assessed today, he would probably have home help instead of being in here. I am glad he is here. He brightens up many of the nurses' days with his huge smile and kind remarks. The staff tend to take a break from a difficult dementia patient every now and then and go to chat with Rob, and he cheers them up.'

'Would a night nurse check on Rob each evening?' asked Alicia.

'Yes, to give him his medication, but that would be all, as long as he is well or unless he rings his bell. The medication is handed out to each patient by the staff. We have a list of what each patient or resident takes, and the night nurses commence their rounds by dishing out each person's pills or injections. Some people have diabetes and need injections, so their injections are done before meals and before sleeping at night.'

'So only the staff have access to the medicine cabinet? The other residents would not be able to get to it?' James wanted to make sure that one resident could not have injected their medication into another resident.

'There is a key to the medicine cabinet, and the only way to get the key is to register with the receptionist, such as me. They have the medicines checked and sign for them.'

'So they take the key and get the medicines out of the cabinet and then hand back the key? Would they be able to take out another medicine and put it in their pocket unseen?'

'It is possible, I suppose. There is a certain amount of trust to go with it, but we check the medicine every week to make sure it adds up. It is the one thing in each care place that is carefully managed. No one wants to be accountable for the death of a resident. Two of us, the receptionist in charge of the office and a nurse, check it out and count it up.'

James looked at Sharon. 'Thank you, Sharon, for all your help. I did not mean to make it an interrogation of any sort, but if we go into Valley Care not knowing about these details, we could be outmanoeuvred by anyone wanting to pull the wool over our eyes. There does seem to be a problem there, so an investigation by others rather than the involved staff is the only way to make the issue go away, one way or another.'

'I am sure the general staff will appreciate your investigation. There were so many whispers going on while I was there that I was happy I did not have to stay any longer than the six weeks.' Sharon sighed. 'Generally, these care places have a happy group of people. That was the only one I have come across to make me anxious to depart.'

After Sharon showed the resident records, they strolled back to Rob and Granny on the front veranda. 'Sharon, when we have finished this case, would you like to visit us on your day off to have dinner or lunch with us, and we will tell you all about it?'

Sharon's face lit up. 'I would love to, Alicia, both to catch up and to hear your final word on the case, as you call it.'

'We are still in the bookshop. Remember, Granny and I lived next door. Rob has given the bookshop to us, and James and I live in his old apartment upstairs, which Granny has had modernised. He is such a lovely old man. He calls me his granddaughter. I thought of him as my grandfather while I was growing up. He was a huge part of my life. I am sure you will hear about the end of the case through the grapevine, but I will ring you and make a date.'

'I will look forward to it, Alicia. The only thing wrong with the care homes is that they are full of old people, and you often wish to talk to a young group, as you feel you are getting out of touch. The staff are usually too busy to chat.'

'We haven't reached that stage yet, Sharon, so we will see you in a week or two.'

* * *

As they drove away towards the town, James said, 'Well, that was worthwhile. We learnt quite a lot on how to manage a nursing home. It was marvellous that we had Sharon to tell us everything. Someone else might have been a little put off with the things we said, but she was very forthcoming, with all sorts of information. I like her, Alicia. Do you think she would suit Harry or Freddy?'

Alicia laughed. 'I thought the same thing myself when I asked her to come for dinner.'

'We will wait until the Valley care case is closed one way or another, and have a repeat dinner. And can you think of any other women who could come along too? Would Sharon have any friends?'

'I do not know about Sharon's friends, but I thought of Bettine Smith. Do you think she is a bit young?'

'She seems like a sensible person, not a flighty type. If we cannot think of anyone else, we could ask her. We could always fall back on

Kate. She is free and her children often go to their father on weekends, so she would not have to hurry back for the babysitters.'

'We shall wait and see. This case may last several days, maybe longer, and it will tie us down. We will be unable to do much else for a while. I am a bit nervous about this job, James. I feel a sense of dread.'

'We shall manage, Alicia. I too have been thinking about it, and I think you and Kate should do only the day shift and check the office out. Kate could do that, and you could mix with the residents and chat with them to get their feelings on things that have happened.'

'I would feel happier doing that. I dread meeting this John Dewson. Just the thought of him makes me feel creepy/

'Okay, we will do that. Percy and I can do the night shift and take it in turns to nap in short shifts so that there is always someone alert. We need to purchase the walkie-talkie machines in the morning. I am sure they come in smaller sizes than the ones I played with as a boy, and we may be able to carry them in a pocket and perhaps have a button we can press so that we do not disturb Dewson and make him suspicious. I will look on the computer tonight to see what is available.'

Granny spoke up. 'That sounds sensible, James. I too have been a little worried about the girls going into an area where a demonic suspect is acting out his vampire dreams. From the history I have heard, it is possible he has been euthanising people for some time, and this Jane person has been the only one brave enough to speak up.'

James and Alicia laughed. 'We haven't heard of any vampires in the area,' James said.

Granny smiled. 'No, but you wonder what the man is thinking at home when he is alone, and when and how he does his planning. If he does not have access to extra medications, he must be holding back on some poor soul's medication and saving it up so that he can have a store to use when he wants to euthanise someone. There must be some method in his madness and some planning ahead, so, Alicia, you will have to ask if he has missed giving some medications to other people. He must get his store from somewhere.'

James's face hardened. 'You are spot on, Granny. I had not got that far in my thinking yet, but it is one answer. You must ask each person you visit, Alicia, if they have received each day's medication correctly. I think Granny is right in her speculation. The medication has to come from somewhere, and if they are all counted and come up correct each week, that has to be the answer.'

'What other questions should I ask, James and Granny? You seem to have your fingers on the pulse. I just seem to keep thinking about John Dewson and feeling dread and being unable to get further.'

'Would you prefer it if Granny did a shift first to try the place out? You could look after Jody and the bookshop for the day, and Granny could go to Valley Care for morning tea and chat with the residents. She could pretend she is looking for a place to go into. That would work for us.'

'What do you think, Granny?' asked Alicia.

'I could do that, as long as Kate is available to help me out. I could pretend she is my carer at the moment. Yes, I would like to help, and it will give me a change of scene for a day. I tend to do the same thing over and over, and I occasionally get bored—not too often, just in melancholy moments. I quickly get over them. Jody has been a bright patch for me. You cannot get too bored answering her questions all day long.'

'You would be a big help, Granny. The other residents will be falling over themselves to tell you everything, and even if Dewson walks in and discovers you, he will not be suspicious, because you are of an age to be looking for care. However, as he works the night shift, I doubt he will turn up while you are there.' James could see Granny chatting with the residents. She would have everybody mesmerised; such was her habit in the bookshop.

By this time, they were almost back home, and James said, 'I am taking you both to the Italian restaurant we usually go to, and I will ring Percy to join us. We can talk it over a bit more over lunch. Percy could not come this morning although he had shown an interest in meeting Rob, because he had a prior arrangement with his son. He went to have morning tea with the family and to see the grandchildren, because they were going out to a friend's house and unable to give him the Sunday lunch he usually has with them. I am sure he would welcome company for lunch.'

He rang Percy to invite him and received a thank you and a response that Percy would meet them at the restaurant.

*   *   *

It was their favourite restaurant, a place where they had grown friendly with the staff and where the cook usually came out of the kitchen to greet them and suggest the menu for the day. The food was always good, and the staff, mostly family members, were always happy. They even liked the background Italian music.

Percy agreed to Granny—or Valerie, as he usually called her—doing a morning at Valley Care, saying, 'I cannot think of anyone more capable to get to the bottom of the story. I agree too that Kate should accompany Valerie. It is possible she may pick up on looks and nuances in the conversations that Valerie may miss.'

He also agreed that Kate and Alicia should go back the next day for Kate to check the paperwork and for Alicia to chat with the residents. They should have a good picture by then. James and Percy would do the night shift together, mainly to watch for Dewson and his reaction to them overseeing him. None of them knew exactly what they would be doing; it depended on what happened during their time there and whether it needed longer scrutiny.

Each of them understood their part and were now ready to start on Tuesday.

18

The necessary warrants came on Monday afternoon, delivered by Alec Overington, who wished them luck and said, 'Do not forget to ring me and let me know how you are proceeding. Jane is very anxious to know what is happening.'

Alicia explained to him the strategy they were going to use. Alec's face showed how pleased he was about being kept informed, and when told that Valerie Newton was going to the residential home first before James and Percy, he showed delight at her inclusion. He had met Alicia's grandmother at the opening party for the office and was quite taken with her and her novel way of seeing the world.

'That is just right for the situation. Valerie is wonderful with people and can talk about just about anything. If she probes and asks about the care that is given there, she will surely be successful. You are lucky with your ladies, James. Both of them are wonderful people.'

'You are preaching to the converted, Alec. I recognised their value when I first met Alicia, and she is just like her grandmother, who brought her up. Yes, I am lucky.'

Alicia was blushing. 'Thank you both for the vote of confidence.'

Alec asked, 'Has Percy worked out where he has met Dewson before? He never forgets a face and can often work things out with merely a description. I am surprised he has not come up with an answer sooner.'

'We have not asked him again, Alec, and he has not mentioned it. Perhaps the penny will drop as soon as he gets a glimpse of Dewson on Tuesday night.'

'Keep me in the loop, James. I will ring Jane Lambert and let her know of your progression and your plan and your description of the care unit you went to yesterday for comparison. I am sure she will be pleased to know of your actions so far.'

'Okay, Alec, our first report will be Wednesday morning. Granny and Kate will be first in the nursing home at about ten tomorrow morning, and Percy and I will go in at 5 p.m. tomorrow for the night shift.'

Everybody was a little subdued after Alec left; they were wondering what lay ahead of them. Alicia left for home a little early to arrange the evening meal, with Aaron expected to deliver the verdict as to whether Sandra would walk again.

Jody jumped up and down when she arrived home, pleased to see Alicia earlier than usual. After a day out with Aaron, visiting her mother, she had been tired out yesterday and had gone to bed early. Now she was full of where they went and what they had done. Aaron had taken her to the London Eye, and they had waited in line for ages to get on. Jody was not scared of the height and had enjoyed the ride. She wanted to tell Alicia everything she had seen.

Aaron came in just when Jody finished her story, looking very weary and a little teary. Alicia made him sit down and gave him a cup of tea in the nook and said, 'Relax for a while, Aaron. Save your story until after dinner, and you will be able to tell it without breaking down. Granny and James want to hear the story too. James will be home any minute, and Granny is now in the shower, freshening up, and will be out soon.'

'Thanks, Alicia. I do not know how we would have managed without you and your grandmother looking after Jody. Sandra chose you well. She would never let Jody out of her sight before her treatment became so necessary. I think if she had discovered you earlier, she wouldn't have been so badly off, but she refused any offers for someone else to look after Jody. It was as if she had been waiting for you to come along.'

'James and I only returned because Granny was almost run over and had shattered her elbow in trying to escape the car coming at her. She needed our help, so we obeyed the call. At first, we thought it would be only a few weeks. It was not until the doctor told us how bad the break was, especially in an older person, that we realised it was going to be some time before we would be able to leave her, so James had to give up his London career and joined Percy in the private investigations business. We have only been here since January, but it seems we will be staying now. The business is doing well, and I am helping out, until it is fully established anyway.

'Sandra saw me in the shopping mall just after we opened the business and did not say anything about looking after Jody, so it was a big shock when we arrived home after a few days after to find Sandra missing and Jody already looking very much at home in the bookshop. She is a lovely child, Aaron, and we have been happy to be able to help out.'

'I feel as if I have failed Sandra and Jody. I was the one driving at the time of the accident. Sandra received the worst from the airbags because she was pregnant, but at least she saved Jody.'

'James investigated the crash, Aaron. You did not cause it, and where you were situated in traffic, there was nowhere to go to avoid the bus coming at you. The fact that you all survived it is a miracle in itself, and to have a perfect baby after it is incredible.

'James is now working out how you can join the class action for the explosion of the airbags. Unfortunately, he has been too busy to finalise it. He does not want to get your hopes up about it, because he thinks it will be some years away, but with it happening worldwide, something must be done about it.'

'You have all done so much for us. We will be forever grateful.'

'Sit here for a while and play with Jody. You can look after the shop while I go and check the dinner. James is due home any minute now, and we will close the bookshop when he arrives. If a customer comes in, Jody knows what to do. She is the ultimate salesperson.' Alicia laughed as she slipped out the door to go to the house next door to check the dinner in the oven and to see if Granny needed any help with dressing.

* * *

During dinner, everybody was cheerful; eating a lovely meal took precedence over any news. After they finished, James made a cup of tea, and they sat back to hear Aaron's news on how Sandra was going to face her future.

Aaron took a long breath. 'Sandra went into the theatre in a happy mood. However, after two hours, the doctor came out to tell me that there was nothing he could do to help her. Any chance of her walking again could be in the future, if science comes up with a way to renew or replace vertebrae that had crumbled. It is all a structural problem, and there is no reason that, besides having to get around in a wheelchair, she should not lead a normal life. He believes her addiction to drugs has abated, mainly because she has been in bed and has not been putting a strain on her back to cause the pain she required the painkillers for.'

He stopped and looked at Jody. 'We will be glad to get her back in any condition. Jody and I will look after her. The doctor said he will write a report for the health department to get us help with a nurse to come in and check her regularly. She will be discharged from the hospital in a week's time. At least that will save us from going on the train every few days. My head has still not got used to the noises on the train. I spend many nights with headaches on the days I go up to London.'

His audience looked sympathetic, and Alicia said, 'At least she will not need the pills any more, or as often. Lots of people manage in a wheelchair and lead normal lives. It may mean a few adjustments to the house so she can reach things. Luckily, you live on the ground floor, and ramps are already in place in your block of units. I think it will be an improvement for you all.'

James concurred. 'Once we get over the adjustment period, there is no reason Sandra should be held back. She can still look after Jody, reading and talking to her. She will still be able to continue her painting, and perhaps she can do a little fashion designing and sell the designs or even make up the dresses and sell them herself or even hire someone to sew them if it is a strain on her. That could make a new career for her. It is remaining positive that is the main thing. Adjustment to the situation will take a little time, but Sandra has had the rest she needed so desperately and will be ready to start a new life with you.'

Aaron looked at James curiously. 'You sound like a lawyer giving his final wind-up to the jury.'

James laughed. 'Getting a bit pontifical, was I? It becomes a habit after a while. Yes, I am a lawyer, but not practising while I am in the private investigations business.'

'I have thought that in the several conversations we have had together. You always sound so level-headed. Now I know the reason.'

'I do not want to sound as if I am an expert to advise you. I have had no experience with disabled persons. It just seems like common sense, and recognising Sandra's abilities and her compulsion to do the best for Jody will help her recover her equilibrium and keep her going.

'I recognised her art, when I saw it in your house, as being very good, and Alicia has told me how she designed and made up her own clothes after she left school. She was admired by everyone. These things could help her readjust to life in a wheelchair.'

Aaron was quick to reply. 'James, I did not mean to criticise you. You always make such good sense. You are completely right, of course. It is only the adjustments to our life that seem humongous at the moment. It will take a little time.'

'Do not delay or dilly-dally, Aaron. You need to get on with the changes and stand up to any delays with force if necessary. It will be a hard thing to do, but you may have to push Sandra a little to overcome the lethargy that could set in. Sandra is a talented human being. Do not let her sink into oblivion just because she cannot use her legs.' This was Granny speaking, quite forcefully. Everyone turned and looked at her. If Granny was giving advice, everybody would listen.

'Bravo, Granny,' said Alicia. 'I agree, Aaron. It is up to you to motivate Sandra. You and Jody together. After spending so long in bed, Sandra may think that is her life from now on. We all know that it is not. We do not want her to waste away but to use her art to keep her mind active and her resourcefulness to design new clothes for the fashion-minded. She has Jody to help her, but it is you that will have to prod her into action.'

Jody, sitting at the head of the table, said, 'Okay, Daddy, we can clean her brushes for her and get her water so she can paint. Maybe she can make little girls' dresses too. I like wearing dresses.'

Aaron looked at her with tears in his eyes. 'You are so right, Jody. Of course, we can do that, and more too. We will work it out as we go along.'

James looked sympathetic. 'I know it may feel insurmountable at the moment, but you have no time to waste. If necessary, get a carpenter in to help modify your home. If your funds are limited, we will loan you the money to move ahead, and you can pay us back as soon as you are on your feet again. You have only a week to do all the modifications necessary, so you have to move quickly on it.'

Alicia said, 'We will have Jody's suitcase packed and ready for when you want her home with you again. Ask Sandra's opinion on this. She may want her immediately, but then again, she may want to wait until she has adjusted to her new life. She is the one to decide this. Meanwhile, we are happy to have Jody with us. She fits right in, and we will miss her when she goes home.'

Jody leaned over and took Granny's hand. 'I will miss you, Granny. Can I come back some days to see you again?'

This time, it was Granny's turn to have tears in her eyes. 'Any time, my lovely girl. You will always be welcome here with us. We love you as if you were our own little girl.'

Aaron said, 'Sandra and I both appreciate what you have done for us. Jody is so precious to us, and it has helped Sandra, knowing she is happy to be here with you. Sandra certainly chose well when she left Jody with you. Life will be different, but I can already see it will be better than it was before Sandra left for rehabilitation. We can also see that what Bull did was a terrible thing, but it was a catalyst to change what had to be changed. Hopefully, we will be better off from it.'

Granny had the last word. 'It is good, Aaron, that you are thinking positive. That is what you both have to do now, and it will not seem so bad. At least Sandra will be home with her family. I will take your daughter upstairs to bed. It is past her bedtime. Say goodnight to everyone and give them all a kiss, Jody, and we will go upstairs to clean your teeth and get to bed.'

James and Alicia started to clear the table, and Aaron said, 'I am ever grateful for your help, not just with looking after Jody but especially with Sandra and me. My life was at a very low ebb when you rang me up and asked me for a pint at the pub. Life had been catapulting me along any which way and was getting out of hand. It started looking up with that pint, and the future looks much better from here. Thank you to you both and to your grandmother, Alicia.'

Alicia kissed his cheek. 'Go home now and rest. The walk will clear your head, and you will be able to sleep better. If you need that money to do any modifications, give us a call. We will catch up soon.'

After he had gone, Alicia said, 'I think it is just about bedtime for us too. I can sleep in tomorrow. I have a "bookshop and Jody" day. You will be up and about late tomorrow night at the Valley Care home, so you need to get an early night tonight to get ready for it. We do not know how much rest you will get between watching what is going on.'

'Yes, it is an unknown. I am not worried about it yet. Time for that tomorrow night. Okay, I am ready for bed. I missed Harry's exercises tonight and may not be able to go on Wednesday if we do not sort things out at the Valley Care place beforehand. I will ring him in the morning and apologise.'

'I thought of that when I organised dinner with Aaron, but I realised we had no choice of days to choose from. We had to find out what was happening with Sandra.'

'Do not worry about that, Alicia. I knew that Aaron came first. It is only that Harry is just getting started with his business, and I wanted to support him. But things will get in the way from time to time, and I will not be free to go. I will go and exercise when I can. I enjoy it. I feel a little slothful some days, sitting in an office all day, and it is good to go out and limber up. It is something you always say to yourself: "You need to exercise." Despite knowing that, you do not do it for long enough when you are alone. But in the company of several others, you do it and enjoy it.'

'I can see it makes you happier, James. I am all for it. It brightens up the brain too.'

19

Percy drove Granny and Kate to the nursing home to start their interviews, and he went into the reception area and handed the warrants over and described what Kate and Granny were going to do that morning. The receptionist acted pleased to see them and showed the ladies into the dining room, where the residents were gathering for morning tea.

Percy asked if he could see staff personnel records, explaining that there had been a complaint against John Dewson and that it was his particulars that Percy was interested in checking. The receptionist explained, 'Everything is computerised nowadays.' She pulled up Dewson's details for him to look at. Percy asked if he could have a copy printed to show his lawyer, and the lady printed it out.

He then explained that he would be back at five o'clock with his partner to check through other paperwork, such as deaths in the community and medications and the reasons for the residents being in care. Both he and his partner would stay for the evening shift to see what goes on.

The receptionist seemed pleased there was going to be an enquiry. She said, 'I have only been here for a short time, but all the whispers going around are disturbing to the whole staff. It is a pleasant place to work, but the way it is going, everybody seems scared of something. I find myself looking over my shoulder each time I am left alone. If it continues like it is, I will be looking for a new job soon.'

Percy smiled. 'I am sure you are safe, but we will try to find the evidence to what we think is happening. Things should be better in the future. It will only take us a few days, but we cannot put a timeline on it yet. While I am here waiting for the ladies, will you show me the records of the residents, when they came in, how long they stayed, et cetera? It will save time tonight and leave us free for our main project, which is to watch what happens when the night nurse comes on duty.'

'No problem at all. We have a paper record of that, and it is updated monthly.' She looked on the shelf behind the desk and produced a thick file. 'This goes back to the opening of the care unit. You will find it all in here. We have it on computer as well, but because it was always done this way, we have continued it.'

'Thank you. You have been very helpful. I will sit over there in the waiting room armchairs and go through it while I am here.'

Percy was pleased. He did not feel comfortable with computers and did not like using someone else's, in case he pressed a wrong button and lost the information. Also, he could examine the file without getting in the staff's way. He sat down and went through the file, noticing in particular those who had died there.

Generally, the old and infirm were admitted and stayed a year or two. There was one group that was there for respite, to gather their strength after an operation or illness. This group only stayed for an average of eight to ten weeks. Then there were some not-so-infirm admitted because they were alone and unable to care for themselves. At first, these were in the majority, but later, more dementia patients were admitted. He did not know whether this was a growing trend, but it appeared to be so.

In the past year, there were four deaths, but the reasons were not logged on the file. Of three of those deaths, the nurse attending was John Dewson. Percy took the file back to the office desk and asked if he could have a copy of the last sheet in the file for his records.

He asked, 'Are post-mortems done on patients who have died?'

'Because the patients are old and sometimes ill, post-mortems are not done unless there are question marks about their deaths. The doctors sign the death certificates.'

'There are not as many deaths included here as I expected. Why is that?'

'This is not a hospital. It is a care unit. If a resident becomes ill, we would call an ambulance and have him or her taken to a hospital or a palliative care unit at a hospital. In those cases, a doctor would sign them out as being too ill to stay here. Our staff are only geriatric nurses and are not trained to look after really ill patients. The deaths you see in the file are those who died in their sleep or of natural causes.'

'I wondered why there were not so many deaths recorded for the number of patients, especially as the majority are aged persons. You have helped me understand.'

'So many of the general public say they would not go into a nursing home, because they would die there. It is not always true. Some only need a respite to gather their strength after an illness or a broken hip or pelvis, or to gain strength after chemotherapy, and these are discharged as soon as they pick up and can manage for themselves. Their stays can be from one or two months to six months, and they are happy to go on with their lives at home. They are usually admitted because there is no one at home to look after them in those early days after an operation.

'I think the general public has a bad image of nursing homes. My father refused point-blank to go into one when he grew too old to manage for himself, and the burden was on our family to cook and clean for him and call him every day to see if he was all right. He became a cantankerous old man, saying we were ignoring him and leaving him alone all the time.

'The truth of it was that we all had our jobs to go to and our families to bring up, and it left little time for him. We had a family roster for visiting and doing jobs for him, which included a week's meals and washing. He would have been much better off here, where he would have companionship with others his own age.'

'You have helped me immensely. I am one of those who would not want to go to a nursing home, but I can now see the value in it for those who need it. I hope I will never need a nursing home. I like the idea of going out fighting, but I can see its value in the community now. Thank you for all your help today. As I said, my partner, James Armstrong, and

I will be back around five o'clock this evening. It will be advantageous for James if I can tell him everything you have told me this morning.'

As he spoke, Kate and Granny came around the corner to the reception area. Granny smiled at the staff member and said, 'Well, that was an experience. I will not need to have lunch today, as I had so much food pressed on me while everybody was chatting.'

The receptionist laughed. 'Food is one thing that is in abundance. With so many tastes to satisfy, the cook tries to do a bit of everything. I hope you learnt something, Mrs Newton. We would like to have the air cleared around here.'

'I will have to tell Percy and James what I heard and let them see if anything was worthwhile. Kate has been taking notes, so if anything is interesting, they can pick it out. I am going home now for a nanna nap. I am exhausted, as they all wanted to tell their stories at once.'

'Life is like that. Everybody welcomes a new face in here to tell their story to. Everybody has a story.'

'I enjoyed myself. Thank you for your help. I will leave the follow-up to someone else.' Granny took Percy's arm for help down the stairs and into the car.

They drove to the private investigations office to bring James up to speed. Kate said, 'I will type my notes up while they are fresh in my mind. Some of the remarks were very interesting indeed, and I am sure you will want to follow them up. Mrs Newton was a hit amongst the ladies. There were some men there, but they seemed more subdued and did not join in the general conversation. It might be better if one of you went to afternoon tea to see what you can find out.'

'I might try that,' said James. 'It is always good to get some beforehand knowledge of the situation.'

Percy laughed. 'I did not think of it while I was waiting around. The receptionist was very helpful and put a different light on what a care home is and what happens there to ill residents. It was totally different from what I had been thinking. Most of the residents are released to hospitals if they are really ill, and many of the residents are only there until they gain their strength after an operation or chemotherapy. It does not have a palliative care unit—they are mainly at hospitals, and a nursing home is not a hospital.'

He continued, 'John Dewson was the attending nurse for three deaths this year. A doctor signed the death certificate in each case, as there had been no need, in their opinion, for a post-mortem. All this I learnt while the ladies were having morning tea.'

'Well done, Percy. I was not aware of any of that. You have done well in such a short time.'

'The other thing I picked up, James, is a copy of John Dewson's CV and personal file. He worked in palliative care at the general hospital when my wife died suddenly and unexpectedly there five and a half years ago. I intend to ask him tonight what part he played in my wife's death.'

'Do not show your hand too soon, Percy. Let us look this fellow over first. We want to find proof of what he has been doing. So far, it has all been hearsay. We cannot convict him on hearsay.'

'Okay, James, I will follow your example. You go for afternoon tea and chat up some of the male residents. They must have a different point of view. I do note that all the deaths that Dewson has attended have been women. Perhaps he has a mother complex of some sort. Maybe we need a psychiatrist to have a look at him.'

'That is up to the police, Percy. What we need to do is find the proof to get him that far. The police turned Jane Lambert away because there was no proof.'

'Okay, I will take Valerie home and come back and have a snooze in my chair in preparation for being out all night.'

*   *   *

Percy came back a little later with two packed meals to take to their job for the night. 'Alicia said they may not realise you are there in need of dinner, so she has made these dishes for us. We can ask to have them warmed in a microwave or oven. Thoughtful girl, your wife.'

'We can always count on her, thank goodness.'

'She was avidly listening to what Valerie had to say about her morning when I left. Has Kate printed out her version of events yet?'

'Yes, I am just now going through it, as Kate suggested. I find it very interesting reading. There is one woman who only wanted to be named Roma, who said that on the evening that the lady died from falling out of bed, supposedly, she heard something. She had got out of bed herself to go to the toilet and heard screaming. She opened her door to identify where the scream was coming from, and as she did so, the screams were muffled and stopped. She could not say exactly where the scream emanated from, so after a few minutes of quiet, she went back to bed.

'Next morning, the news of the death of a patient circulated, and she realised it was that person's room that the scream had come from. She was too afraid to own up to hearing the scream and has not spoken to anyone about it, but she is leaving to go home after lunch this afternoon after the doctor had been to check her out. She wanted to tell someone. Roma said she was pleased that there is to be an enquiry. She had planned to write a notice for the newspaper when she got home, to alert the public that everything is not right in this place.'

'Did she say anything about the night Winifred Lambert died?'

'No, but she said she had kept a low profile after that dreadful night when she heard the scream and never told anyone about it because she did not want to be the next one to go. Kate asked her about Winifred being very vocal, and she said yes. She complained a lot about various things and, in particular, about the night nurse coming into her room at night. She did not like a man just walking into her room. It did not pay to complain about the night nurse, or you would be missing the next morning when everyone else got up for breakfast.'

James sounded most indignant. 'I can imagine many of them would not like it. It seems strange to have a male nurse in a women's section, especially at night, with no other staff around. I suppose it is a matter of using experienced staff. Sharon said they were short-staffed at this place. I can imagine women cowering in their beds at night.'

'One of the other women said that Dewson strolled around the place as if he owned it, going into rooms without knocking first, and many of the women said they did not like it. Remember, most of these women are not sick, just recuperating from operations. To have a man wandering into your room unannounced would be horrible for them.' Kate had joined them and went on, 'I do not think there was any woman there who did not express their dislike of Dewson. With your report on this, I am sure Valley Care will ditch him.'

'It is still not actual proof. We have to find something to prove he has helped these women die,' said James.

'Maybe the opportunity will come up this evening. He will be aware as soon as he enters the wards that we are there to watch him. It may tip his hand.' Percy looked thoughtful. 'Perhaps I will help it along tonight when I ask him about my wife.'

'Be careful, Percy. Keep the beeper close in your pocket. It just needs a touch. I was unable to get walkie-talkies delivered on time, so I bought these beepers instead. Just press it, and it will make a noise. I will be close by to hear you, and I will come running.'

'Thanks, Kate, for the typed sheet. I will pass it on to Alec tomorrow. It could come in handy as evidence. I am off now for afternoon tea. I will see you when you arrive, Percy. Go and have your rest now. Kate, can you mind the office and lock up?'

*   *   *

Chatting with the male residents at the nursing home was not fruitful. Each man said he minded his own business. A couple of them said it was not right having a male nurse on night shift in the women's section, although none of them had any idea what went on other than in their own section, which was down a passageway from the lounge and dining area; the women's section was in the other direction, in the L-shaped building. The only communal areas were the lounge and TV rooms and the dining room. James was disappointed. He had hoped to have some backup from the men, but they only wanted peace and quiet and to be left alone.

He saw a lady waiting in the reception area with a suitcase beside her and realised this could be Roma, waiting for her lift to go home. He sat down beside her and introduced himself, saying he had read

Kate's notes from this morning's interviews in the dining room. He asked Roma whether she was willing to sign a copy of her statement to Kate and Valerie.

She looked at him for a moment. 'Yes, as long as my name is not mentioned for the public arena. I do not want this nurse fellow to follow me up and try and silence me like he silenced Winifred Lambert. Poor woman. She could not help herself. She was used to expressing herself and everybody taking notice of her. I tried to hush her up a couple of times, but she would not listen. She had a bone to pick with the night nurse, and it did not do her any good in the end. He fixed her.'

'Are you sure of your details in the report, Roma?' asked James.

'As sure as I am sitting here,' she said adamantly. 'I have kept this to myself until now, and I will not go back on my words. I have gone over what happened that night over and over again to see if I could think of any alternative to the story, but no. The same verdict comes up again and again. I heard a scream, and then it was muffled. But I could still hear it in my head. By the time I reached the door, it had been muffled, and I could not positively identify where it came from. Screams are not something you hear in this place. By nine o'clock, it is silent, and the lights are put out. Only bedside lights are allowed after that time. We have to think of others wanting to sleep or rest. Most of the residents are recovering from an illness and need extra sleep.'

'Why was it someone else did not hear the scream? You say it is rare, so it would have been noticed.'

'Winifred Lambert heard it. Several of the residents who were here that night have been dismissed and gone home. Others, like me, have kept quiet, afraid of repercussions if word got around that they had heard something. Some may have been asleep with covers over them to baffle the sound. There are many reasons, but my opinion is, because it was late. I had been reading a book by my bedside light and got up to go to the toilet, and that is why I heard it. Definitely, most would have been asleep at that time of night.'

'Yes, that makes sense. What time was it?'

'Eleven o'clock. I do not stay up so late usually, but I had a book I could not put down until I finished it.'

'Would you mind if one of my staff called to see you tomorrow at your home to take a statement from you? It will probably be Kate. You already met her this morning.'

'That is fine with me. I was going to go to a newspaper sometime to tell the same story. That nurse needs to be stopped, and you seem to be the man to do it. It will lift a burden from my chest to hear he has been charged with murder and taken off the wards. I will look forward to seeing Kate tomorrow for morning tea.'

A tall man came into the reception area and took a seat nearby, sitting quietly to hear the end of the story between James and Roma. Roma stood up. 'This is my son, Alistair, who is here to take me home. He has not heard this story yet, so I will tell him of it later after dinner.'

'God bless you, Roma, and I hope your recovery continues. We will let you know what happens, to put your mind at rest.'

'I can only say that I am glad you came today. If it had been tomorrow, I would have been out of sight and still simmering.'

Alistair picked up her suitcase, and she took his other arm. They walked out of the room just as John Dewson came in the door. He said, 'Goodbye, Roma.' She did not lift her head to look at him or say anything and continued on her way out the door.

'That is gratitude for you,' Dewson remarked as he went past James to the reception desk to sign in.

20

ercy arrived a few minutes later. They waited for Dewson to go into the staffroom, and James brought Percy up to date on what he had done during the afternoon and his discussion with Roma. They agreed to wait until Dewson came out of the staffroom to go into the dining room. They planned to be there ahead of him to see the residents' attitude when the night nurse walked in. Some of the residents would be having injections before the meal. They wanted to be there in time for that, as they presumed Dewson would be a few minutes collecting the right medications before arriving in the dining room.

James said, 'As you picked up copies of all the relevant paperwork this morning, I suggest we approach Dewson together and stay in sight of each other for safety. He will realise that it is him we are after. I am not sure what else we can do except have our dinner and watch him. He must make a move sooner or later to shake us.'

'I want to ask Dewson about my wife.' Percy looked grim. 'Now that I have seen him and confirmed he was nursing at the general hospital, I am sure he was the fellow on duty the night my wife died. I have a bone to pick with him and it may get dirty, so keep close by.'

'Do not put yourself in any danger, Percy. This is a man who is not right in the head. He is a mass murderer, the way I see it. He thinks he is doing society a favour in getting rid of the infirm, but the last two deaths put down to him appear to be worse than that. He has now tipped the scales in the other direction, and he is reacting because he is angry at people for recognising him for what he is. He is sick. Watch out for any strange move on his part. He may retaliate about being watched. We do not want to be the next persons missing in the morning.'

'Yes, James, I agree with what you have said, but we have to do something to bring him down. I think I have the catalyst in my wife's death. I spoke to her doctor that same afternoon that she died, and he said there was no reason she should have left us until at least three or four weeks later. The only reason he had put her in palliative care was to relieve me to go to work and being in palliative care would help her when she was in pain.

'Because of the long hours I worked, I was unable to be with her as much as I would have liked, and my son suggested the hospital ward for her. I was going to take leave from the department towards the end of her time with us, but I never got the chance. She died the first night she arrived at the hospital, to our great shock.

'Our new granddaughter was only a week old, and my wife was looking forward to bonding with her. It was her belief that if you bond with a new baby, they will remember you. That was her hope anyway and what was keeping her going.

'So when we were told she did not survive the night, we were in total shock. My doctor son rang the duty doctor and was told he was baffled also. He could have sworn she would stay around for three or four more weeks, maybe longer, with the special care she would be getting in the palliative care unit. It has rankled with me ever since. I wake up in the night and think about it. Something did not add up. I have the chance now to find out what really happened to her.'

'All right, Percy, just make sure I am close by. I will look out for the opportunity for you to tackle him. I will give you the nod, and I will stand by out of sight.'

Percy laughed. 'I am sure I can handle him, James. He is only a skinny bloke.'

'He may be skinny, Percy, but he will be fighting for his life and he is crazy. Being crazy can give you extra strength. Just remember that, and make sure I am close by, ready to come save you. Do not forget the buzzer to alert me to any danger from him.'

'Okay, James, I will do my best.'

*   *   *

They waited while the meal and medicating were over, wondering what would happen next. However, Dewson disappeared into the staffroom and did not come out again for an hour or so. He walked past the two men waiting him out and visited each bedroom, turning off the lights as he went, until all the overhead lights except in the lounge, where James and Percy sat, and the passageways were darkened.

James said, 'It looks like your opportunity is about to come, Percy. When he comes in, I will walk out, saying I have to go to the office to check the books, but I will stay outside of the door so I can hear what is going on.'

Dewson appeared in the doorway. James stood up and excused himself and went out the door in the direction of the reception area, then circled back, standing quietly outside the door.

Dewson started the conversation with Percy, sounding antagonistic. 'What is your brief? The note left for me said you are investigating the nursing home. What do you think you are going to learn, staring at me all night?'

'I am staring at you because I have met you before. You were the night nurse on duty at the general hospital palliative care ward when my wife died. You decided in your wisdom that she did not deserve to live until God decided to take her. You decided you would play God, and you killed her.'

'That is nonsense. Why would I do that?'

'That is what I am asking you. Why did you do that? We were told that same day that she would live comfortably for three or four weeks, and that made her happy, as she would see and hold her brand-new granddaughter daily for that time. But you, in your special status as God's helper, did not see it that way, and you injected her with something to end her life that night.'

'I say you are foolish to say that. It is words like that that can end your life. You must not say anything like that again.'

'Why, because what you are doing is sacred? Because God has sent you to do his will?'

'Yes, as a matter of fact, God has spoken to me and told me that all these old and helpless people are a burden on society.'

Percy looked curiously at him. 'You really believe that? When did he speak to you?'

'I woke up early one morning after a dream. It was still dark, and I had this vision of a man in white standing in a glow of light beside my bed. He told me to relieve society of those who were heavily holding society back by living too long. That was not his intention. Those people needed to have the lives terminated to allow growth in the community.'

'You felt you were the chosen one?'

'Yes, I was working in the ideal place to obey his order. It was easy to make a choice. Anyone over sixty-five would go. Your wife was only fifty-nine, but I made an exception of her because she had cancer. I was doing her a favour by ending her pain for her.'

'It did not matter to you that my wife did not want to die yet. She knew she was going, but she needed to finalise things for herself and say goodbye to her family.'

'She did not say anything to me. She was asleep. It was an easy decision to make for her.' Dewson sounded so sure of himself.

Percy felt like gagging. His wife was thought of as a non-entity by Dewson instead of as the wonderful person she was. 'And you managed to live with yourself after each person died, because they were old or were sick.'

'I never thought of it again. I was carrying out my orders. Like a soldier, I had no choice.'

'And what about Mrs Lambert, and Mrs Cummins who fell out of bed and died? They were old but well. Why did you target them?'

There was a flicker in Dewson's eyes as he looked at Percy with a sulky downwards look and a pause before he went on. 'Mrs Cummins fell out of bed.'

'What made her fall out of bed? Did you frighten her?'

'I walked into her bedroom, and she woke up and saw me standing over her and scrambled to get away from me. But I was only delivering her night-time medication. That is all. I do admit that I then got angry with her and yanked her back on to her bed, and she hit her cheek on the corner of her bedside table. That was stupid, and I hit her, because how was I going to explain her face to the day staff in the morning? She made me so angry. I tripled her pills and she died in the night, so she could not complain to the day staff about me. It was all an accident, really.'

For a few seconds, Dewson looked agitated. Percy did not feel sorry for him and pressed on. 'Hitting a helpless old woman and tripling her pills does not sound like an accident to me. And what about Mrs Lambert?'

The nurse was getting confident again and spoke almost boastfully, confidence in his voice sure of himself and his ability to get away with his crimes. 'She went around telling people I hit Mrs Cummins, and she died. Silly old witch. She would have had the police here if I had let her go on talking, so I gave her an injection to shut her up.' He had gained his equilibrium again and was back on track.

'How many women have you euthanised, John? How long since you received God's order?'

Dewson looked sombre. 'Only about twelve, eight at the general and four here. I cannot do it any faster, because it is hard to get the drugs. They look after them so carefully in these places, counting out every little pill, so I have to work slowly. But I have started to look for other drugs that are more easily available. Then I will be able to work faster for God. It has been five years now. Your wife was my first. I need to hurry up the work. It is far too slow. I do not want God to forsake me for someone else.'

'Why have you confessed to me, John? You know I will take it to the police, don't you? I remember you were flustered to find out that I was a policeman when you killed my wife. How did you get over that?'

'It was God's will, and he looked after me. No one suspected me.'

'But now you have told me, John. I more than suspect you. You have given yourself away to me, and I have a list of all the women you have euthanised and killed. You have told me yourself!'

Dewson was slowly moving closer to Percy, little by little, and was now virtually standing at his side. Percy attempted to move away, step by step, but found an armchair boxing him in. Suddenly Dewson lunged at him. 'You will not be telling anyone, old man. You will not survive the night. No one will know what I have told you at all, and I can go back to God's work. You are one of the old people we do not need around.'

He had pulled a syringe from his pocket, and before Percy could move, it was jabbed into his neck. Percy hit his pocket, and his beeper sounded loudly in the quiet. James burst through the door and hit Dewson on the jaw with his fist, which made Dewson let go of the syringe and fall to the floor, dazed.

James pulled the needle slowly out of Percy's neck, handling it carefully, and with his other hand, he dialled 000 on his phone and urgently asked for an ambulance at the Valley Residential Care home and for the police to attend also. He did not have time to say any more, as Dewson was climbing to his feet, very groggy from the blow to his jaw. James laid Percy down in the armchair, with a cushion behind him so that he was semi-upright.

James grabbed Dewson, bringing his arm up behind his back so that he could not get away without breaking it. He pushed Dewson to the wall to hold him. James felt that the man was very light, not heavily built in any way and not used to being manhandled. He seemed dazed that someone could do this to him, but at least he was silent. He did not say a word.

James dialled Percy's son using his other hand and told him to go to the general hospital because Percy was going to be admitted there. He picked the syringe up from the floor, where he had placed it out of the way of being disturbed by anyone coming in, and wrapped it in his handkerchief to give to the ambulance people, just as they burst through the entrance door.

He called out to them, and they hurried to the lounge room. James explained that Percy had been given an unknown quantity of the drug in the needle wrapped in the handkerchief, and he did not know what drug the syringe held. They bundled Percy quickly but gently on to a stretcher and ran with him out of the centre to the waiting ambulance. Percy was unconscious by this time, and James worried that he had been too late in pulling the needle out of his neck. The drug would have gone straight into his bloodstream.

A police car arrived a few minutes later, and once again, James described what had gone on. The policemen handcuffed Dewson and led him away. Dewson did not say any more. He appeared dazed at what was happening and kept stroking his jaw where James had hit him.

James heard a rustle of feet and clothing behind him and turned to see an audience of about ten elderly ladies, dressed in their nightclothes and dressing gowns, clapping their hands.

He laughed and asked, 'How long have you been standing there?'

One dear old lady said, 'We heard the beeper sound and knew something was going on. It was marvellous to watch, much better than television. He is a wicked man, and we are all happy you have worked this out and had him taken away. We were all frightened of him. He would get angry at any little thing. I think he was mad.'

'You could be right. I notice there are no men here with you. Could they hear the beeper where they sleep?'

The same elderly lady said, 'It is the same distance to their rooms. They are not interested in anything that does not concern them, and half the time, they do not notice us. They just want to lead a happy, peaceful life. But us ladies in this wing were not leading a happy, peaceful life with the thought of that nurse coming back each evening. One positive thing about it is, we all had very early nights and feel better for it.'

'Will you all be okay if no staff comes in till morning?'

'Sure, we will. We have each other. And if anything comes up, we can call out, and someone will obey the call. We might be old, but we are experienced with life's twists and turns. If we really get into trouble, we will call an ambulance to take care of it. By the way, there is a night nurse in the third wing of the hospital. She looks after the dementia patients. She could come in a pinch if anything gets too bad. But we are okay, aren't we, girls?'

There was a chorus of 'Yes, we will be fine. Do not worry about us. Go and see if your friend is all right.'

'Well, I am glad you are on my side, ladies. Thanks for your vote of confidence earlier. I must go to the general hospital to find out how my partner is doing. We did not mean to have that sort of thing happen. We thought it would be nasty, but not fatal.'

'Tell your friend when you see him that we are all praying for him. Prayers can help.'

'I will. Thank you all.'

James rang Alicia. He thought he may be waking her up, as it was getting very late, but she answered the phone immediately. He told her everything that had happened and that now he was going to the hospital to see how Percy was doing. He could hear the tears in his wife's voice as she said, 'Give him our love, James.'

When he arrived at the hospital, he asked for Percy and was told he was still in the emergency ward. Dr Gray, his son, was with him, and he was doing as well as could be expected. James recognised the ploy to pacify enquirers and asked for the way to the emergency ward. He found Percy's son by the sound of his voice saying, 'What the hell were you doing, provoking a madman?'

Percy's voice was not as loud; in fact, it was quite weak and wavered as he answered his son. 'It was the only way to find your mother's killer, and he admitted it to me. It all happened so quickly. I did not realise he was gradually boxing me in, and I could not get away. It was worth it to remove that crazy man from the hospital system. He admitted to twelve deaths—all for God, in his mind.'

James was standing by the end of Percy's bed by then before they noticed him. Percy said, 'Here is the hero of the hour. He moved so quick we did not see him coming, and he bowled that skinny crazy fellow over and pulled the syringe out before it all got into my bloodstream. How good is that?

That fellow is a real crazy. It is amazing how he got away with so much. We are all so busy minding our own business nowadays so someone as crazy as him slips past, and everybody says someone else will fix him up, until he is so crazy he has killed twelve people. Can you believe that? All in front of dozens of other medical people, and no one noticed!

'You survived tonight because the lady residents of Valley Care are praying for you, Percy. Your beeper called me and also called most of the female residents, while the male residents did not hear a thing. As you were taken away and the police arrived to take Dewson into custody, I turned to the sound of clapping, and there the women all stood, delighted in our night's work. I do believe that if we had not managed to tie Dewson up, those old ladies would have done it themselves. They said it was much better than any show on television.'

Dr Gray had his turn. 'I think you are both a little crazy, putting yourselves up against a mass murderer. You could have been number thirteen, Dad. Without any backup, you could have been added to Dewson's list of the "God-given".'

'True, son, but nothing ventured, nothing gained. This fellow got away with twelve deaths without anyone challenging him. The one lady that did challenge him paid for it with her life. If it were not for her daughter, Jane Lambert, whose mother's death started this investigation, he would still be plying his trade for God, as he sees it. We had to have proof to keep him in remand, and now we have it.'

'Okay, Dad, I will stop nagging you. I thank you, James, for being so quick getting to my father. The needle only went into his neck partially, because when you knocked over Dewson, it partly pulled the syringe out. That is why we are able to talk to him tonight. It will give him a good sleep for the rest of the night, and he will be back at work tomorrow, a little slow but at least alive, thank goodness.'

James felt himself shaking; it had been a scary moment to see the syringe stuck in Percy's neck. 'I must admit, I got a fright all the same, Percy. One minute, he was talking to you, and the next, the buzzer went off. I am so glad you are okay. I will go and have a sleep now too, if I can get to sleep after all the excitement. You did very well, Percy, getting him to admit to what he was up to. He certainly sounded crazy to me.'

Percy laughed. 'He is as mad as a hatter. Goodnight, boys. I am getting very drowsy. I will see you in the morning, James, to write it all up.'

*   *   *

James went home to Alicia, glad he had not roused Valerie to tell her Percy was in hospital. He fell asleep immediately, without any dreams.

Alicia did not wake him early in the morning; he looked so peaceful that she did not want to disturb him. She waited until it was almost time to leave for the office before she did, reasoning that if he could sleep as deeply as that, Percy must be all right.

21

J ames made it to the office in time to greet all the others arriving and delegated Kate to have tea with Roma and to take a statement from her. Percy, still looking very shaky, was told to sit down and write his report. James did not want him to collapse.

He rang Valerie Newton and asked if she could have Percy sit in the nook at the bookshop until he gathered his strength; James would bring him at morning teatime, after he wrote his report. Percy needed to rest until he recovered, with somebody watching him in case he collapsed. If necessary, and if Valerie thought she needed extra help, Alicia could come home. Granny said she could manage; if she needed Alicia, she would ring her to come, and if Percy did collapse, she would ring an ambulance.

James was satisfied that Percy would sit quietly in the bookshop and snooze, knowing he would be watched over. James rang Alec Overington next to report on the happenings of the last twenty-four hours. The lawyer was amazed they had developed the case so quickly but was sorry to hear of Percy's clash with the mad night nurse. He was astounded that Dewson had claimed twelve deaths to his credit. When James, Percy, and Kate put in their reports, he would visit the police station to make sure crazy Dewson was kept locked up, away from continuing his life as God's helper.

James felt washed out; he had been on a high for the last twenty-four hours and was glad it was all over, except for the paperwork. Alicia looked at him and went to make him a cup of coffee. 'Sit down, James.

This has taken its toll on both you and Percy. You need to relax for a while. Now that you have told Alec Overington, you can take it easy for the day, sitting quietly and writing your reports.'

'That is good advice, Alicia. This report may take some time. I do not want to miss anything in it. That crazy nurse fellow needs to be put into a psychiatric hospital and never be let loose on the public again. I still cannot get over the fact that he has killed twelve people and nearly got away with it again. Percy was lucky this time, but I would not like to see him face Dewson again. It was lucky I was there. We did not know what he would do, but we never expected him to bring out a syringe. I wonder if he carried it around in case he saw someone he thought should be euthanised, or perhaps he prepared it for one of us, on the odd chance we would accost him.

'Actually, the ward he was in would have slowed down his business quite a bit. They were not sick women, just convalescing. I suppose that was why he was making up excuses to himself for carrying on his vendetta, like killing the ladies Cummins and Lambert. He wanted to keep his hand in. Except for those two, all the ladies he chose were in the last months of their lives. Cummins and Lambert were not ill. That is why he came to our notice, and we eventually took him down. Otherwise, he would still have been working away at God's plan for the aged and perhaps got away with it.'

'It is clever of you, James, to have worked out that difference. I suppose he missed what he called in his madness "God's work", and when he grew angry, he flipped and murdered those other two women. I presume that if he had got away with those murders, he would have progressed to more, so no one would have been safe from him.'

'Yes, that is my opinion, Alicia. While I was listening behind the door to the lounge room, he seemed very proud of what he had done and what he hoped to do in the future. His move on Percy was not unexpected, but it was the quickness that I was amazed at. Percy had not been expecting anything when it happened. It happened so fast, and Percy had not realised until the last minute that he was boxed in and unable to move away.'

'Percy will be fine after a little rest, James. The drug may still be working in his system, and just like you feel washed out, Percy must still be feeling its effects as well as by his connection to Dewson. Time is what is needed for you both to recover.'

Kate came into the office, waving her sheet of paper. 'That was the easiest statement I have ever written. Roma was aware that her memory of what happened when Mrs Cummins was killed was very important, and she left nothing out of her story. A very intelligent woman, I thought, as she signed the record of what happened at the nursing home. Now you have to tell me all about your evening's work. I only caught bits and pieces of it before I went out.'

James related to her the evening at the Valley Care home, up to his talk with Percy at the hospital with his son.

'Whew, James, I am glad I was not there with that madman. I have been in some sticky places with peculiar people, but that beats them all. I hope Percy is going to be all right,' said Kate.

'He will be fine, Kate. It may take him a little time to come to terms with the fact that the crazy man killed his wife. That will be the hardest part for him to go over in his mind. Percy will adjust. He is a steady person, but he may need a day or two. We have sent him to the bookshop for Valerie to look after him. He will not be down long.'

'What a great idea! Relaxation with something else to take his mind off Dewson. Young Jody will be a help in getting him to pick up.'

Alicia and James laughed. 'He might be glad to come back to work.'

Alicia said, 'We are losing Jody next week. Her mother is coming home from hospital on Tuesday, but she will be confined to a wheelchair for the remainder of her life. Jody's brightness will be a big consolation for her. Now that we know more of the story, there are no reasons for keeping Jody with us. Her place is with her parents.'

'Yes, I can see that, but I am sure you will miss her. She is such a bright little girl, so accepting of what is going on around her, and she has not lost her way.'

Alicia smiled. 'We expect to see her from time to time. Granny will miss her company. In a way, Jody came at just the right time for us. She has helped Granny be cheerful despite the pain in her arm, and she helped many times with little things so that Granny thought of the little girl instead of her handicap.'

Kate looked sympathetic. 'What a difference in their lives. I feel sorry for Sandra. I now realise she had been on the edge of falling into an abyss, but disaster in the shape of Andrew Bullock was an angel in disguise for her. She would not have had the care to recover if she had not been in the hospital. She cannot walk, but a lot of people accept that burden and make good lives for themselves.'

Alicia replied, 'We can only wait and see and offer help if it is needed. We will use Jody as an excuse to visit to see how thing are progressing. Sandra was not one of my teenage friends, but that does not mean I would not help her, if she will accept my help. She was the type of person who was very proud, never mentioning the things that could have held her back, such as alcoholic parents and being put into care and having to run away from the homes she was put into because of the men in the household fondling her. I only learnt all this since visiting her in hospital, and it all came out when I asked if she wanted me to visit her parents to tell them she was in hospital.'

Kate was aghast. 'All that in her childhood, and the car accident too. Poor girl. You have to admire her. Remembering her when she came into this office, I would never have thought I would say that.'

'She had reached the end of her tether by the time she came in and left Jody with us. It was only that we knew very little of her background at that time.' Alicia was thoughtful. 'James and I will try to be a friend to her, if she will accept us. Granny too can be helpful by taking charge of Jody when Sandra needs a break. She trusts us with Jody now.'

'It will be interesting, watching how things work out.'

Alicia turned to James. 'Why don't you give Aaron Dunstan some help by giving him the story of Dewson to write up as a scoop for his newspaper? That could give him a big boost.'

James looked astonished. 'What a good idea. Why didn't I think of that? It would give him something towards the expenses on the work for his house alterations. I will give him a call straight away, although I should ask Percy what he thinks first. I can't see that he would object.'

He rang Percy to discuss it and then rang Aaron, who was very glad for the call and said he would be right over to look at the reports, thanking James and Alicia for thinking of him.

While showing Aaron the reports, James said to him, 'Aaron, I want you to make this Percy's story. Give him the kudos for bringing this man down. The truth is, I hit Dewson pretty hard with my fist, lifting him from the floor. If that gets out, I could be in trouble. I did not think of it at the time, as I was so intent on getting him away from Percy and the syringe he had in Percy's neck. If you leave that part out of the story, it could save me from an assault charge. Quite frankly, I did not realise how light Dewson is. He is not tall, about up to my shoulder, and has quite a light build, I found. I was surprised when he flew across the floor after I hit him. I had only meant to knock him away from Percy and his hold on the syringe.

'This is Percy's story. His wife was the nurse's first victim, and he was the one that drew the story from the crazy fellow, making him confess to having twelve victims over five years after he saw a vision of God telling him what to do. Build Percy up as the chief in the investigation, and if you need an extra person, do not name me. Just say "the partner" or "business partner". That should cover it. You have to be careful nowadays with the way in which you treat even the evilest of predators, and this man, John Dewson, is a serial killer.'

'I can make this a big story, James, and it should sell newspapers. I will leave your name out of it, as you wish. It is a shame, as it could bring good advertising.'

'Using Percy's name will make a bigger impact, as his wife was murdered by Dewson. The same impact will be made by using his name for the business. It does not need to be shared with me. I am happy to stay in the background.'

'Okay, James, as you wish. I will not mention you, other than as Percy's partner, and will not use your name. I must say, this is different, as most people would jump at the chance to have their name in print.'

'I have my reasons, Aaron. I have a former crime boss looking for me. I only heard of it in the last two days, and I am still trying to work things out to avoid him. My name up in lights at the moment could give this criminal my contact details. This includes my wife, so I am considering what to do about it to keep us safe.'

'I would like that story, James. It sounds interesting.'

'Perhaps I will give you the story later, Aaron, when it is resolved. At the moment, I feel nervous about it, especially as it involves Alicia's safety. For the time being, I want to stay under the radar. It is easy to find people on the computer nowadays, so I cannot stay out of this criminal's way forever.'

22

James had received a diplomat package the day before going to the Valley Residential Care home. He had put it aside until he had time to assimilate the contents, and he had opened it a few minutes prior to Aaron appearing. The package was from his friend Jameel in India.

It was a friendly note with a nasty twist. Jameel had looked up the details of the airline officials in the passport-and-jewellery theft case that Alicia and James thought had been finalised the previous year. He had included a photograph of Ralph Dalton in the package. When James looked at the photograph, he felt very disturbed.

Ralph had been picked up by the police when he arrived home in Mumbai after leaving the UK. Following his release by the police, he was grabbed by members of the gang. Sahib ran and was tortured so they could find out who had captured him in London. He was forced to give up the name of James Armstrong to the gang. He was then kicked and bashed and left for dead in a back room of a hovel in Mumbai. It was very lucky for Ralph that his brother went looking for him, or he would not have survived. The result of the bashing was in the photograph Jameel sent.

Ralph's younger brother went to the police to see what had happened to his brother, as he had not arrived home as expected. The family hunted and asked people if they knew where Ralph was, until they found him lying in the hovel, unable to move, and took him home. When Jameel turned up at the Dalton family home, they showed him into a bedroom, where Ralph looked close to death.

Jameel had him transferred to a hospital, and he was looked after until he revived and was able to write down his story for Jameel and the Dalton family. The main reason for his bashing had been to get information about the person responsible for breaking up the successful scam; Ralph had eventually been forced to give up James Armstrong's name.

Jameel also said that he found Dalton a job away from Mumbai and that he was safe, hidden in a smaller city. He was now well, and although still bruised, with the breaks to his arm and leg still improving, his writing skills were still there.

The gang was found guilty of the passport deals, and the jewellery was retrieved in many cases where it was still in shops and returned to the owners in the UK. The main man in the airline in Mumbai was the younger brother of Sahib.

The family had grown up in Mumbai with the same father, an Englishman who was an unsavoury person. Sahib, was Edward Moorland, and he had a brother, William, who was five years younger than him. The elder brother was the instigator of the scam, which had been dreamt up when he went to live in London, and his younger brother worked the Mumbai side of recruiting airport officials and airline personnel to run the scam for them in both countries.

Jameel warned James and Alicia to be careful, as these criminals would stop at nothing to get revenge on them for disturbing their very successful scam; James should beware of any strange-looking fellows of Indian origin.

*   *   *

After Aaron left the office, James rang Jack Whistler in police headquarters in London and said, 'Look for a fax regarding my friend in India, which arrived yesterday and which I have only now opened because of other business I needed to finalise first.'

'What other important business could it have been to put your friend's mail aside, James?'

'We picked up a serial killer in a nursing home last night, Jack. Most important work. Percy was injected with drugs by him and is resting today. This man has killed twelve women in the last five years, including Percy's wife as his first victim.'

'You do get around, James. Well done. I would like to hear the full story. It sounds like a good one.'

'I will send you a copy of the newspaper story, Jack. I get the feeling this one will go nationwide. I have asked the journalist not to include my name and to make it Percy's story. You will see the reason when you read Jameel's letter. The break only opened up this week, and we are all still a bit strung up from our all-night vigil and arrest last night. It may take a day or two for us to get over this one.'

'The fax is arriving now, James. I can hear the machine tapping away. I will get back to you later when I have looked at it.'

'We thought this was all over for us, Alicia and me. To have it raise its ugly head is disconcerting, to say the least. We will watch our backs and stay out of the limelight as much as we can.'

'I would say that is the best solution, James. However, it cannot keep you a secret for long. With social media on the computer, most people are traceable. You will know that by your business dealings, finding runaways and such. We will have to work out a solution for it. I will think about it. Perhaps I will talk it over with my boss, Harold Griffiths. We will work something out.'

'It is still a new thought so far, Jack. I have only had the letter open an hour or so. I will talk about it with Alicia. She might have a few ideas of what to do.'

'Yes, clever girl, your wife. I will get back to you later, James, when I have talked it through with Griffiths.'

'Thanks, Jack. I will look forward to your input.'

James put down the phone and called Alicia into his office and showed her Jameel's letter. She sat down in front of the desk to read it and, when she finished, looked up with alarm in her face. 'This is terrible news, James. Do you really think we will be targeted by the passport scam people?'

'I am afraid so, Alicia. The way they treated Ralph Dalton shows they are intent on recriminations, even to finding us to vent their unhappiness that we spoilt what was a very huge money maker for them. I have rung Jack Whistler, and he agrees we will have to be careful. I have asked Aaron to keep my name out of the Dewson case when he writes it up. I told him to make it Percy's story.'

'That will be okay until it goes to court, James. After that, your name will be known all around the country. This is a story everyone will be interested in. I can see it will be not only nationwide but international also. You know how people like serial killer stories. The sensational ones always hit the headlines. We get American ones in our news, so this story may get that far in return.'

'Hmm! Yes, I can see our sensational story piece may go international. I had not got to thinking of newspaper reports yet and their impact on us. I still feel numb from the evening's work at the care house. I rang Jack Whistler and passed Jameel's letter on by fax, and he said he would discuss it with Harold Griffiths and get back to us. That is all we can do at the moment, other than watch out for unknown shady characters loitering around the office.'

'That is not a nice thought, James. We were feeling safe and happy, and now it is starting all over again.'

'Do not worry, Alicia. Stay close to me when you are outside the office. I did not know my own strength when I hit Dewson last night. He flew across the room. I must have picked up my strength doing the exercises at Harry's classes. I should be capable of knocking the block off anyone who attempts to do something to us, if that is any consolation, although they would have to get close enough for me to manhandle them first.'

'Perhaps I can go to Harry's lessons as well. Jody will be going home to Aaron and Sandra on Tuesday morning, so I will be free in the evenings from now on. I have envied your exercise class, James. Sometimes I feel very unfit, although I walk to the office and back home in the evenings. Sitting around all day in the office makes me feel unfit. While I was a flight attendant, we used to joke that we walked to

India and back in two days. We did not get time to sit down except on landing. I miss the walking, but I would happily replace it with Harry's self-defence exercises.'

'I will ask Harry at the next session if he would take women. He did mention it to me once.'

'Kate might be willing to come along as well if Harry would have us. I will ask her.'

Alicia went out to Kate, and she looked up, smiling. They both came back into James's office.

Kate said, 'I would love to learn self-defence. Will you ask Harry for us? I would prefer eight o'clock in the evening if possible. I have a going-to-bed ritual for my children, and I would hate to change it or miss it, for their sake. They love it. However, if that is too late for Harry's lessons, I will adjust it.'

'I will ring Harry and see what he says, as I have missed this week's lessons. I will have to excuse myself. I will not be seeing him until Monday.'

He rang Harry's number, and the call was answered immediately. 'Would you have room in your classes for two ladies, Harry? Alicia and Kate, my assistants in the office, would like to come along.'

'I could start up a ladies' night, James. Several of the men have said that their wives would like to come. We might get enough for a "women's only" show. Some of the wives apparently said they preferred that rather than taking on the men. I could do Tuesday or Thursday. What does Alicia say will suit her?'

James turned to the two women looking at him and said, 'Would you prefer Tuesday or Thursday?'

They said together, 'Tuesday, at 8 p.m.'

He spoke to Harry. 'It was unanimous. Tuesday, 8 p.m.'

'Good, I like quick decisions. I will put up a note on Monday night to the men to send their wives along on Tuesday at 8 p.m.'

'Thanks, Harry, we will look forward to next week. This week has been busy for us.'

'I understand that you cannot come each night, James, because of your business. I will look forward to seeing you on Monday.'

'Yippee! Thanks, James! Will the cost be an office expense?' Alicia looked very pleased.

'I do not see why not. I will ring Barry Cross, our accountant, and ask him. My lessons could also be put down as an office expense. I surely used my knowledge last night to get Dewson out of circulation. If we are going to need skills like that, we will certainly get it as an office expense, I would think.'

'This has been a good morning's discussion, James, and now we will be able to take on anyone who thinks they can outdo us.'

'Whoa, Alicia. You have not had a lesson yet. Do not get too cocky, and keep your eyes open for strange men.'

Kate asked, 'Have we a new case for watching ourselves?'

'Yes, Kate, and because you are associated with this office, you too could be in danger. Alicia and I solved a case last year before starting up this business. Alicia was involved because she was a flight attendant who had been scammed into delivering passports to India, unbeknown to her. The passports were being sewn into her flight bag by the concierge of Alicia's apartment. In the department I worked for, I was in charge of finding out who was stealing passports from Indian and British homes—also gold jewellery.

'We solved the case but have now heard that we are possibly being searched for by the musclemen of these scammers for retribution for breaking up their very lucrative scam. We only heard about it today from my friend, Jameel, whom you met on the Isle of Wight earlier in the year.

'I have explained it to my friends in the police force in London, and they say they will look for a resolution. Do not worry yet. It may never happen, but just be extra careful when there are strange people around. This is one reason for the self-defence lesson and I enjoy the lessons, so I thought you may also.'

'I haven't seen anyone yet that fits the bill, but I will watch carefully, as you suggest.' Kate did not sound deterred by the thought of strange people around her.

Alicia said, 'I will ring Granny to see if Percy is okay. I do not want to put a big burden on Granny.'

'Good idea, Alicia. It has been very busy here this morning. No new cases, but old ones rearing their heads. Just as well we sent Percy to rest. He does not need any more worries at the moment, so do not mention anything about these Indian scammers wanting retribution. If he asks, tell him that Alec Overington is coming in the morning to pick up our reports. That will give us a break before we have to go into it again.'

When Alicia rang the bookshop, Granny said, 'Jody has been looking after Percy all morning, and now he has gone upstairs to the second bedroom of your apartment to lie down for a sleep. Jody organised this and tucked him into her bed. He appeared quite sleepy all morning but had no adverse effects from the drug that I could see, just sleepiness. I send Caroline upstairs every half hour to check that Percy is all right. I suggested that Percy stay the night in the apartment's second bedroom and Jody can sleep in the house with me, just so we can watch Percy and be available if he is in trouble. It will also save Percy from finding something to eat.'

'Thank you, Granny. That is a big problem off our minds. We have been thinking we will close the office a little early tonight, as James is tired and needs a sleep also. We will come home about four o'clock and leave a note on the door of the office. I will run into the supermarket and get something easy for dinner.'

'I heard that, Alicia,' said James. 'As a precaution, take Kate with you to the supermarket. We do not expect trouble yet, but as I say, "as a precaution".'

'You really do expect trouble, James?'

'Jameel is not one to issue a precaution if there is not a possibility of trouble. He is a very cautious man, and I believe trouble will come sometime. We just do not know when and by whom.'

Alicia looked worried. 'All right, James, we will be careful. If I hear Urdu or Hindi being spoken, I will look around to see who it is.'

'No, Alicia. If you hear Urdu or Hindi being spoken, look around casually. Do not act as if you expect to see anyone in particular. It will draw attention to you.'

'I understand, James, like when I was carrying passports to India. If I had known, I would have drawn attention to myself.'

'Exactly. We have to protect you, and we do not want to see you rush off into the lion's mouth. Kate will be watching for you. Trust her, she knows what she is doing.'

'Okay, James, I get the picture. Come on, Kate, we are going shopping.'

After the ladies left, James received a phone call from Jack Whistler.

'I have talked over Jameel's letter with my boss, James, and he agrees we could have a problem. He suggests we send Ken Johnson to you. He can work in your office and follow you when you go out. Harold suggests you pay half his wage, and you can set him to work. This would be more natural than having someone standing around, watching you. We will pick up the tab for the other half of his weekly pay and for his travelling expenses. The only problem is finding him accommodation. Would you have any ideas for that?'

'Percy lives alone in his house, not too far from us. He could be around within ten minutes, even after pulling his boots on. I would have to clear it with Percy, of course. He has lived alone since his wife died five years ago. I do not know if he would like a live-in guest.

I like the idea of Ken. We got on well together when we went to the Isle of Wight, and he seems a capable fellow. The only problem is, we do not know how long it will be that we are in danger.'

'We can try it for a year, James. Harold Griffiths also seems to see the danger to you and your wife being ongoing. Ken can work out the rent with Percy for himself. He can pay that. He is a handy man to have around, I have found. Very intelligent and quick to action. We called him into the office and put it to him, and he agreed to the year with you. Check with Percy and get back to us tomorrow so we can make arrangements.'

'I have not told Percy about Jameel's letter yet. He was struck with a syringe of some unknown drug last night by our serial killer, and he has been asleep much of the day. He is at our apartment, being watched over by Alicia's grandmother, and he will be staying the night in our spare bedroom so that we can watch over him. I will get to talk to him sometime before lunch tomorrow, and I will call you.'

'Good! We can change things as we go along, if necessary. Your friend, Jameel, seemed sure someone will come to find you sooner or later. We also always thought someone may turn up. Sahib's methods of keeping people in line are like a tribal chieftain issuing edicts. I did not think he would give up easy.'

'You certainly know how to scare a person, Jack. It is not just me. Alicia is on their radar as well, and that is what frightens me.'

'With the extra person in the office participating in your day-to-day business, it will be easier for you to control, James.'

'Yes, thank you, Jack. Give my thanks to Harold Griffiths also. It will put our minds at rest for a while.'

After James put the phone down, he sat thinking of Jameel's letter. It seemed that Jameel was sure that someone would attempt to harm them. The gang had moved fast on Ralph Dalton when he arrived back in Mumbai. It seemed they did not hang about. Sahib had ordered recrimination, and the gang was moving on it. It had been at least a month since Ralph had been forced to give up the name of James Armstrong. Looking for someone to do a job for them could take a couple of weeks, and then looking up *Armstrong* on the computer could take another few days. In James's estimation, they would be ready to move against him by now. Alicia's name would come up at the same time, as the wife of James Armstrong and the courier under suspicion at the time of Sahib's arrest, so she would be involved too.

Thanks to Jameel, they had warning of something happening in the near future. They would discuss it with Percy tonight. He had been asleep most of the day, so he would be ready to listen and discuss the thought of letting out a room in his house and having extra surveillance in their office.

James sighed. Extra surveillance was needed for Alicia. She believed everybody was good underneath, and she would try to talk her way out of a confrontation with an aggressor. He did not think these were the type of aggressors who could be talked to. He would have to ask Kate to watch over Alicia, both in the office and out of it. There were many occasions when Alicia was left alone in the office while they were out on a job. Kate would have to stay back from these jobs to let Ken do them for a while.

Alicia and Kate arrived back from the supermarket. Alicia said she would go home now to check on Percy and to cook dinner. If anyone came near her, she would hit them with the leg of lamb she had in her bag. Kate and James laughed and let her go alone.

James asked Kate how they managed in the supermarket, and Kate said, 'Anywhere Alicia goes, people turn to look at her. She is a very attractive lady and has a certain poise and friendliness about her that everybody sees, so she is watched by men and women alike, and especially young ones. She is totally unaware of her personality and warmth. It is so natural to her. I can see that anyone wanting to find her would catch on very quickly that this is who they are looking for.'

'You have her in a nutshell, Kate. Yes, I have experienced the looks she gets, which then turn to me, as if to say "You are a lucky fellow". We will have to appoint you as her permanent watchdog until the danger is over, Kate. Would you mind that? We are getting help from London. They are sending Ken Johnson down to work with us for a year to help the situation.'

'That is fine with me, James. I will have to work out a plan though for outside the office—for instance, to stay a few feet behind her rather than walk side by side—so that I can watch to see if anyone is too interested in her or is following her. I can always move up quickly to warn her.

'Staying in the office with her is a good idea, as you and Percy are out quite often. It does mean that some of the computer work will be kept up. It tends to be put aside when there are other things to do. Ken Johnson is a nice chap. He will come in handy and as a backup for you, to keep you safe. I imagine that these people, whoever they may be, are mainly going to target you, James?'

'It would appear so, Kate. I thought we had got away from it. It has been nearly twelve months since the arrest of Sahib. It has been the sort of thing that stays in the back of your mind, so I am glad it is going to come into the open now. We will finish it altogether if they appear. These are nasty people, Kate, so be very careful how you handle them.'

'You would think that with having the top men of the scam arrested, it would go away. They are a very determined mob, James.'

'Very. It seems to be in their makeup. Go home now, Kate, and I will lock up. We have done enough for the day, and your kids will love having you home early. We will see you tomorrow. Thank you for all you do, Kate. We appreciate having you on our side.'

'That is a nice thing to say, James. I love working here. The atmosphere is great, like one big happy family. I enjoy coming to work each day.'

23

Percy woke up when Alicia arrived at the apartment. He looked fresh and bright-eyed; the sleep had done him good. Alicia suggested he have a hot shower to freshen up and handed him a pair of James's pyjamas and a dressing gown, saying he could go back to bed after a good meal and would then be back to normal by morning. She was cooking roast lamb and vegetables for dinner in Granny's house, so he had the apartment to himself for a while. James was coming home early to have a rest, and there were things to discuss after they had eaten. Percy was expected to stay the night in the apartment so they could watch over him a little longer.

Percy grinned. 'Thank you, Alicia. You are great people, all of you. I feel like you are my family now, and I think you are getting the message. No one else would have looked after me as you all have. I have been a one-man band for so long, my family thinks I can do anything for myself. My son did ring me at lunchtime and was very glad I was here recovering and asked me to convey his thanks. He was worried I was alone and could have a relapse. He has a long list of appointments for the day and was going to come see me when he finished work, but I told him how well I was being looked after and to go on as usual.'

'It is our pleasure, Percy. James has a new lot of problems to discuss with you tonight, and I will let him explain it. It is quite complicated.'

'Well, my mind is clear now. It was very cloudy this morning. I would not have got through the day at the office.'

'We could see that, Percy. You even looked quite green, and we were sure Granny and Jody could look after you better than anyone else until the drugs wore off. I am off to add the vegetables to the baking dish. James will be here any minute now.'

Granny was getting ready to close the bookshop, and Jody was packing up her things in the children's area, prior to going to the house. Alicia stopped and watched Jody and said, 'We are going to miss you, Jody. You will have to come and visit us again next week to tell us how you are managing at home. We will always love to see you.'

'I will miss you too, Alicia, and Granny and Caroline. You are my best friends forever.'

Alicia smiled. She was such a lovely child. There had never been any complaints from her, even though she was separated from her parents. She had fit in as if it were ordained that they were now her family. Alicia thought, *How could you not love her?*

James walked through the door. 'It feels strange to come home this early, but I am so tired. I was not doing much work anyway. It is nice to be home with our family.' He hugged Alicia, and Jody came to be hugged too.

Granny smiled. 'If my arm was not sore, I would join the four-way hug.'

'Come, Granny,' said James. 'Have a hug for yourself. You deserve it, being great-grandmother, bookshop manager, and now nurse to Percy.'

'Maid of all things, eh, James?'

'Appreciated and a boon to have around, Granny.' James grinned.

James went upstairs, and Alicia, Granny, and Jody went to the house next door, with Jody chattering about what she did all day, including how Percy had read a book to her and how she had put Percy to sleep in her bed.

After dinner, Granny put Jody to sleep in the bedroom upstairs and came down again to listen to James tell the story of Jameel's letter. James passed the letter to Granny to read. Percy had read it while she was upstairs. There was silence until Granny finished the letter. She placed it down and said, 'What does this mean, James? Are you and Alicia in danger from these people?'

'I think, Granny, that we are all in danger. This group of gangsters are very dangerous people and will stop at nothing to do us harm. You, because you are part of our family. Percy, because he is part of the business. Even Kate, because she is associated with us.'

He turned to Percy with a grim look on his face. 'Percy, the London police are sending down Ken Johnson to help us. They will pay half his pay, and we will pay the other half. We can get Barry Cross to pay our part from my wages. It is not fair to thrust you into danger and then have you pay the bill too. I have been thinking about this all afternoon, and here are some of my suggestions.

'Firstly, Percy, you will move into the spare room upstairs, here in Granny's house. That will give her safety during the nights. We have the doorbell downstairs in the bookshop to alert us to any problems, and we can ring you if we get nocturnal visitors.

'Secondly, Ken Johnson will stay at your house and pay you rent—a nominal amount. He can look after himself there—cook, wash, et cetera—and can work office hours, except for any jobs we have at night. He will be joining our staff for a year, and the police will pay half his pay for that year, with alterations as we go along, as necessary.

'Thirdly, Kate has agreed to be Alicia's minder during office hours. Ken will take her place with me on jobs out of the office. Kate will work on all the computer jobs while she is in the office. By the way, Kate and Alicia will be learning self-defence from Harry starting from Tuesday, at 8 p.m. They are both looking forward to that. It comes at a good time, you will have to agree.

'Lastly, we will go on as usual, with Ken taking Kate's place on outside jobs until further notice. Any comments, anybody?' He looked at the others sitting around the table. 'Granny, what do you think about Percy moving in for a while?'

'Yes, James, I can see that would be helpful, if Percy is willing. We need not get into each other's hair too much. I will be in the bookshop all day, and we enjoyed Percy's company when he moved here while you were detained in London, James.'

'What about you, Percy? You will be the one most inconvenienced.'

'If I can join you at mealtimes, James, it will not be an inconvenience to me. It will be a pleasure. Also, there is no need for you to pay Ken Johnson's wages. He will be working for our business after all, besides his guardian role. This will be a good arrangement, with us all guarding ourselves at night. I will try to fit in and not cause Valerie too many problems.'

'Thank you, Granny and Percy. Do you have anything to add, Alicia?'

'I think it is all a good idea, James. Will you accompany Kate and me to the Tuesday evening classes?'

'If you want me to, Alicia. It may be a good idea for a while, until we are satisfied that it is all clear.'

'When do you want me to move over, James?' asked Percy.

'Over the weekend, if you find time. Jody usually sleeps in the bookshop apartment, so the bedroom upstairs will be free. She is going home to Aaron and Sandra on Tuesday morning anyway, so she will then be out of the danger zone. Thank you, Granny and Percy, for believing in Jameel's letter and his thoughts for our safety. Maybe nothing will happen, but Jameel was alarmed by the situation with Ralph. Who also thought we may be in danger, so it would be unwise not to take notice of them. They know their own countrymen, so we will take their warning to heart and at least wait the thugs out.'

Alicia said, looking sad, 'It is all my fault for carrying those passports. I am sorry, everybody.'

'No, no, Alicia. You were unaware that you were being used by the gang, so we cannot put it on your shoulders. We would never have met, except I was sent to you to find out if you were involved in the gang, and I found that you were definitely innocent. This is not your fault but Sahib's. We always knew it was not going to end with putting him in jail. He is the sort of serpent that can grow many heads, a truly evil man. His attack on Ralph Dalton proves that. Poor Ralph, he was coerced into doing their dirty work for them, and look how it has turned out for him. Thank goodness Jameel found him in time to save his life.'

'Have you any idea what we have waiting for us, James?' asked Granny.

'It is an unknown at the moment, Granny. When Ken Johnson arrives, we will have a conference in the office to talk it over. Ken might have more ideas about what to expect. This will not be an English way of thinking, so it is harder to look into the likely methods our thugs would use. Ken may have a better idea because he currently works in the larger city where they normally operate. Alicia and I will go to our favourite Indian restaurant tomorrow night and quiz the staff there for their ideas. Every little thing could help us know what to look for.'

Alicia looked pleased. 'Good, at least we will get something good from this story. I love Indian food.'

James laughed. 'You are delightful, Alicia, seeing good in everything.' He leaned over and gave her hand a squeeze. 'I thought that they could do a bit of scouting for us. Any Indian, even if he is a thug, will hunt out an Indian restaurant. They do not like non-spicy food, like what we eat. The staff of the restaurant could also speak to their friends and ask about a new man or two in town, who they will notice for sure.'

Percy looked interested. 'That is a good thought, James. Perhaps we can eat there once a week to keep up to date, and Alicia can help us with the menu. I find that when I go to an Indian restaurant, because I am not familiar with the food, I always seem to choose the hottest dish on the planet and then cannot eat it.'

James laughed. 'I know what you mean. I would go to buy Indian food when I was at university with Jameel, and he would guide me as to what was just hot and what was spicy and delicious. Alicia helps me choose the right dishes, and I am a big fan nowadays.' He yawned. 'Sorry, folks, I need to have a sleep. I have been tired all day because I only had three hours' sleep last night, after an eventful evening at Valley Care. Today has been eventful also, so I am off to bed. I will help clear up here and then go.'

'You go, James. I will clear up, and I will come over with Percy when it is done,' said Alicia.

*　*　*

Everything at the office ran as usual. Ken Johnson arrived and went off with Percy to look at the house where he would be staying. Alicia and Kate settled into the front office, with both of them at the reception desk, which was long enough to accommodate them and Ken took over Kate's office.

The restaurant people were appalled to hear that a violent person, or even two, would be arriving to make trouble for James and Alicia, and they agreed to watch out and also to alert their friends.

Alec Overington called in to pick up the paperwork for the detention of John Dewson and said he would alert some of his friends to the forthcoming problem. He said he regularly went to a different Indian restaurant, so he would go to this one that night and talk it over with the friendly staff there. He also advised that they should notify the police of the situation; they had policemen on the streets all over town who may detect strangers in their midst.

James explained the help that the London police were providing to advise the locals through Ken Johnson, who had an appointment with the top man at two o'clock. James would be going with him for any explanations for the cause of the problem, taking Jameel's letter to show him.

James was satisfied they had most avenues covered; as Kate had said, forewarned is forearmed. They could go on with their daily work, keeping an eye out but acting normal.

They only had to wait two weeks for the action to start. A petrol bomb was thrown into the office one morning. It flared up, and Kate yelled at Alicia, 'Get under the desk quickly!'

The siren of the fire alarm went off, making a very loud noise. The automatic sprinklers came on, saturating the room and its contents. James and Ken were out of the office, and Percy came rushing out to look for the ladies. Seeing them under the desk, he turned off the sprinklers, as the fire had not spread and had been extinguished.

Alicia and Kate crawled out from under the desk. Kate ran to look out the door to see if there was anyone suspicious still standing around, but she was met with the general public who had been passing by, saying, 'Is everybody okay?' Someone said, 'I have called the fire brigade.' Another said, 'I have called the police.' And someone else said, 'Do you need an ambulance?'

Kate faced them and said, 'You people are a breath of fresh air. It is good to know we still have good citizens around us. Thank you all for your thoughts and actions. We shall be okay for now. Would any or all of you be happy to make a statement next time you are passing by? I cannot take it now, because everything is drenched, but if we have your statements and if we catch the person who did this today, we will be able to prove his or her guilt in the court.'

'No problem, miss. We pass by regularly to go to the mall. We will call in next time we come.'

Kate went back into the office. Percy and Alicia were assessing the damage. All the paperwork was wet and now useless, mostly just magazines and what was lying on the desk. However, Alicia had grabbed a handful of it when she went under the desk, and these were dry. The papers kept in the files in the file cabinet were fine. The chair cushions were saturated but would dry in time. The sprinklers had been on only a few minutes, long enough to extinguish the original blaze, and Percy had jumped on the remaining flares. The damage did not look so bad.

Percy rang James and Ken; they were on their way back and would be there in ten minutes, depending on the traffic.

The fire engines arrived. The firemen were pleased that a sprinkler system had done their work for them, and they congratulated Percy for putting out the fire before it spread.

Percy said to them, 'This is a reasonably new set of offices, and I asked for the sprinkler set to be put in when they were building it, as you never know what sort of person is around to do something silly. Between the fire alarm going off and the water coming down, we wondered where we were for the moment, but things do not look too bad. It is lucky we have a tiled floor, so besides a few scorched areas as souvenirs, we may not even have to apply to our insurance company. It could have been worse if their aim had been more direct and landed on furniture. The bomb landed on the tiled floor, and there was nothing there to burn. So most of the damage is water. We can dry it out.'

'Your mindset is good, sir. Do you have enough in your insurance policy to cover if the fire had spread?' asked the man in charge of the firemen.

'Yes. You do not start up a business such as ours without covering your back for all contingencies, like the sprinkler system. We hoped never to need to use the insurance policy, but you cannot see into the future. Who knows what the crazies will do?'

'That is a good way of looking at things. You are in a good spot here, but it could be inviting to anyone wanting to prove themselves. While we are here, we will check your fire alarms and make sure the batteries are still working.'

James and Ken arrived just as the police turned up. All these things happened within ten minutes, and by that time, Kate and Alicia had mopped up the floor, wiped over the walls and furniture, collected all the wet paper, and taken the covers off the cushions and had them airing in the rear of the office. Things did not look too bad now. The girls were not wet except for their feet. They had taken their shoes off and walked around barefoot.

James walked in and said, 'So it has begun. Did anyone see who did it?'

Kate said, 'Percy was in his office. I looked up when the door opened, but only the petrol bomb took my notice. I am afraid I missed who threw it in.'

Alicia said, 'I saw this little man or boy, I cannot be sure, with dark hair and about my size, average-looking. I do not know if he was Indian or a dark-haired English person. It was all so quick. My mind swung to the bomb and flames before the picture of the person became clear. I may be able to remember more after I sit down and try and recall him.'

'Come back to the conference room, everybody. Alicia, you and Kate sit down, and I will make some coffee. You two had the box seat, so sit down and try and recall the details. Just relax for a few minutes, Alicia, and it may come to you. Do not worry if you cannot remember it. Things may come back to you later.'

A fireman and a policeman had been talking to each other, and the fireman said, 'I will be off. Tony here will let me know if he needs my report, but you folks can tell him more than me. You had the fire out already, and the sprinklers were turned off before I arrived. I wish more of the public took such care.'

'Before you go, can I have a word with you?' James asked.

'Certainly. How can I help?'

'It is possible the same people may try to burn the bookshop and house where we live. Alicia and I live above the bookshop, and it could be a tragedy if they set a fire while we are asleep. Would you mind taking a look at the bookshop and house next door to see where a fire could be started, so we can prepare a way to extinguish a fire before it takes over?'

'We will go straight there now, James, and will call you back after we have assessed it.'

'Thank you. I greatly appreciate your help.'

Kate said to James, 'I rushed out of the door to see if I could catch a glimpse of the perpetrator, but he was nowhere in sight. However, by that time, we had quite a crowd outside the door. One rang the police, one rang the fire brigade, and someone else asked if we needed an ambulance. At that moment, I was not in a position to take details from any of them, but they said they will call in next time they come past us, as they shop in the mall often. It is possible one of them saw a dark-haired person lurking around to see if his work was successful.'

'That is good, Kate, well done. I realise that you would have been wet, and all your paper as well. Let's hope someone does call in during the next few days. It would be good if we can identify this man. It is possible someone took a photo on their cell phone. Everybody does that now, so why not one of them?'

Alicia said, 'James, could you get me a pencil and paper, and I will see what I remember?'

He handed her a pad and pencil, and he turned to Percy and asked about insurance.

'I do not think we have enough damage to make a claim. There is a high excess needed to make a claim, and there is not enough here to warrant it. The cushions will dry up, and we can take the covers home to wash them. Most of the important paperwork was in the file cabinet, so it did not get wet. Alicia grabbed the book we use for appointments, so that was safe. There is a small burn mark on the tiles, but we can put a mat over that to cover it up. Everything else will dry up in time. Besides the shock of it, there was no real damage done.'

'Thank goodness there were not any customers waiting. Are you girls all right? It must have been a big shock to you. Would you like to go home, Kate, and have a rest?'

'No, thanks, James. I am fine, though I think we will have to close the front office for a while, as it is still a bit damp and smelly. We should prop the front door open to get rid of the smell. It should be okay by tomorrow. I can work in one of the other offices, and we can put a note on the front desk for customers to call out to us for attention. Do you want to take Alicia home? It was a big shock for her, and she has managed very well, taking it in her stride.'

Alicia looked up. 'I am fine, Kate. It shook me up a bit, but I am over it now. What do you think of this?' she said, holding up the notebook she had been poring over. There was a dark-haired boy grinning back at them. He looked to be about fifteen, not yet grown into manhood, still a child, a young teen. 'This is the boy I saw at the door,' she said.

'I did not know you could draw, Alicia!' exclaimed James. 'I have never seen anything like this before.'

'Granny did not want me to be like my mother, so she never encouraged me. But she could not stop me in my bedroom at night or at school. She would not buy me any paints, so I was unable to try them. I only did pencil drawings.'

'This is excellent, Alicia. What do you all think about this drawing, guys?'

They crowded around, looking at the picture. Percy said, 'I have seen that face somewhere.'

The policeman, Tony Walton, said, 'That is the son of the Indian stallholder who appears every weekend in the square. Sometimes he is working. Mostly he is hanging around with a crowd of other boys. Perhaps he has nothing to do with your Sahib fellow after all.'

'I think Sahib's men gave him cash to do this. At fifteen, you are easily induced by cash,' said Percy.

Ken spoke for the first time. 'This needs looking into. How do you find these stallholders, Percy? There must be a record of them. They pay the council fees, don't they?'

Tony said, 'I will get on it straight away.' He pulled out his cell phone and made a call, and then he wrote an address and a name and hung up. 'Here you are. Thanks to the likeness you drew, Alicia, you now have your man—or in this case, your boy. What do you want to do about it?'

James was sitting, drinking his coffee, and looked absorbed in his thoughts, so Percy answered, 'I think this needs a visit from us. Who is volunteering?'

James looked up. 'Me, for a start. What about you, Ken? You may come up with something you recognise from your London experience. The characters will not be local. They met this young fellow in the square and talked him into throwing the petrol bomb. That is why he is grinning in Alicia's picture. He thinks it is a joke!'

'Some joke!' said Percy. 'If it had not been for Kate's quick thinking and Alicia following her, we could have been burnt to the ground, and by the time the fire department arrived, the fire could have spread. That would have been a real disaster!'

'A fifteen-year-old does not think that far ahead, Percy. You and the girls, with their quick action, saved the office block. It could have spread without your quick thinking. I also agree with James's version of the story,' said Ken. 'This boy thinks it was a joke and will be at school by now, boasting about his exploits. We should wait till four o'clock, when he will be home with his parents, to quiz him. We need to have a parent with us when we interview him. Can you make that time, Tony? Perhaps we can bring him into the station for you to threaten to lock him up if he does not at least give us a description of the men who employed him.'

'I will tell them at the precinct to expect a crowd. They may insist that a lawyer accompany them,' said Tony. 'Okay, I will turn up at their home in a police car. That always frightens the average person. Will you, James and Ken, be there at the same time?'

'Yes, we will take an office car in case it is needed to carry everyone,' James said, looking disturbed. 'Percy, will you be all right here, looking after the girls? You were all amazing this morning, but we now have to wait for the next instalment. We do not know what direction it will come from, other than that we have been given our warning.'

'We will manage, James,' said Alicia. 'Kate told me to get under the desk. I was busy looking at the boy, and if I had hesitated much longer, we could have been in trouble. But as you say, we have been warned, and I will keep my eyes open in future.'

24

When the boy was interviewed that afternoon, he was very cocky, until his father reprimanded him. After that, he willingly told the policeman his description of the two men who had chatted with him in the square several days before and who had paid him £50 to do the job. He had been told to get the bomb description and how to make it from the Internet.

They could see how disappointed the parents were that their son had done what they called 'this terrible deed'. The mother was in tears and said to her son, 'I have asked you to amend your behaviour. If you do not stop your silly ways and settle down, we will send you to India to your grandparents, and there you will stay. The first time we hear of any more nonsense about you, there will be an airline ticket the next day.'

By this time, the boy looked very crestfallen and was released into his parents' custody. He had given a good description of the men. At least they could possibly recognise the perpetrators if they showed up. As they walked away, the boy turned again to James and Ken. 'I overheard them talking. They probably did not realise I understand Hindi, so they did not try to lower their voices. They plan to set fire to the bookshop in a day or so, they said, and were off to look at the possible plan right away so they could prepare.'

Ken had been writing these words down as the boy spoke, and then he looked at James. 'I would say that you asking the firemen to have a look around came just in time. When are they going to ring you?'

'I gave them our email, so there may be a message when we get back to the office. I knew we were coming out to meet Samuel and his parents, so I told the fireman to email us instead of calling. Let's go and find out what he said.'

James turned again to the boy. 'Thank you, Samuel. You may have redeemed yourself with those few words. We may owe our lives to you. If the bookshop is burnt, we will go with it, as we live above it, in an apartment. Now we will be able to close these hoodlums down before any more damage is done.'

Samuel's father said, 'Thank you, sir. Samuel is not a bad boy. He is always looking for something to do to keep his mind busy. We will watch him carefully from now on.'

James handed him his business card and wrote on the back of it the details of Harry's fitness class and a phone number. 'This is one way to wear a young man out in a healthy way. Give Harry a call and go along to a class to see for yourself.'

* * *

On the way back to the office, James said to Ken, 'I will take you to where we live now and show you the bookshop and house next door and get your appreciation of the difficulties ahead of us. Meanwhile, I will ring Alicia or Kate and see what the firemen had to say. The email should have arrived by now.'

The email had arrived. Alicia read it out to him, and James said, 'We are going now to have a look at the bookshop, Alicia. We will be back soon.'

James introduced Ken to Granny and Caroline, only telling them that he was showing Ken around to get the lie of the land in case their intruders arrived sometime. Granny was intrigued that the firemen had done the same, and she asked James, 'Do you expect them to set fire to the bookshop?'

'It is only a precaution at the moment, Granny. We want to be ready if they do. We do not know from what angle they will come at us, so we are checking out all possibilities.'

'The firemen told us about the petrol bomb in the office. Are you all okay?'

'You would have been proud of Alicia and the way she, Kate, and Percy handled it. Ken and I were out on a job, so we missed the fun. By the time we got back to the office, everything had been mopped up. We are now looking at the possibility that they may try to set fire the bookshop, but we cannot see how it would be successful. The window is made of heavy-duty glass and would be impossible to break. The new doors and locks on the front and back doors are made from heavy-duty material as well.

'The firemen see that the only way they could accomplish a fire is to pour petrol or kerosene into the mailbox on the door and set fire to it. The only other way is to firebomb the window in the apartment. That would be a hit-or-miss operation. It is high, and they have no way to get up to that level. But it is a possibility. You did a good job, Granny, when you renovated the bookshop. It would be difficult for any intruders to enter.'

'That was exactly my intent, James. I spared no expense to do it, because I was living alone here at the time and thought I could be a target sometime in the future. A little old lady all alone is vulnerable.'

'I admire the job you have done, Mrs Newton,' said Ken.

'Thank you, Ken, for those kind words.'

'We will go back to the office, and I will let all the others go home. Alicia, Percy, and I will be home in twenty minutes or so, Granny. We will see you then and talk it over after dinner.'

*   *   *

When they arrived back at the office, they found it looking normal again. Alicia had the cushion covers ready to take home and wash.

This time, James said they would take the car to carry the cushion covers. He told Percy to take his car as well, for backup. Percy looked at him strangely. 'You have a plan in mind, James?'

'Sort of, Percy. We will talk it over after dinner. Alicia, is there enough to eat tonight for Ken to join us?'

'I can add another spud to the pot, and there will be plenty. Are you planning a nocturnal adventure to mind the bookshop, James?'

'Something like that. With all our minds working on it after a nice meal, we should come up with a plan of action.'

'Good,' said Alicia. 'I feel as if we are sitting ducks, waiting to be popped off by the next passer-by. I look at everyone as they pass, to see if they are the ones coming to get us. It is a strange feeling.'

'I do not think they will try the office block again, as there are too many people around, passing by the door. That is the reason they used Samuel to try it. I think they will try the bookshop next, as it is a much quieter area, especially at night. I presume they would have checked it out during the day without getting too close, in case they are recognised. By not getting too close, they would not realise the window is safety glass of a very high standard. You would need a bulldozer to break it. And the new doors and locks we had installed last year are practically break-in proof. Let's go home, and I will show you what I mean.'

Kate said as she left the office, 'I feel like I am letting you down by going home to my children and missing out on the fun and games you are concocting.'

'Kate, you were very impressive today. You have done your bit, so relax with your children. It may not happen tonight, and it would be a lot of sitting around for nothing. Enjoy your evening. We will see if we can get some sleep. We will update you in the morning.'

The others went in the direction of the bookshop, and Alicia went straight into the house to organise the dinner and add that extra spud.

Alicia was amazed how calmly her grandmother was taking the news of the office petrol bombing and a proposed bombing of the bookshop. Granny said, 'They cannot do it, Alicia. When we upgraded the bookshop, we went overboard on making it a safe place to be. At that time, I was thinking I would be alone here, and a little old lady living alone is a target at any time. So my helpers in renovating made sure it is almost impenetrable. I believe we only have to block the mailbox up, and we will be safe!'

Alicia stopped what she was doing and looked at her grandmother with her mouth open. 'Is that what the firemen said, Granny?'

'Yes, Alicia. They were very impressed by the renovations and said that as long as the doors are locked and the mailbox covered so nothing can be pushed through, we should be safe. So relax. Let the men do the worrying about how to catch these people. You and I will be safe here in the house, and they can watch the bookshop from their cars.'

'Have you said all this to James, Granny?'

'There is no need to, Alicia. He is a smart young man, and he will work it all out for himself. I am betting this will be his idea when we talk about it after dinner. He is quick off the mark, your James. I feel completely safe with him around.'

Alicia still looked amazed and said, 'You have completely gobsmacked me, Granny! I do not know what to say.'

'Have a little faith in your husband, Alicia. He is very smart.'

*   *   *

After dinner, when they talked through James's plan, this was exactly what he said. Alicia watched all the faces and could see that they hung on to James's words. Yes, it was obvious that they agreed with his plan and that he came up with it so quickly and that they had not come up with it themselves. She looked at her grandmother and wanted to ask the question 'How did you know?' but did not say it.

At seven o'clock, the doorbell rang, and James answered the door. 'Come in, Tony. I expected you to turn up. You can't keep a good man down. Welcome! The only person you have not met is Alicia's grandmother, Valerie Newton. You will make up the foursome to sit in the cars, two in each. One can sleep, and one can watch. Change over every hour so we are awake if the call comes to move fast. Does everyone agree with that?'

Everyone nodded. Granny said, 'I have organised for some pillows to use for your sleep periods and a snack if you get hungry and a drink bottle each. I have also got some blankets too, as the nights are getting cold and, sitting in the car, you may need a blanket.'

Alicia saw the look that passed between her husband and her grandmother. These two recognised each other's abilities. At that moment, she wondered what sort of man her father had been. Granny seemed to have accepted James as his replacement, and they certainly had rapport with each other. She wondered if she had thought of her father when she met James. Her father had died when she was five years old. Perhaps there was a memory of him that had been hidden all those years when she was growing up and that had surfaced when she met James. Her grandmother said he looked like Jason, her son. Alicia would have to look up some photographs of her father at some time in the near future. She had been attracted to James as soon as she saw him, and that was unusual for her. Perhaps there was recognition there after all.

The group sat around chatting until nine o'clock, and James said, 'Are you ready, everybody? It's best you all go to the bathroom before we leave the house. We do not want to attract attention getting out of the car to use the bathroom when the action is about to start.'

They gathered up the goods Granny had prepared. Tony said, 'We do not always get this much looking after on our nights waiting around. Thank you, Mrs Newton.'

The others all grinned. 'You will find that coffee and cake will be ready when this is all over, I bet,' said Percy, looking at Granny.

'Of course, Percy. I am sure you did not doubt it. Alicia already made the cake while she was cooking dinner.'

Percy looked triumphant. 'There you go, boys, something to look forward to after a night in the car.'

They went out to make themselves comfortable in the cars, feeling cheerful.

*   *   *

It was midnight before James noticed two men walking down the street. He had told the other men earlier to put their phones on vibrate so he rang the other car and nudged Ken awake. They watched as the men drew closer. James had noticed a car an hour previously, driving slowly past and looking at the bookshop. He had put a light on timer in the upstairs apartment, and it had now turned the window dark, as if they had gone to bed. The arsonists must have parked further down the street. Both men carried a parcel, and as they drew nearer, James heard the clink of bottles. They must have bought kerosene from the supermarket. James presumed that out-of-towners did not have much choice. It would be difficult to take anything more to their hotel rooms without it looking obvious, such as a plastic container of kerosene would.

The four men waited until the proposed arsonists stopped at the bookshop. They saw one man glancing at their cars, and they dodged down for a few minutes. But the arsonists' interest was not in the cars. The men had been parked there from early in the evening, and anyone would have assumed that they were there for the night and that the owners were inside the houses, fast asleep by now.

James felt elated. It was going to be as easy as he expected. He had worried that more men might turn up, which would have made things hard to handle. Now he signalled to his crew to get out of the cars quietly and make their way to where the men were fumbling with the letter box opening, which James had boarded over earlier. The four men were very close before one man looked up at their movement and said something angrily in Hindi to the other man. It was too late for them to run. They were outnumbered. They turned and put their hands up.

James asked Tony, 'Is there room in the lock-up until morning?'

'I am sure we will find a space, James. I presume you will be along first thing in the morning to question them. At the moment, we only have an intent. They have done no more than that, so we will not be able to hold them too long.'

'We will be there at nine in the morning, Tony, for the interview. Ken and I particularly want to be present to see what the score is and whether there may be more men following up to have a go at us.'

Tony grinned. 'I will look forward to seeing you there. I will take Ken with me now to assist in the delivery, and I will drop him off at his house. I left the police vehicle down the alley at the back of the bookshop.'

'Thank you, Tony. You have been a great help. I was so pleased to see you at the door when you arrived. We did not know how these fellows would be to handle. A bit of a fizzer, really, but I am pleased it was as easy as it was. We can all go home and get some sleep safely.'

*　*　*

James and Percy went into the house. The ladies were watching television in the lounge although it was 1 a.m. 'You did not need to wait up, ladies. We managed it okay.'

'Did you catch them, James, before they could do any damage?' asked Granny.

'Two men are wrapped up and are on their way to be booked in for the night, and we will interview them tomorrow at 9 a.m. I have a feeling that, like Ralph Dalton, they are not professional crooks. They will be some of the people caught up in Sahib's web, in the country on a false passport. They seemed to be fumblers, inept amateurs, not really knowing what they were up against. However, if they had caught us unawares, we would have been barbecued by now, despite their inexperience in crime.'

'What a thought, James! I will wipe that picture from my mind. Thank you!'

'Sorry, Alicia, I should have put it a bit nicer. I guess I am a bit tired. Let's go and get some sleep so I am bright and alert when I meet these gentlemen in the morning for an interview.'

Percy said, 'The same for me. I am not usually up this time of night. I need to sleep.'

Alicia said, 'We will have the cake I made for morning tea tomorrow, and you can tell the story of the interview while we eat it.'

*　*　*

When James met the two Indian men in the morning, he knew at a glance that they were not the usual criminals that set fire to buildings. He was not surprised when they admitted that their orders had come from someone representing Sahib. They had been blackmailed into coming to this place to fire the business and home of James Armstrong. They would never have done this of their own accord, but Sahib's representative said he would notify the immigration department of their entry into the country on false passports if they did not obey.

James turned to Ken. 'Could you escort these two men to London? I will come also, and we will take them directly to your department and notify Sarah Hudson in the immigration department to follow them up. They will be extradited to India, where at least they will be away from Sahib's influence. Both your chiefs said that Sahib would carry on his business from his jail cell, and it seems he has someone acting for him. We will have to continue to watch our backs, as there may be more coming at us.'

'It is not often you get retaliation like this. What exactly did you do to him?'

'He was using Alicia as his courier. The concierge in her apartment block was sewing passports into her suitcase before each flight to Dubai and Mumbai. Alicia and I had an argument one day, and Alicia resigned from her flight attendant job and came down here to be with her grandmother. I followed her down, and it was then that Percy and I discussed it and sent her bag to the forensics down here to prove once and for all whether passports had indeed been carried in her bag.

'The result was positive, and it was easy from then on to check on the airline personnel. We found Ralph Dalton, who had been passing information about Alicia on to Sahib. It was easy to find Sahib because of his voice, which was described by Ralph, who had never actually met him. Sahib had an easily identifiable voice on the phone. Your department took over from there, but I had handed Sahib—Edward Moorland—to them on a plate. Jameel found all this out from Ralph when he arrived back in India. He had been picked up and tortured to give me up.

'This is the result of me meeting my friend on the Isle of Wight and telling him the story. He followed it up from the Indian side. He looked for Ralph and found him at his parents' home in a state of enormous stress, as he had been forced to tell the thugs about me. He was close to death, having been bashed and left to bleed. My friend, Jameel, took him to hospital, and he is now better and working in a different city and safe.'

'That is some story. It is possible you may never be safe. Next time, he may send a more experienced criminal to get you.'

'That is what I think also. Do not mention it to Alicia. She worries that this is all her fault, but she had no idea that she had been carrying passports to India and Dubai. They were a very clever lot of thugs. I had been living with Alicia for a year and could not find any evidence. They were so good at their job of hiding the passports.

'Come, we will take these men to London and call into the office on the way, to tell Percy, Kate, and Alicia what we are doing. Perhaps there will be a piece of cake left to go with our coffee. Percy is particularly partial to cake, so there may only be a small slice left. We can lock the men into the car with handcuffs while we eat it. When we get to the office, I will ring Jack Whistler to tell him that we are coming. Do you want to stay on with us, Ken?'

'I feel as if I have only just arrived, James. I have been so busy I haven't even looked up the boating and the fishing I was hoping to do. I think there is a chance that there may be more strange people looking you up. You will need a backup at some time, so I think I should stay on for a while.'

'Let us push for the twelve months Jack promised us, Ken. We will be glad to have you. I will confirm it with Percy before we take off to London. After all, it is his house you are staying in.'

Percy was happy for Ken to stay in his house and said, 'We will have to talk it over with Valerie to see if she wants me to stay in her house. But there are three bedrooms in my house, and Ken was allocated the second bedroom. So I can always go home at any time.'

25

J ames said to the group sitting around the table in the conference
room, 'Thank you, everyone. We had an easy night last night. We
are now taking the two men to London to meet with the London
police. They will question them on where the instructions to burn us
down came from. We will leave them to it. Ken and I will be back by
five this afternoon. Carry on.' He gave a grin and waved to them and
went out to Ken's vehicle with its prisoners.

Alicia looked at Percy. He looked white and was yawning constantly.
'Percy, I think you should go for a check-up to find out if those drugs
are out of your system. You do not look well. Perhaps your son can give
you a look-over. It may be because you were up late last night, but I
would like you checked.'

'I am okay, Alicia. Thank you for your concern on my account. I
think it may be that I am getting too old to handle all this late-night
work. I never thought I would say that! I don't seem to be pulling up
like I usually do.'

'I do not think you are past your use-by date yet, Percy, but what
if you took a back seat for a while? If Ken is staying, you can do more
office work or casual work outside the office. Leave the dangerous work
to the other two men. I will talk to James about it tonight, and we
can discuss it after dinner and see if Granny agrees. I am sure she has
noticed the difference in you as I have.'

'I will think it over, Alicia. You may be right. It may only be a
temporary condition after the drug I had at Valley Care, but I do feel

listless. I think I will go and see my doctor, not my son, and have a check-up.'

'Good! I am pleased about that. Ring right away. I know how you men are about going to the doctor. I want to see you make the phone call.'

'Okay, little mama, I will do it right away.' Percy laughed.

* * *

Percy was able to get to his medical centre at noon, and after he returned, Alicia asked him the result of his check-up. He said, 'The doctor could not find too much wrong with me but said that at my age, it takes longer to pick up from an illness or from being attacked by a maniac with a syringe and being injected with a strong drug. I should have rest and several days off work.'

'I agree with that diagnosis and the advice, Percy. You certainly are not the jovial fellow we know and love. What will you do with your time off?'

'I am not taking time off, Alicia. This business is what keeps me going. I do not want to be one of those fellows I see mooching around in the mall, looking for someone to talk to.'

Alicia laughed. 'No, Percy, I cannot see you doing that. How about you do my reception work at the front desk, and I will do some of the computer research from your office? That would be more restful for you.'

Percy grinned. 'I will try that for a while. If I need a snooze, I will let you know, and we can change places.'

'Done deal, Percy. Kate has gone out on a job, checking out a shop that has complained about young kids stealing from them and that says there seems to be a vendetta against them. They telephoned in because they are afraid to leave their shop with only one attendant. They say the police came and took the details, and they have not seen them since. So they are calling us in to investigate.'

'Kate should be able to manage that on her own if it is only kids stealing. We will see what she has to say when she comes back to the office.'

'It might be a job I can do with Kate next time she goes to the shop, and you can manage the office on your own to get your hand in, Percy.'

'I think I can manage a little shop-watching, Alicia. Both sorts. I may have a little trouble chasing kids though. My running skills are running out on me.'

'Since going to the exercise classes with Kate, I have learnt just how out of condition I am. I am starting to pick up, and I think I can catch a child or two, depending on their age. I was good at running at school and have a few ribbons to prove it, but in recent years, I have not had the need to run. So I replaced it with walking. I am still a great walker—not fast, but able to go good distances before I have to sit down.'

'If you go to the shop with Kate, work out a strategy first. Separate as soon as you go into the shop, and one of you stay near the doorway. That is the time-proven method. By now, Kate will have the layout of the shop in her head, and you should go over it with her before you leave the office. After-school hours are the peak time for children stealing, so you will have to be in position by four o'clock.'

'I think I will be good at it. After all, I am being coached now by a master of the game. Thanks, Percy, for your advice. You could take my place if we are not successful today. You could go tomorrow, or with James and Ken here, when we get to the office. Kate, you, and I can go tomorrow. You do the looking, and we can do the running.'

'That sounds like a good deal to me, Alicia, and James can look after the office. That will be a big change for us all.'

'I will get ready to go this afternoon with Kate if that is what she wants. It looks as if it is going to rain all afternoon. It is getting very dark outside. It may not be a good time to chase children, as the pavements will be wet and slippery. Tomorrow may be a better day.'

Percy came and looked out the window. 'It looks as if we may have a thunderstorm. Not a good time to be running around, as you say. Wait and see what Kate has to say.'

* * *

Kate had noticed the thunderstorm brewing and said, 'The rain always seems to come as the children come out from school. They may not go to the shop today, because of the lightning. I discussed this with the shop owner and she agreed, so we are on tomorrow for shop-stealing. It is a confectioner's shop, and the owners say the children go for the most expensive items, as if they have been trained on what to look for. She has put some of these things in glass cabinets but says this has not stopped the children from stealing them. Her opinion is that the children steal things and the goods are sold somewhere.'

'How big is the shop, Kate?'

'A little larger than the general confectionery shop, as they sell handmade chocolates as well. These take up a whole counter, and one assistant stands there, making the chocolates. The other lady stands at the till area. Because they cannot watch all of them at once, if someone comes in and takes their time choosing what they want, it leaves a vacuum in which the stealing takes place.

'I think it is sad, because most of the things are handmade by the two ladies, and so much time and effort are put into it, only for someone to come in and steal the best bits. They said they have tried moving counters around, but it has not worked for them. Things still go missing. They seem to think a Fagin like game is being carried out. They do get a lot of children in the shop.'

Percy looked as if he had picked up and was interested in what Kate was describing. 'Let us leave it until tomorrow. It should be a better day, and the three of us can go and see what is happening. If we take the car and go a little earlier, we can park the vehicle somewhere close, and we may see what is happening around the shop. These children must pass off the goods quickly. They are breakable items and would not be any good all broken up, so I would say there is an adult that waits close by to collect them and pay the kids off.'

'We will need the car anyway, Percy. It is quite a distance away, in Newtown. I caught a bus, but if the weather turns inclement, we may have to watch from the car to catch this adult anyway. I am glad you see it, Percy, like I do—some Fagin figure, maybe even a woman, sending in kids to steal. The children cannot carry very much at a time, as this would need quite large bags, so I think there would be three or four at a time that enter the shop. One makes a diversion by openly choosing sweets, while the other two or three each pick a good-looking piece they can carry under their woollen cardigans and walk out.'

'That sounds feasible, Kate. I think that could be what is happening. The shopkeeper cannot chase anyone, because that would leave the shop open for the kids to grab more. The other attendant is at the chocolate counter at the other end of the room and would not be able to stop them.'

Alicia said, 'I am ready for this adventure, Percy. Count me in. It will be easier with the three of us.'

'It may be as well to take Ken with us too. He still has a licence to arrest someone. I do not think it is just kids in this operation.'

Alicia said with glee, 'That will leave James to mind the office. It will be his turn to wonder what we are up to.'

Percy looked at her and smiled. 'We will make it a fun day, Alicia. I will buy you a chocolate to say thank you for all your lovely meals.'

'I will look forward to that, Percy.'

*   *   *

James and Ken came back into the office. James went straight to Alicia and hugged her and said, 'Jack Whistler and his boss both said hello to you.'

'That is nice of them, James. What is going to happen to Sahib and his lawyer that is doing his dirty work for him, organising thugs?

'That is a different story altogether. Sahib is going back to court, and first of all, the lawyer is going to get a drubbing. They will investigate all his credentials and check on his passport to see if he is an illegal immigrant. They will make a big deal of the fact that all the people working for Sahib are illegals and bring up the fact that he acted as procurer and instigated the arson attack on us. We will be using our arsonists as witnesses.

'Secondly, the police lawyer will ask the judge that jail time for Sahib be extended and, if further damage is done to us, extended again.

They told me Sahib is not in good health at the moment. I suppose he does not like jail food. I do not think there will be any need to worry about him for a while.'

'That is good news, James. What about Ken? Is he allowed to stay with us on the earlier terms?'

'Yes, both Jack and his boss said they would not go back on their word. He is here for the year.'

'That is good news. We need him tomorrow to possibly make an arrest for us,' said Alicia.

James laughed. 'What have you been doing today, Alicia, to need someone arrested?'

'Not me, James. Kate has a new job we are all going to work on tomorrow—except for you, James. You have to stay and mind the office!'

'We have changed places. You have turned investigator, have you, Alicia?'

'Just this once, James. The job calls for someone to pretend to go shopping, and you know I am good at that job. I will not need to pretend too much.'

'More information, please, someone!' said James, looking around.

Everyone laughed, and Kate explained what they were doing the next day.

Percy interceded. 'Kate and Alicia have planned this sting by themselves. Ken and I will only be going along as observers.'

'Sounds interesting. It is a shame I cannot come and observe too, but someone has to watch the office.'

'Never mind, James. We will tell you all about it when we get back to the office tomorrow.' Alicia laughed.

26

After dinner that evening, everyone was too tired to chat, so James and Alicia went straight to the apartment to go to bed. It had been a long night and a long day following it. Before they went to sleep, James asked, 'Whose idea was it for you to go out on a job tomorrow?'

'Percy was not feeling his best yesterday, and I made him go to a doctor for a check-up,' said Alicia. 'The doctor said he is still getting over the needle jab at Valley Care, and at his age, it takes longer to get over such traumas to the body. He should have two or three days off work to rest.

'Percy said he did not want time off from work, so I suggested I go with Kate tomorrow. I can be the runner, and Percy can watch from the car to point the way. I am a bit worried about Percy. He has seemed subdued since the nursing home episode.'

'Yes, I have noticed that. I think that besides being injected with a drug, the fact that he learnt his wife was killed by that evil fellow and that Dewson told him that his wife's death had been more or less an experiment, because she was the first, was not easy for him to hear. He is still trying to absorb the news.'

'Poor Percy, it must be terrible for him. We can help by being around for him for a while.'

'While he is staying here, with Granny to watch over him, he should get over it in time. Have a word with Granny in the morning, Alicia, out of Percy's hearing, and ask her what she thinks about it. We may have to invent some easy jobs for Percy until he recovers.'

'I suggested he look after the front desk for a while, and I will do some of the research work from his office. He seemed okay with that.'

'That sounds like a good idea for a while. We will watch and see how it works out. He is almost seventy, a little old to be chasing around after people, but his mental faculties are still intact. We cannot retire him, as he is the senior partner in the business. Perhaps the front office is a good place for him.'

'I like to think it will be good, James. In fact, I have been working myself up to say that I think I should resign. I have not had a holiday in years. There are some things I would like to do but have not had a chance at, as there always seems to be some job or other that I should do first. I have loved doing the reception work at the office. I have enjoyed the camaraderie amongst the team. But since Ken arrived, it has not seemed the same. It now seems more business-like. I think Percy being at the front desk and doing the odd job with you will keep him happy, and Kate can step into the reception job when Percy is out of the office.'

Alicia waited, with her breath held, for James to reply. She knew her announcement would be a surprise for him. She watched his expressive face, seeing his thoughts go over it.

'We have loved you taking part with us in the office, Alicia. You have been our centre since we began, and we would miss you if you were not there. I agree that Percy could take over the reception. It is a good way to keep him occupied and is not too tiring for him. But he is not you, Alicia. You make the office a happy place to be. Each time I walk into the office after a job, I look forward to seeing your beautiful, happy smile. What will you do with your time if you are not in the office?'

'First of all, the Christmas holiday break is coming up, and Caroline has told Granny she would like time off to be with her son during the vacation. Otherwise, she will have to send him to after-school care, and she has always tried to avoid that so she can spend time with him herself. That means we will have to find a replacement for her, or I could help Granny.

'Secondly, I would like to learn to paint. I have always wanted to try painting, but Granny was against it after my mother's experience. However, I am not my mother, and I cannot even remember her. She made so little of her time with me. I want to try it because of something in me. I know I can draw, but I want to see if I can paint. It is a strong compulsion. I may not be any good at it, but I want to try. I have been thinking that Sandra may like to teach me. I could go to her house for one day a week to see her and Jody. I find myself missing Jody when we come home from the office.'

She stopped talking and looked to see how her speech affected James. He was smiling. She felt as if a weight had been lifted from her. 'What do you think, James?'

'Why don't you try a month off, Alicia? It is coming up to the Christmas period and our first anniversary in the business. See if you miss the office. I would hate to see you leave us. Percy's face is not as good as yours at the reception desk. However, I understand you have not had a chance to wind down from everything in the past, and you need a break for yourself. Let us sleep on it. It is getting late, and we can talk more about it tomorrow. Perhaps you could come into the office on a part-time basis. Anyway, whatever you decide, we will go along with it. I want you to be happy, not resentful that all your time is taken up with private investigations work.'

Alicia sighed. 'I am grateful you do not think I am pulling out because I am unhappy, James. I love working with you, but somehow Ken coming has changed the office atmosphere. Everything must change, I understand that. As you say, we will think more on it. It is a new thought for me also, so there may be a way around things.'

* * *

Alicia went off to sleep, feeling happier than she had been for the last two or three weeks. Ken had made a difference in the atmosphere in the office. Somehow she felt they were under scrutiny from the London policeman. Perhaps it was only her who felt it. James seemed to have accepted him wholeheartedly, and there seemed to be no attitude change from Percy and Kate.

Maybe it had added something to the way Percy felt. Maybe he felt left out of things. James and Ken had been doing things together, and until now, it had been James and Percy doing things together. She would probe things a little more to see if she was right in her assumption. It was Percy's business after all, and it would not be right for him to be left out of things.

*   *   *

The next afternoon, they set off to Newtown to visit the confectionery business under siege from thieves. Percy sat in the car while Kate and Alicia went into the store, and Ken went for a stroll along the shopfronts to see if he could see their quarry. At the bus stop, he waited until a bus came in, and then he turned and followed a young woman pushing a pram, the type that folded down, with her were four children, possibly aged between three or four to eleven or twelve. They walked towards the confectionery shop slowly, chatting as they went. Ken stayed several feet behind them.

As they approached the shop, Ken gave a thumbs up to Percy. Percy climbed from the car and walked over and entered the shop to speak with Kate and Alicia, and then he purchased two boxes of chocolates and left the shop as the children entered. He went back to the car and read a newspaper. Meanwhile, the girl—she appeared to be fifteen or sixteen, no older—and the smallest child stood a few feet from the door of the shop, watching the door.

Inside the shop, Kate was wandering around, looking at the luscious-looking confectionery, and Alicia was chatting with the chocolate-making staff member, talking about the methods of filling up the chocolates, but positioned so that she could see the shop's customers. Percy had alerted them, saying children were approaching. She saw a little girl, about Jody's age, in a school uniform, standing at the counter with a shopping list, which she handed to the other staff member. Two boys—one aged about six or seven, also in school uniform, with his rucksack on his back, and a bigger boy, about eleven—were wandering around the shop to take up positions, looking at the sweets as they went around the shelves. Alicia saw the younger boy bend over and take his haversack off and open it. She watched as he took out two apples and gave one to his elder brother and filled up his bag with pieces of confectionery that the elder boy passed to him. They then walked to the checkout, the older boy handing a sweet to the little girl and saying loud enough for all to hear, 'We will take this one too, Ellie. Mum will like this when she comes home from work.'

Ellie, the little girl, took the sweet from her brother and showed it to the staff member watching her and said, 'Add this one too, please. I think we have enough money.'

The child looked so pretty and cute in her oversized school uniform that all eyes were on her. The three walked to the door and went through without anyone apprehending them, and Alicia and Kate followed them, giving the staff a wink as they went out the door.

When they arrived at the car, they could see Ken talking to the older girl as the children came up to them. He looked towards the car, and Kate nodded to him. He then asked permission of the girl to examine the child's haversack. She was obviously taken aback and asked Ken for his authority to ask.

Ken showed her the identification he carried, and the girl opened the bag for him. Kate wandered over to ask if he needed help. The girl looked defiant, and the children started crying. Ken looked as if it was all too much for him when the young woman started crying too, and Alicia slipped out of the car to help with the group of crying children.

The girl was quite voluble in her information. She said her father was in jail because he had hit another man at the pub; they had both been drinking, and the other man started a fight. Her father had hit the fighter to shut him up, and he hit him too hard. The man fell to the pavement and hit his head and died.

With her father in jail and missing from the family, her mother needed to find work to support them and worked from four till eight at the local pub where it all happened. The manager at the pub felt sorry for her and gave her a job, but it meant that the girl, Hilary Thompson, was then in charge of her younger brothers and sister every day, between four and eight. She was not paid anything for looking after the children, so she dreamt up the sweets-stealing deal to earn some pocket money. They took them around to people's houses in a basket and sold them every Saturday morning. Nobody ever questioned where the sweets came from, and they sold out every week.

The little girl, Ellie, piped up. 'Don't forget the flowers, Hilary. We sell all of them too.'

Hilary hushed her little sister, but it was too late. Kate asked about the flowers they sold.

'The same as here, really. We go to florist shops and take a few bunches from each. They put buckets of bunches of flowers outside their doors in the street. No one has ever noticed us, and they sell quite well.'

Kate said, 'I think we will have to take you all into the sweet shop so you can give back the sweets you picked up today, and you will need to apologise and see what those ladies want to do about you. We need to have your full names and address and a phone number. We will have to tell your mother all about this. It will probably be up to her to punish you.'

They took the children back to the shop to apologise. The ladies were stunned that they never noticed these particular children stealing; their method of getting Ellie to go up to the counter and request sweets had always worked for them. Kate asked what they wanted done to Hilary and the children, as some redress was needed to stop them from doing it again. The ladies behind the counters thought about it for a few minutes, then one of them said, 'I suggest that Hilary bring the children here twice a week to make sweets. We will pay them for each piece that we are able to sell on the counter. That should work two ways: Hilary will get a little pocket money, and so will the other children. And they will not be tempted again to steal someone else's work when they find out how hard you have to work to make the sweets.'

She thought some more and added, 'If Hilary and the children are willing, they could go on selling from their basket to their neighbours, but with our permission. We could split the money three ways. One-third for the materials to make the sweets, one-third to us for making the sweets, and one-third to Hilary for selling the sweets. Does that sound fair to you?'

'That is a very kind judgement you are handing down. Take note, Hilary, of all that these ladies will teach you, and thank them for not sending you to the police station. We still have to tell your mother what you have been doing and about the judgement these ladies have given, as they will need your mother's permission.'

Hilary looked relieved that she was not going to prison, even smiling at the thought of making sweets.

The group of investigators went back to the office, taking James a sweet each for leaving him alone in the office. Alicia was very happy with their announcement that the job had gone as Percy planned.

27

James announced, 'There will be a dinner to include all of you at our favourite Indian restaurant on Friday night. The office will pay, on the expense account. The main reason for this evening together is to tell the restaurant people that we have caught the chaps we were looking for and also to discuss the future of the investigation business with the holidays coming up.'

Percy said, 'Good idea, James. I have been given a few ideas as well. That will be a good opportunity to air them.'

James continued, 'All ideas are welcome, so get the brain cells working so you can all air them. The business has done well for its first year. We are in front, so we can afford holiday pay. I suggest a month's break, closing the office down from the week before Christmas until the new year.

'I am sure you would like some time off to be with your children over the Christmas period, Kate. We would love for you to continue with us in the new year. Ken will be with us until November next year. That will be a plus. He is a handy fellow to have around. Percy and I go with the business, so you cannot sack us. We will be around too. If next year continues as this one has, we will be happy. So arrange your Friday evening to include dinner with us.'

Kate was the first to answer. 'Thank you, James. Yes, the time off will be gratefully received, and I will look forward to starting work again in the new year.'

Ken said, 'I may have time to do some fishing over the break. The weather will be cold, but that is the time to get the bigger fish, I am told.'

Alicia did not say anything. She knew James would bring it up at the dinner after they had discussed her part in the business affairs further in private and discussed it with Percy. She had made her mind up; she wanted a break. It had been so long since she had a holiday, and now she wanted to be able to do what she had desired for a while.

Perhaps she would feel different after a few months off; she may miss the constant coming and going from the office and when the others would return with stories to tell. Each story was interesting, but at the moment, she wanted to do her own thing. James could tell her about the interesting cases over dinner each night.

James wound the day down by saying, 'Percy and I thank you all for your work with us this year. We appreciate each of you very much. We will lock up now and go home and think things over about what we can do to improve things in the new year. Goodnight, folks.'

*   *   *

Over dinner that evening, Alicia said, 'I am looking forward to being able to cook something more innovative trying out new recipes for a while. There is nwo time between office and home to come up with more interesting dishes.'

Percy looked at her. 'You mean you can do even better than you do, Alicia? Each meal has been delicious. I have brought your chocolates I promised, and also a box for you too, Valerie, to say thank you for your wonderful acceptance of me in your home.'

'James and I have been discussing my having time off from the office, Percy. I feel as if I have been running all year to keep things up, and I want a break. It has been so long since I have had a holiday to do the things I want to do, so we have discussed me resigning from my reception work at the end of the school year, as Caroline will be having the school break off from the bookshop to be with her son. I can fill in for her until she returns in the new year. After that, there are several projects I have been wanting to do for some time, and I have not had time to pursue them.'

'Ahh, so that is why you wanted me to practise as receptionist,' said Percy with a grin.

'Actually, I did not think of it at that time. It was only after that conversation with you that I decided what I wanted to do. I am sorry to leave you in the lurch. It will be easy enough to find a receptionist if that is the way you want to go, but you and Kate can do it between you, Percy. You know you need to slow down a bit. We cannot do without your expertise in the office, and for some small jobs, I could be available to help out, if required. I do not want to work every day. It gives me no time for other things.'

'I accept that, Alicia,' said Percy. 'I know also that I need to slow down. That injection I received gave a big jolt to my way of thinking, and I now accept that ageing means slowing down. My mind is still alert, but my body has slowed. I am lucky I do not get some of the arthritis and knee problems that a lot of people in my age group get, so I am still able to do some things without any problems. But yes, I can help out in the reception area and still keep up with small jobs outside.'

Granny said, 'I am pleased you have both spoken out loud about these things. I have been watching Alicia for the past couple of months and have seen how restless she has become. Why not try her out as part-time—say, Tuesday and Thursday, or Wednesday and Friday—for a while? That would give her a little pocket money and Percy time to do his outside jobs.'

'That sounds fair to me, Granny,' said James. 'What do you think, Alicia and Percy?'

Alicia looked around the table. 'That is a good compromise. What do you think, Percy?'

'I think you should be in the office for the Monday morning round-table conference, Alicia. So much comes out of that meeting, and after the weekend, there are usually jobs to do. What do you say, James?'

'I have been trying to stay out of the conversation to let Alicia make up her mind about what she wants without me interfering, but since you ask, I agree that Monday is an important day. And perhaps one other, depending on the work we get. She can decide as she goes which day it will be.' James looked as if he did not want to say any more.

Alicia understood how James was feeling. She knew he enjoyed her being in the office each time he returned, but she would be home when he arrived after work, to listen to him, as he liked to bounce his ideas off her to see what she thought, from a woman's point of view. She would still be here for him.

'Okay, Monday and one other day, as you propose, Percy. We will try it out in the new year and see how things go. Granny, I suggest you close down the Monday children's time until after the school break. Many of the families will be going off to their grandparents and other places for holidays over that period, so you would not have enough to bother about. Take a break for yourself, and I will be available if you want time off. It sounds as if we are all going to slow down a bit.'

James said, 'I was wondering if you would consider going to Spain with me, Alicia, to visit my parents for a few days.'

'That would be nice, James. Yes, let's do that.'

Percy asked, 'Do you want me to stay on here until your return from Spain, James?'

James looked at Granny and received a nod. She said, 'Yes, please, Percy. That is thoughtful of you. It will be handy to have you here if anything comes up. Also, I think I should close the shop for that month and have a break. Caroline will not be here, so I would have to manage alone. I could use a break from the everyday bookshop chores, to catch up with things.'

James clapped, and Percy and Alicia joined in. 'Way to go, Granny,' said James.

Alicia let out a long-held breath. They would all get a break, including James. At last, she would meet her in-laws. She had been writing to them but was yet to meet them face-to-face. It would be nice.

A month off over Christmas would freshen them all up again before they started the new jobs that were sure to come when they reopened the private investigations office in the New Year. It had been a very successful first year, with a promise of more work to keep them going in the next year. They had made some good friends, and the future looked good for them.

Made in the USA
Coppell, TX
30 November 2019